A Birthday Wish

Gladys Polson feels led to help a crotchety widower who is wealthy in material things but poor in spirit. Haydn Keller comes to Calico at his grandfather's request and wonders what Gladys's purpose is in reaching out to his grandfather. Will the two young people fulfill the old man's birthday wish?

Miss Bliss and the Bear

Annie Bliss decides to knit hats and mittens for soldiers at a nearby fort, knowing they must be as lonely for their families as her brother, also in the army, is. But fort chaplain Jeremiah Arnold isn't sure he wants a woman hanging around the fort—even one as beautiful and well meaning as Miss Bliss.

Buttons for Birdie

Birdie Landry, former saloon girl and new Christian, can barely make ends meet on her income from her sewing. She needs additional funds to buy supplies to make everyday dresses for other girls wanting to leave the saloons behind. When storekeeper Ned Finnegan pays her more for her extra eggs than they are worth, she rejects his help. Will Ned's project, "Buttons for Birdie," prove the depth of his love?

A Blessing for Beau

Schoolteacher Ruth Fairfield knows the three orphaned Pratt children well. When their uncle Beau arrives to take care of them, he refuses any offers of help. They clash over what is best for the children, but will the blessing Ruth plans lead to disaster. . .or true love?

CALICO BRIDES

FOUR-IN-ONE COLLECTION

DARLENE FRANKLIN

BARBOUR
PUBLISHING

Cover design: Kirk DouPonce, DogEared Design

Published by Barbour Publishing, Inc., P.O. Box 719, Uhrichsville, Ohio 44683, www.barbourbooks.com

Our mission is to publish and distribute inspirational products offering exceptional value and biblical encouragement to the masses.

 Member of the
Evangelical Christian
Publishers Association

Printed in the United States of America.

Dedication

I dedicate *Calico Brides* to the staff and residents of Wadley Care Center in Purcell, Oklahoma. They have helped me heal and followed the progress of this book with great enthusiasm. The staff are the people who put "care" into the center's name.

Prologue

Calico, Kansas, 1875

Gladys Polson opened the door to her two lifelong friends, Annie Bliss and Ruth Fairfield. "Come in out of the cold. Welcome to the first meeting of the year of the Calico Ladies Sewing Circle."

"From what Ma says, we can expect equal parts sewing, missions, and gossip." Annie removed her wool-knit cape and hung it on the coat tree.

"Someone is standing on the opposite corner but isn't coming any closer." Ruth, a little older than Annie and Gladys but a good friend, cleared a small spot on the window to the right of the door.

Gladys peered over her head. "It's hard to tell, wrapped up in all those warm clothes, but I think it's Birdie Landry."

Annie drew in a shocked breath. "*Birdie?*"

Ruth slipped her arms back into her coat. "We must welcome her. I'll invite her to sit with us; she's about our age."

Before Gladys or Annie could respond, Ruth opened the door and headed across the street. Casting an amused glance at Annie, Gladys put on her coat and opened the door. "You can welcome anyone who comes before we get back."

Ruth's impulsive action didn't surprise Gladys. The pastor's daughter did her Christian duty with a full heart, even in unpleasant circumstances. Gladys had learned to follow her friend's lead and let her heart catch up with her later.

Welcoming Calico's saloon-girl-turned-saint to the Sewing Circle qualified as one of those uncomfortable times. Using a trick she had learned from singing in choir—thinking of happy things so she could smile no matter how she felt— Gladys smiled and prayed silently. *Thank You, Lord, for Birdie's salvation. Thank You for bringing her here today. Help me be a good friend.* When Gladys reached the near corner, Ruth waved and crossed the street with Birdie close behind. "Good news. Birdie will be joining us today."

So Ruth had already coaxed the reluctant woman to accompany her. Gladys extended a hand. "I'm so glad you came, Birdie."

A faint smile played around Birdie's mouth. Though not painted like the scarlet woman Gladys's parents warned her about, Birdie's lips were so full, so naturally red, that she looked overdressed. Gladys attributed the pink in her cheeks to a brisk walk in the cold, or maybe her uncertainty about her welcome. "Mrs. Polson encouraged me to attend, but I hope the good ladies of Calico don't object to my presence."

"You are a new creature in Christ. The Bible says so. Don't let anyone tell you differently." Ruth's tone took on the scolding aspect that earned her respect in the classroom where she taught Calico's children.

Annie opened the door and helped Birdie remove her coat. "We'd best hurry in. Mrs. Sparrow is ready to begin the meeting."

Gladys held the door open and slipped in last, behind Birdie. There weren't four empty chairs together, so she went to the dining room to get extra ones. The friends were too old to giggle and chatter through the meeting the way they had when they were younger, but they still preferred to sit away from their mothers' sides.

A few women exchanged looks at Birdie's unexpected presence. Mrs. Fairfield smiled a welcome, and Ma, God bless her, carried the tea service to their corner. "So glad to see you, Annie, Ruth. And Miss Landry, I'm delighted you could join us."

"Please call me Birdie." The newcomer spoke in soft, melodic tones. She accepted a cup of tea, holding it at precisely the correct angle.

Mrs. Sparrow presided over the meeting, updating the group on the success of their collection over Christmas— an impressive one hundred dollars raised for missions in China—before introducing the project for the new year. "My husband has been in contact with the director of the Indian school. He said they are in need of everything, from school supplies to books to warm blankets and suitable clothes. I told him I was certain our sewing circle would be glad to help meet that need."

"Miss Lucy Langston in China said they are still in need of bandages." Ma wrote regularly to the missionaries the church supported. "I have already requested that the mercantile order additional wool for bunting."

Annie frowned at the pictures of the children Ma passed around. "They look like the Smith children."

Gladys's mind wandered. Ma loved reading about God's work in other lands. But Annie's words made her wonder why they didn't do more to promote the gospel and good works closer to home. There were plenty of people in Calico in need of a loving touch or a helping hand. She skimmed through the possibilities while the women began sewing. She loved quilting, and she had started her marriage quilt. But today she was working on a smaller piece.

Conversation flowed as the ladies worked. Ma offered everyone her sugar cookies, but most ladies declined. They didn't want to get their fabric soiled. Beside Gladys, Annie's knitting needles clicked. Birdie was hemming a square of bunting with tiny, meticulous stitches. She was a skilled seamstress, whatever other skills she possessed.

Gladys tied off the end of her thread and began a new square. "I have an idea for a mission project."

"Another one?" Annie double-dipped her knitting needle into her stitch. "It sounds like we already have enough to keep us busy."

"I would like for us to help people who live close by. There are people here in Calico who have never heard the good news of God's love." Gladys laid the quilt square in her lap and looked at the three women seated near her. "Ruth, you're in the best position to observe which families are in need. Maybe they lack a mother's touch."

Ruth nodded. "I can think of a few. There's always at least one family that's dirt poor."

Birdie opened her mouth but closed it without speaking.

"What are you thinking, Birdie?" Gladys bet the former saloon girl knew which men spent their family's money on liquor or which men gambled it away at the Betwixt 'n' Between.

"Some of the other girls at the saloon would like to get away from that life, but they can't go around town in the dresses Nigel Owen gives them." She lifted her shoulders a delicate fraction. "If I could make them modest dresses. . ."

"Oh, I love that idea!" Annie tucked her yarn back into her knitting bag. "Let's do it."

"One special project for each of us, to be finished this year." Gladys made a note in her tiny diary. "Let's pray and ask God what He wants each of us to do."

"Here's to the junior members of the Ladies Sewing Circle." Annie grabbed Birdie's right hand and Ruth's left hand, and Gladys finished the circle.

"Amen!"

A BIRTHDAY
WISH

There is one alone. . .yea, he hath neither child nor brother;
yet is there no end of all his labour;
neither is his eye satisfied with riches. . . .
Two are better than one;
because they have a good reward for their labour.
ECCLESIASTES 4:8–9

Chapter 1

Gladys checked the baskets on the kitchen table. Red calico bows she'd festooned with small white flowers peeked out between juniper branches. Such cheerful decorations should improve even crotchety widower Norman Keller's spirits in the middle of the miserable Kansas winter.

Ma carried a couple of baskets to the family wagon, together with garlands of fragrant juniper branches. "Maybe it would be good if I came with you."

Gladys came close to agreeing when she remembered the last time she had knocked on Mr. Keller's door. The growl with which he had greeted carolers could have passed for Ebenezer Scrooge's. "I'll see how it goes today. I'd like to do this on my own, if I can. I'll be back in time to help with supper."

Grateful for the January thaw that made an outdoor project possible, Gladys buttoned up her winter coat and drew on her mittens before heading out to the wagon. When she'd decided to reach out to Norman Keller, she hadn't considered how to keep her activities a secret. To avoid attention, she would keep her wagon off Main Street.

A few minutes later she came to a stop in front of the

imposing three-story structure that Norman Keller called home. As far as Gladys knew, he was the only one who lived there. His wife had died, and his children never visited. Rather than knocking on the front door and risking Mr. Keller's rejection before she even started, Gladys approached the house from the back. She tied the horse to the railing and carried the baskets to the wraparound porch. A closer inspection of the once-magnificent structure revealed sagging boards and peeling paint. Such neglect by the richest man in town befuddled her. She hoped he would feel better after she'd hung enough baskets for him to see one no matter which window he looked through.

As she walked down the porch, a basket in each hand, she realized she had miscalculated the number needed to adorn the rafters. She'd start from the front and work her way back. She tiptoed to the corner and put the baskets down. She returned for her stepladder, and as she carried it to the front, it bumped along the floorboards. She froze, expecting Mr. Keller to shuffle out the door to check on the noise. When he didn't appear, she continued until she had unloaded everything in the wagon.

From the corner, she studied the overhang. With a hammer in one hand and two nails in the other, she climbed the stepstool, reached high overhead, and tapped a nail into the wood. A thin crack appeared. Would a section of the overhang split and fall? Mr. Keller wouldn't appreciate it if she destroyed his property in the process of decorating it.

Tucking her tongue behind her teeth, Gladys waited and

the nail held. Next she centered the basket handle on the nail. She stepped down to study the effect. *Good.* Setting another arrangement on the railing, she climbed the stepstool to hammer the second nail in place.

As she adjusted a couple of ribbons around the berries, she wondered what else she could do for Mr. Keller. Fashioning a few bows hardly qualified as a mission project, and she wanted to do more. She tapped the nail in and reached for the basket.

Behind her, the front door banged. "What are you doing?"

The edge of the door caught the stepstool, throwing Gladys off balance. Her arms windmilled, her feet slipped, and she fell backward.

Into two strong arms.

"Oomph."

The arms lifted her and held her steady while she regained her footing. The basket had fallen, crushing the bows and scattering the juniper branches across the floor.

Falling into Mr. Keller's arms wasn't the introduction Gladys had hoped for.

Slowly she turned around to meet the man she wanted to help. And looked up. . .and up. . .and up. Long legs, straight limbs, strong arms. . .brown hair.

Definitely not Norman Keller.

Haydn stared at the person who had been making all the noise. Her cheeks gleamed bright red beneath a green knit cap, and brown curls bounced on her shoulders. Her mouth

17

opened just far enough to reveal straight white teeth. This little thing didn't weigh much more than a hummingbird. "Are you all right? Did you hurt yourself?"

"No." She brushed her hands on her coat and glanced at the porch, covered with greens and ribbons and straw baskets. What was this stranger doing on the porch on a ladder in the middle of winter? The Old Man hadn't mentioned any guests.

"I apologize for making such a mess." She gestured helplessly at the scattered items on the floor. "If you give me a broom, I'll clean it up."

The Old Man's pride demanded Haydn refuse. As he stepped to the side, a board moved underneath his foot, a reminder of all the repairs needed on the house. Whoever this stranger was, at least she wanted to help. "Let me get one for you." He paused at the door. "But who are you?" *And what are you doing here?*

"I'm Gladys Polson." Shivering, she slipped on a pair of gloves. "Who are you? I haven't seen you before."

"I'm Haydn. . ." He hesitated in mid-introduction. "Haydn Johnson." He used the name he often gave in his newspaper work.

Miss Gladys Polson was as pretty as a Christmas angel, standing there against the backdrop of the winter-white world, and whatever her purpose in coming to the house, she surely meant no harm. He smiled. "Look, it's a miserable day. Come in and get warmed up before you do any more work."

Her mouth opened, and he thought she was going to refuse. Tilting her head, she touched her lips with a mittened hand. "I'd like that."

Haydn held the door open.

"Who was it making all that blasted noise?" The Old Man's petulant voice carried across the living room.

"It's Gladys Polson."

"Don't know her."

Gladys crossed the room to greet the man sitting in the straight-backed chair by the low-lying fire. "Good afternoon, Mr. Keller. You may not remember me, but I want to introduce myself. We're members of the same church."

Haydn hid a smile behind his hand. The Old Man didn't know how to respond to this force of nature. "So you were the one making all that racket out there?"

Pink tinged Gladys's cheeks. "I apologize for the noise. I had hoped you might not hear me inside. I wanted it to be a surprise."

She shivered, and Haydn remembered how cold the living room had seemed when he first arrived. He added a couple of logs to the fire, and soon the flames leaped merrily. "I'll fix us some hot tea while the room warms up some."

Gladys nodded. "Thank you."

As she unbuttoned the top button of her coat, he started forward. "I'm sorry. Let me help you." He stood behind her, his arms easing behind her slim shoulders, ready to take the coat as it slid from her back. This close, she smelled like rosewater and cedar needles. Draping the coat over his arm, he pulled the chair closer to the fire. "Sit here by the fire until the room gets warmer."

She glanced at the man in the chair, huddled beneath a thick blanket. Noting her silent interest, Haydn scooted the Old Man's chair closer to the fire.

"What the fool do you think you're doing?"

"Putting your feet to the fire. Doesn't that feel better?"

Scowling, the Old Man stared at the fireplace. "It's a waste of good firewood, that fire is."

Yes, Mr. Scrooge. "We want our company to feel welcome, don't we?"

Gladys stared at her hands, folding and unfolding them in her lap. "Go ahead and fix the tea while Mr. Keller and I visit." She flashed a smile full of genuine warmth at Haydn, and he relaxed.

"Three cups of tea, coming up. I wish I could offer you some cookies, but all we have is a couple of slices of bread." He grinned.

Walking into the kitchen, Haydn questioned why he had offered tea instead of coffee. Maybe because tea seemed like the kind of thing he should offer a lady. Hot cocoa sounded even better on a cold day, but he didn't know how to make it, some slow process of heating milk and adding cocoa powder and sugar. He'd prefer coffee, but they only had the dregs of the pot from the morning.

He couldn't mess up boiling water and adding tea leaves. He opened the cabinets to the usual collection of blue enamelware but then changed his mind and headed instead for the china cabinet. If he was going to entertain a stranger, even one up to an unexplained errand on the front porch, he might as well do it in style. A silver tray nestled at the back of the china cabinet; he brought out three cups and saucers that looked like they hadn't been touched in a month of Sundays. He cleaned them with a dishrag, filled a sugar bowl, and poured fresh cream into a small pitcher.

While he waited for the water to boil, he listened to the quiet murmurs of conversation from the living room. Gladys spoke in a pleasant cadence, and the Old Man answered in short, one-word answers.

After the water came to a boil, Haydn poured it over the tea leaves in the pretty china teapot.

"I have a question of my own." A querulous voice broke the quiet murmurs. "What are you up to, disturbing my peace and doing all that hammering on my front porch?"

Chapter 2

The tray tilted in Haydn's hands, and he righted it. Waiters and hostesses might handle trays with a single deft hand, but he kept all ten fingers on this one. His host would never let him hear the end of it if he dropped any of the china. Through the open doorway, he watched the tableau unfolding before him. The Old Man had his hands on the arms of his chair, his face set in an angry mask.

Across from him, Gladys leaned forward, perfectly at ease in this awkward social situation. "Why, I'm obeying our Lord's command."

"Speak up, young lady. I can't hear you."

"I'm obeying our Lord's command." The girl spoke louder and slower, as if used to speaking to someone who was hard of hearing.

"Which one is that? The one that says to trouble a man in his own home?" The Old Man waved Haydn into the room. "Come on, young man. Stop hovering."

Haydn laid the tray on a small table with a marble top.

"Shall I?" Gladys reached for the teapot as if she was the hostess, ignoring the outburst. "What do you like in your tea, Mr. Keller?"

"A teaspoon of sugar."

She stirred in the sugar. "The command to love our neighbors as we love ourselves."

"You don't live next to me." He looked through the windows on either side of the parlor. "I would recognize you."

"No, I don't. How do you like your tea, Mr. Johnson?"

The Old Man looked up sharply at that, an appreciative gleam in his eyes. He covered his chuckle with a sip of tea.

"I'll take it black, please."

Handing the cup to Haydn, Gladys continued her explanation. "But everyone in Calico is my neighbor, don't you see? God brought you to my mind. I realized I don't know much about you except your name. And I thought I should remedy the situation."

"Busybody." The word came out under the Old Man's breath.

If Gladys heard him, she ignored him. After she fixed her own cup of tea, adding both sugar and cream, she leaned forward and chafed her hands together in front of the fire. "A fire cheers up a room, doesn't it?"

The temperature had risen a few degrees. The Old Man no longer looked so drawn. It was a surprise he hadn't come down with a cold before now. Haydn would keep the fire going after Gladys left.

"You still haven't explained all the hammering."

Gladys's face turned bright pink. So this question came closer to revealing her true purpose for showing up this morning. Haydn leaned forward, awaiting her answer.

"I had some bows left over from last Christmas that look

good against greenery." She dabbed at her mouth with a napkin. "From what I could see from the outside, you didn't have a Christmas tree. I thought some hanging baskets might cheer up the house."

The Old Man harrumphed. "Seems a waste to cut down a tree just so's to decorate a house for a couple of days a year."

"We each may celebrate the birth of our Lord in whatever way we wish, that is true. But I didn't notice you at church any time during December." She batted her eyelashes, making her stinging statement into innocence reborn.

"I don't have to go to church to know the Savior."

"That's true. But God wants us to love each other. It's hard to do that if we never see each other. That's why I'm here." Gladys smiled, having brought her argument full circle.

Haydn felt the indictment. He, who had good reason to love the Old Man, hadn't bothered to spend much time with him at all since he started college four years ago. This slip of a girl was practicing the heart of the law: to love the Lord God and to love one's neighbor as one's self.

She poured both men a second cup of tea before standing. "Now, with your permission, I will return to hanging the baskets." She slipped on her coat and headed outside.

"Well, go after her. Make her stop."

A smile sprang to Haydn's lips. "What, and stop her in her God-given mission in life? You have to admit, it's kind of sweet." He stood behind the curtain, watching Gladys move the precarious stepstool. Soon the banging of the hammer resumed.

"Sit down, why don't you," the Old Man said. "We haven't yet had that conversation I promised you."

"Very well, Grandfather." Haydn settled in his chair. "You do have some interesting neighbors."

"Sweet, I think you said." A calculating look brightened his dark brown eyes. "That's just as well, given the nature of my proposition to you."

Haydn arched an eyebrow. "I thought since I graduated from college, it was high time I came for a visit."

"Your father and I have been in communication. Believe it or not, we do write to each other."

Haydn did know. Something in the Old Man's most recent letter had scared his father enough to insist his only son come straight to Calico. Haydn leaned forward. "I'm here to help in any way I can, Grandfather."

"Humph." Grandfather's gnarled fingers tapped the arm of his chair. "It's more what I can do to help you. I understand you're interested in the newspaper business."

Haydn nodded. "I was the editor of my college paper my last two years at school. I've applied for an internship at the *Topeka Blade*. The editor who interviewed me said I have a good chance." That news had brightened Haydn's Christmas holidays considerably.

"What would you say if I told you that in spite of its amenities, one thing Calico sorely needs is a newspaper?"

Was the Old Man suggesting. . . ? It was out of character from what Haydn knew of him. "That's good news for someone who has capital to invest." He closed his mouth before he mentioned his financial constraints. From what his father had said, the Old Man believed each man should make his own fortune.

"Or someone who has an investor willing to back the enterprise." The words fell into a dead silence in the room.

Haydn slowly leaned forward, clenching his hands in his lap. "What do you mean?" He reached for a log, ready to add it to the fire.

"Don't do that. Can't waste good money."

Haydn tamped his impatience. The Old Man's idea of a warm room barely kept water from freezing. Why he wasn't sick remained a mystery, but they could talk about that later.

"Sit back and look me in the eye."

Haydn did as his grandfather requested, resting his hands on the arms of the chair while the silence lengthened.

At last his grandfather put on a pair of glasses he only used when he was reading his Bible. "There's a folder on top of my desk. Bring it out here."

Haydn walked down the hallway, growing chillier the farther he moved from the parlor. A single thick folder sat on top of his grandfather's desk, newsprint curling over the edges. He started to pull back the cover then decided against it. His grandfather had taken effort planning this surprise; Haydn wouldn't ruin it.

The Old Man gestured for Haydn to lay the folder on the end table by his arm. "They're all in there." He opened the folder and pulled out a piece of paper about a foot long and two inches wide—a newspaper article from the looks of it.

Grandfather peered over the top of his glasses then brought it in closer and read from it. TRENTON RUNS FOR TOWN COUNCIL.

The words sent a shiver of shock through Haydn. He had guessed that the file held his articles, but not that one. He had been so proud when his first piece appeared in his hometown paper when he was sixteen years old. He had been joyfully surprised when the *Topeka Blade* picked up the story.

"You weren't expecting that, were you?" The Old Man chuckled. "Your father sent everyone he knew a copy. He was so proud." He cleared his throat. "So, for that matter, was I. So I asked him to keep me apprised if you had anything else published. I have watched your burgeoning career with interest. You have a gift with words, my boy."

He paused, inviting Haydn to respond. But what could he say? "I didn't know. . .thank you."

"It seems that Calico's need and your talent intersect." The Old Man hammered his fist on the arm of the chair. "So, tell me, are you interested?"

Haydn drew in a deep breath. His dreams, handed to him on a silver platter. "Yes."

Grandfather's dark eyes so like his own glittered in the darkening room. "Since you are my heir, it is a fitting use of my capital."

Haydn hadn't thought he'd ever hear those words. "I would appreciate the opportunity, sir."

"Wait until you hear my conditions." The Old Man scowled. "It is only right for me to help you. Frankly, I'd like to see how you handle money. I had to earn mine the old-fashioned way."

Haydn had heard the same song when his father insisted Haydn pay for his own college education. "I've kept my books balanced while I worked my way through college, sir. Running a business can't be much more difficult than paying tuition and bills on a part-time salary."

"Perhaps." The Old Man grunted. He had left school after eighth grade and didn't hold much use for college education. "Be that as it may. I will help you launch a newspaper in Calico and give you twelve months to make it a profitable enterprise. But I do have one condition. One that is nonnegotiable."

The Old Man gazed at the fire's glowing embers. Haydn waited patiently, his mind awhirl with possible demands Grandfather might make of him. Starting with the fact that he would have to live in Calico to run a newspaper here.

"I'm not getting any younger, and I have regretted the distance separating me from my family since your father moved away. The newspaper would allow me to spend time with you, but I want more." The Old Man looked at Haydn, mirth dancing in his eyes. "I want to see your children before I die. My one requirement is for you to become engaged before my next birthday and to marry before year's end."

Of all the. . . Haydn's father had warned him the Old Man could be unreasonable and demanding, convinced he knew what was best for everyone. But surely Haydn's future wife was a matter between Haydn and God—and the young woman in question, of course.

Grandfather looked expectant. Haydn schooled his features not to reveal his shock at the demand.

"Are you courting anyone at the moment?" The Old Man managed to make it sound like a job interview.

"No." Haydn thought about the coeds who had caught his eye during college. None of them returned his interest, however. The debutantes his mother paraded for his inspection lacked intelligence or beauty or spunk. Haydn was in no rush to marry; he figured God had exactly the right person out there when the time came.

Gladys Polson's face floated through Haydn's mind. That one had plenty of spunk, climbing stepladders and hanging baskets on a near stranger's porch in the dead of winter. Her comments suggested both intelligence and spiritual hunger.

Don't be ridiculous. Only Grandfather's suggestion brought Gladys to mind.

"Well, what do you say to my proposition?"

Haydn stood and looked down at his grandfather's upturned face. "The price you demand for your gift is too high. I will marry if and when the right woman crosses my path."

"There's another thing." The Old Man continued as if he hadn't heard Haydn's refusal. "I'm not going to tell anyone that you are my grandson, and I don't want you to tell them either. I don't want any money-grubbers making eyes at you just because they think you'll get my money." Cackling, he settled back in his chair with a self-satisfied grunt.

What arrogance.

If only finding a wife was so simple.

Chapter 3

"You went inside the Keller mansion?" Annie asked as soon as she arrived at the Polsons' home.

Gladys groaned. "I might as well have announced my plans at church. I made so much noise hammering that everyone knew I was there. Why don't I think things through?"

They heard a soft knock on the door. Gladys opened the door to Ruth, Birdie standing behind her.

Gladys hadn't known whether Birdie would join their mission projects or not, but she rolled out the welcome mat for her guest. Birdie took her seat, placing a bag filled with yellow flowered calico beside her. Since she had left the Betwixt 'n' Between Saloon, she had taken up sewing to earn a living.

Gladys brought out a cup and plate and fixed Birdie a tea serving. Dressed in a quiet slate blue dress and with her hair pulled back in a simple bun, the former saloon girl looked much closer in age to herself than she had guessed. Gladys resolved to make her feel at home.

"I was just telling Annie about my disastrous attempt to meet up with Mr. Keller." Gladys took out her quilt block.

"I wouldn't call it disastrous." Ruth was hemming tea

towels. "You met Mr. Keller. That's more than any of us have ever done."

"And you met a handsome stranger." Annie wiggled her eyebrows. "A *young* handsome stranger."

"Haydn Johnson." The name tripped off Gladys's tongue in a single breath. "He was very kind."

Annie's knitting needles continued clacking together. She wanted to send more socks to her brother who was serving with the cavalry up in Wyoming. "He caught her when she fell off the stepladder. And he built up the fire—"

"Brrr, it was freezing in there. I'm surprised Mr. Keller hasn't caught cold." Gladys shivered.

"—and he fixed tea. A man serving tea!" Annie giggled.

"He sounds like quite a gentleman." Birdie took out a length of calico and began working on a seam.

"I doubt I'll see him again. I hope Mr. Keller doesn't slam the door in my face when I go back." Gladys tied off a quilt knot beneath the fabric.

"God led you to Mr. Keller for a reason. I'm sure He'll show you the way." Birdie spoke with a quiet faith.

"Thank you for that reminder. I'm not doing this all on my own, am I?"

"At least you've started. So far, God hasn't answered my prayers for guidance." Ruth flattened out the bottom of the towel and changed the thread in her needle to embroidery thread.

Conversation flowed back and forth while they continued work on their projects. Gladys finished her quilt block first.

"It's time for me to get to the diner for my shift. Is anyone in the mood for some of Aunt Kate's pie?"

"I've got to get home. Ma's expecting me." Annie finished her row and put away her knitting needles.

"I'll come with you." The upper half of a fancy *F* appeared on the tea towel Ruth was working on. "Birdie, would you care to join us?"

Birdie shook her head. "No, not this time, thank you."

Before they left, Gladys rinsed the dishes and slipped into her coat. Soon the four of them walked down the street, the ground beneath their feet the perfect firmness of a sunny winter day. At the corner, Gladys and Ruth bid good-bye to Annie and Birdie and headed for the town square. The Keller mansion was on the way.

"It looks very festive." As always, Ruth found something nice to say.

Gladys stared as they approached, trying to decide. "It looks half finished." As they neared the house, the front door opened, and Mr. Johnson stepped out.

Although Gladys immediately turned her attention aside, he bounded down the lawn to the street. "Miss Polson! How nice to see you again." He joined the two of them without asking permission.

Gladys slowed down. She couldn't outrun him. "Good day, Mr. Johnson." She managed a weak smile. "This is my friend Ruth Fairfield. She's our local schoolteacher."

"Nice to meet you." Mr. Johnson dipped his head to acknowledge the introduction before turning his attention back to Gladys. "I hoped you were returning to finish hanging the baskets. When you do, I want to help."

Gladys's cheeks grew warm enough that the cold air stung her heated skin. "I would love to. When would be a good time?"

"My—Mr. Keller is an early riser. Anytime during the day is fine."

"Are you staying with Mr. Keller, then, Mr. Johnson?" Ruth asked the question that was weighing on Gladys's mind.

"Yes." Haydn didn't offer a reason for his visit.

They reached Aunt Kate's diner. "This is our destination." Gladys paused, unsure if Mr. Johnson planned to join them.

He opened the door for the ladies and followed them inside. Gladys headed for the counter and draped an apron round her neck.

"Who is that tall drink of water?" Aunt Kate, Gladys's plump, pleasant relative, inquired while she exchanged her apron for a coat. "Is he someone you know?"

Rather than get into a lengthy explanation, Gladys simply said, "He's staying with Mr. Keller." Aunt Kate headed out the back door, and Gladys brought a copy of the menu to the table where Mr. Johnson had taken a seat with Ruth. They looked so cozy, she wished she could join them. But she helped at the diner to give Aunt Kate a break. The pocket change was welcome as well.

"What do you recommend?" Mr. Johnson lifted his eyes from the menu. "I wouldn't mind a meal. I've been fixing most of our food, and I'm not fond of my own cooking."

Gladys laughed. "You fix a good cup of tea, at least. I believe Aunt Kate has chicken and noodles left over from lunch."

"I'll take a bowl, then, with a slice of dried apple pie with sharp cheese."

After Gladys waited on the other customers in the diner, Mr. Johnson called her to the table. "Are you allowed to sit with the customers?"

"For you she'll make an exception," Aunt Kate said as she bustled back into the room. One of the friendliest souls in Calico, she would gladly encourage Mr. Johnson's acquaintance with Gladys. She refilled their coffee cups.

Gladys brought a cup of coffee for herself as well as food for Ruth and Haydn. She slipped onto a chair next to Ruth, across from Mr. Johnson.

Goodness, he was handsome. And to think she might never have met him if she hadn't decided to hang baskets on Mr. Keller's house.

❧

To think he would never have met these two lovely ladies if he had never come to visit the Old Man. Some good had come out of the journey, after all. With a shake of his head, Haydn chided himself. Thinking like that would put him right in his grandfather's clutches. Find the girl he wanted to marry, indeed, before the middle of April.

"Do you want anything else to eat?" The owner—Aunt Kate?—reappeared at their table.

Haydn couldn't help smiling. "Just the pie. My—Mr.

Keller doesn't keep many sweets in his house."

Aunt Kate retreated behind the counter.

"No wonder he's so thin." Miss Polson shook her head. She looked apologetically at Haydn. "His hands and fingers were so bony."

Haydn chuckled.

Miss Polson covered her mouth. "Oh, I'm sorry. I didn't mean any offense."

"None taken."

Aunt Kate returned with a slab of pie big enough to be a quarter of the whole. "Here you go, Mr. . . ."

"Johnson. Haydn Johnson." Haydn dug his fork into the tip of the pie and took a bite. "Mm, this is good. Is it possible to buy a whole pie that I can take back to Mr. Keller?"

Miss Polson's beam matched Aunt Kate's. Any woman he knew liked to have her cooking praised. She motioned for her aunt to lower her head, and she whispered into her ear.

"I have an extra peach pie today," Aunt Kate said. "I'll send it along with you. It's the neighborly thing to do."

Haydn shifted in his seat. He had concerns about his grandfather's health as well, but the old man had insisted he was fine, nothing worse than old age. "He might not be sick if I could convince him to keep the house warm."

Miss Polson shook her head in an exaggerated shiver. "I hope you didn't suffer any ill effects from your exposure to the cold yesterday," Haydn said.

Her cheeks grew pink. "Of course not." She sipped her coffee.

Miss Polson's curls spilled down her neck and dusted her cheek. She looked very different from her friend the schoolteacher. Even without their earlier introduction, he would have guessed Miss Fairfield's occupation by the precise bent of the tie around her neck and the exact fixture of her hair on top of her head.

The schoolteacher might know the answer to his question. Haydn thought it a good time to ask what was on his mind. "Is there a place in town where I can pick up a newspaper?"

Miss Polson curled her nose. "Calico doesn't have a paper of its own."

"But you can get the *Topeka Blade* at the mercantile," Miss Fairfield said.

Haydn relaxed. He hadn't realized how dependent he was on his regular dose of news until he'd landed in Calico. He might have to start a newspaper just to give himself something to read.

Miss Polson tapped her fingers on the table. "I believe the library carries the paper as well."

A library but no newspaper? Haydn raised an eyebrow. "I didn't realize Calico has a library."

"Yes." Miss Polson threw her shoulders back like a crow fixing to tell a story. "When Calico was settled, the founding mothers decided to put all their books together so they would have a larger pool of books to choose from. Now we pay a small fee if we want to join. It's the best library in the county."

Small-town pride. "Kansas would still not be much more

than a string of trading posts if it weren't for those founding mothers." Kansas actually had a good education system, and Haydn had enjoyed the coed education at the university.

Miss Polson nodded enthusiastically. "What is your occupation, Mr. Johnson?"

Haydn hid behind his last bite of pie while considering his answer. "I just finished my university education. I've been helping with the family firm back in Kansas City."

"So does your family conduct business with Mr. Keller?" she asked.

"Some." "Business" described the state of relations with his only grandfather better than "family." "My father authorized me to spend time here in Calico, to improve communication with Mr. Keller."

The bell above the door jangled, and several people came in. Miss Polson glanced around the rapidly filling diner. "Aunt Kate needs my help. It's been lovely to see you again, Mr. Johnson. Will there be a time when Mr. Keller isn't home? My presence seemed to upset him, but I'd like to finish what I started out to do." Her eyes pleaded with him.

Haydn opened his mouth to say yes before he thought about the true answer. "He almost never leaves the house." Haydn's fingers drummed the table. "But I've learned he usually takes a nap right after lunch. Can you come by then?"

"I'm working at the diner all day tomorrow, but I'll be finished after midday the next day. I can make it then."

A few minutes later, Aunt Kate came out with the peach pie tied up in a box. She refused payment. "Consider it my welcome present to you, Mr. Johnson. I hope we'll see you again soon."

Miss Fairfield excused herself, saying she had papers to grade from school, and Haydn headed back to the Old Man's house. The baskets of greenery welcomed his approach, although the porch looked half-dressed with baskets hanging on only one side of the steps. Gladys's colorful baskets would bring cheer to the cold house. But if she returned, the Old Man might decide Haydn took his condition to find a wife seriously.

Of the two of the women he had met today, Ruth Fairfield was much more what Haydn sought in a wife: a heart for children, well educated, soft spoken.

So why did his traitorous mind keep returning to Gladys Polson?

Chapter 4

After Gladys returned from work the next day, she started on a buttermilk pie.

Ma took out the rolling pin. "Who are you baking for? I planned on the leftover applesauce cake for a sweet tonight."

Gladys continued stirring the custard for the buttermilk pie. "It's for Mr. Keller."

Ma rolled out the pie dough. "For Mr. Keller—or for his guest?"

Gladys's cheeks warmed. "Mr. Johnson did say he liked having a slice of pie with his meals. But Mr. Keller doesn't keep any in the house." She poured the mixture into the waiting dish and slipped it in the oven. "I've got a basket ready. Do you mind if I add jars of honey and apple butter?" After she washed her hands, she joined her mother at the table.

Ma's laughter rang across the kitchen. "Of course not. They always say the way to a man's heart is through his stomach." She sniffed. "Something smells good. But it's not the pie. It smells like. . ." She turned back the cloth covering one of Gladys's baskets. "Needles from a cedar tree?"

Gladys took small squares of fabric out of the basket.

"His living room smells musty, like no one has opened any windows for years. I thought about making cedar sachets. He didn't have a Christmas tree, either." She held a sewing needle up to the window light and pushed a thin strand of green thread through the eye. "It's sad, really. That big house and no one to share it with." Except for the surprising Haydn Johnson.

"I think it's wonderful how you're reaching out to Mr. Keller. I've only seen him once or twice since his wife's death. I admit, he struck me as a grouchy sort."

"He wasn't that bad." Gladys ran small, even stitches down the sides of the fabric. She used a soup spoon to fill the small pouch with needles before cutting a length of cheery red ribbon to tie it closed. "One down, nine to go."

"Do you plan on redecorating the entire house?" Ma lifted the sachet to her nose. "Such a lovely scent. Can God smell things?"

Gladys was used to her mother's sometimes whimsical thought processes. Her mind ran through the five senses. "The Bible says He sees us. He hears us. We're told to 'taste and see that the Lord is good.' Jesus told Thomas to 'touch and see.' Smell, hmm, I remember something about prayers smelling like incense." She picked up the Bible Pa read from every evening and leafed through the book of Revelation. "Here it is. 'And another angel came and stood at the altar, having a golden censer; and there was given unto him much incense, that he should offer it with the prayers of all saints upon the golden altar which was before the throne.'"

Ma laid the sachet back in the basket. "Of course God was using words we could understand to explain things. I wish I could have been a fly on the wall at creation."

Gladys finished another sachet. "I want to finish these tonight. I told Haydn—Mr. Johnson, I mean—that I would come over tomorrow to finish hanging up the baskets."

"It's Haydn now, is it?" Ma's eyes twinkled. "I'll have to meet this young man. I've never seen you this interested in one of our local boys."

Gladys chewed her lip. "I'm doing it for Mr. Keller, Ma. But Ruth and I ran into Mr. Johnson at the diner. After I made such a nuisance of myself the last time I went to the house, I thought it was best to warn them of my visit."

Ma only nodded and smiled.

Gladys finished the last of the sachets after the evening meal. The pie was cooling on the window sill. When she finished, she cleared off the table. After she dressed for bed, she found Ma studying the contents of the baskets she had prepared. "Why don't you fix them some fried chicken while you're at it?"

Gladys's heart sped at the thought of fixing her special cinnamon chicken for the two bachelors at the Keller house. Then she caught herself. "I've done enough already. As far as I know, they have plenty to eat, even if they are basic dishes."

In the morning, Gladys checked the knot on the back of her head—no one wanted hair served with their food—and headed out the door. "I'll be back after lunch to pick up the food."

"I'll make sure the children leave the baskets alone," Ma called after her.

"Thanks, Ma." As Gladys headed for the diner, she hoped a brisk walk would clear her head of troublesome thoughts of Mr. Keller's young guest. Instead, her anticipation grew, hoping he might return to the diner while she was at work. *Shame on you, Gladys Polson.* She wanted to engage Mr. Keller, not his guest, with people.

Even though the walk didn't take care of her wayward thoughts, it did provide a nice break between the kitchen at home and the kitchen at work. She wasn't sure which she enjoyed more, cooking a good meal or sewing, especially quilting. Ma said Gladys was practicing for a whole passel of children someday. The only problem was she needed a husband first, and not one of the eligible young men in Calico had ever caught her fancy.

Her thoughts strayed again to Haydn Johnson. He interested her because he was someone new, that was all. A college graduate and city dweller wouldn't look twice at a small-town girl like her.

After lingering during the walk, she sped up to reach the diner on time. As she opened the door to the jingle of the bell, she spotted a familiar profile, head thrown back in laughter. She smiled at the sound.

Aunt Kate spotted her first. "Come over here and sit a spell." She winked. "Don't worry. It counts as work."

Since the diner was emptier than usual for this time of day, Gladys took advantage of the offer. "If anyone comes in,

I'll wait on them. Why don't you join us?"

"Don't mind if I do." Aunt Kate sat down with a *whomp*. "Mr. Johnson—"

"Haydn, please. And Miss Polson, please, call me Haydn also."

"And you may call me Gladys." *Haydn*. Gladys loved the way his name sounded. She noted with amusement that Haydn was eating the breakfast special. Did Mr. Keller only serve toast?

"It's lovely to see you again. I understand you have business with Mr. Keller. How long do you expect to be in town?" Aunt Kate asked.

Her aunt sounded like a cross between a busybody and a father interrogating a suitor, but Haydn didn't seem to mind. He pulled his attention away from the newspaper at his elbow. "Do you mind if I take this with me?"

"Of course not."

He folded the paper and tucked it beside his plate. "I expect to remain in town several weeks. We are discussing our arrangement."

"Norman always did like a good bargain. He was active in the community when he was younger." Aunt Kate nodded. "Don't look so surprised. Something happened with his son that created an estrangement between them. He took it hard, and then when his Minnie died, he took to staying by himself. It was sad. He turned away from the very people God intended to help him through hard times."

❧

The food lodged in Haydn's throat at Aunt Kate's statement. The only grandfather he had ever known was the aloof and forbidding Old Man, someone who seemed to have no interest in his only son and grandchildren. But perhaps the estrangement could be blamed on both sides. Haydn determined to start thinking of him as "Grandfather."

Coughing, Haydn swallowed some water. He took up another spoonful of stew and blew on it, pretending that the heat of the previous mouthful had caused his spasm.

"How is his health? Is he faring well?" Aunt Kate asked.

The grandfather Haydn knew wouldn't welcome that question, not even from his grandson.

Gladys said, "I confess I wondered the same thing. You will let us know, won't you, if he could ever use some help?" She smiled.

"He does have a bad cough. I asked him about sending for the doctor, but he refused."

Gladys exchanged a look with her aunt. "I'll fix chicken soup for him," Aunt Kate said.

Grandfather would throw the soup across the room if he learned that Haydn encouraged the people of Calico to intrude on his privacy. "That may not be such a good idea."

"I'll bring it with me when I come over this afternoon. He doesn't have to know where it came from." Gladys glowed with goodwill, and Haydn couldn't say no.

Aunt Kate snapped her fingers. "Even if he objects, maybe you can coax him to eat the soup. That will put some meat on his bones." She disappeared into the kitchen.

Gladys giggled as the door shut behind her. "If I know Aunt Kate, tomorrow she'll come to your place with two loaves of bread and a fresh crock of butter and claim she made too much."

"You're the one who showed up at the house ready to hang baskets. I guess helping others runs in the family."

"Whether they want it or not." She paused, sipping on her coffee. "I confess, I baked a pie to bring today. And I added jam for corn bread or biscuits." A pretty pink infused her cheeks. "I sensed you have a sweet tooth and don't get much to satisfy it."

"Bread and water, that's it." Haydn winked at her.

Mischief shone from her eyes. "You're making fun of me."

"No, I admire your reasoning. You were able to deduce my sweet tooth from only a few clues."

The kitchen doors swung open, and Aunt Kate appeared carrying a box. "Now, you can't refuse. It's only a small crock with hot stew in it."

A snicker escaped from Gladys. Haydn didn't dare look at her for fear he would break out laughing. "I'll have a hard time convincing him these are leftovers." He knew she would ignore his feeble protest.

"Nonsense. Mr. Keller knows I'd feed an entire cavalry if they stopped by. I love feeding a man with a good appetite."

The bell over the door jangled, and Gladys slid out from the booth. "It's the mayor. I'd better put my best foot forward."

❧

Haydn finished his food, but it didn't taste nearly as good without Gladys's company. Rather than going to the register, he calculated how much he owed for today's meal and left three times the amount—for today, yesterday's free meal, and the basket of food Kate had prepared. He would have left more if he thought he could get away with it. Tucking the box under his arm, he headed out before either Gladys or Kate could catch him.

Haydn stole home as quickly as he could and headed straight for the back door so he could leave the food in the kitchen.

"Haydn? Is that you?"

Haydn spun around at the sound of Grandfather's raspy voice. "Yes, Grandfather?"

"What's that?"

"I didn't finish all my food at the diner. Aunt Kate sent it home with me. Let me dish some out for you." Haydn's speech was rushed, but Grandfather didn't seem to notice.

"Kate, huh? That woman is never happy unless she's cooking for someone." Grandfather chuckled, as if he knew the cook well. He sniffed the bowl. "Beef stew. Smells good enough to make me hungry." He sat down and dug into the bowl, finishing quickly. "I'd like some more." His eyes brightened at Haydn's surprise. "I know the woman. I'm sure that crock is full."

Laughing, Haydn refilled his grandfather's bowl. "Do you want me to heat it up for you?"

"Nah." The word scraped the bottom of Grandfather's throat. He spooned more stew into his mouth. "Her stew is good even when it's cold."

Haydn sat down across from his grandfather. Questions

spun through his mind, ones he didn't know how to ask.

Grandfather took longer on the second bowl. Haydn pushed a piece of pie across the table. "Help me eat the pie she sent over yesterday."

Grandfather lifted the plate and stared at the filling. "This calls for some cream." His eyes gleamed with pleasure, and he went to the icebox. He brought out a small bottle of cream. "Betcha thought I didn't know where to find it."

"You sound like you've had her pie before."

Grandfather set down his fork. "She kept the house going when your grandmother was sick." The bleak expression on his face told Haydn not to intrude on his memories. Sure enough, he changed the subject. "Keep going to the diner. That place is gossip central. A good place for a newspaperman to pick up on local news."

Haydn hadn't accepted his grandfather's offer to start a newspaper—yet. But it wouldn't hurt to learn more about the town. Gladys had occupied so much of Haydn's attention that he hadn't noticed much happening around him. The next time he returned, he would have to open his eyes and ears.

Grandfather began to cough in midbite, spitting out crumbs of pie in the process. He gestured wildly. Haydn poured him a glass of water, and he gulped it down. "More." The word came out as a croak. Haydn emptied the pitcher before the coughs subsided.

Grandfather pushed away the plate, the slice of pie half-eaten. "That teaches me to accept handouts."

"You can't blame your cold on the stew." Haydn bit his

tongue to keep from saying any more. If Grandfather got worse, he would send for a doctor. For now, he heated water. Tea with honey and lemon should help.

Grandfather scowled. "Maybe not. But it didn't make it any better either."

Chapter 5

Confidence bolstered Gladys as she prepared for her second visit to the Keller mansion. Knowing that Mr. Keller was probably resting and that she had an ally in Haydn made the afternoon's task less like a siege and more like a social call.

"I've used all the baskets. I need to get some more with my next pay." The only basket left in the pantry was the one Ma used for summer picnics.

Ma waved away her concern. "Go ahead and use the picnic basket, I can get another one before summer. Now get the sachets out of here before our lunch smells like cedar."

Laughing, Gladys carried the first two baskets to the wagon. As she packed them in, Haydn came up behind her. "I thought you might need help carrying your pretty baskets, but I see you have it all organized."

"You can help me bring things out from the kitchen." She walked with a light step as Haydn held the door open for her.

Ma greeted Haydn with a bright smile. "You must be Mr. Johnson."

"And you must be Gladys's sister."

Ma colored prettily at that bit of flattery. "That's kind

of you to say, Mr. Johnson, even if it is a bit of foolishness. Gladys is our eldest."

Gladys handed Haydn the heavier baskets with glass jars and then lifted more greenery baskets.

"You'll have to come for dinner one night while you're in town. You and Mr. Keller must take a break from your business discussions from time to time. Can you make it Saturday evening? Or perhaps Sunday after church?"

Ma was clever to give Haydn a couple of choices and make it harder for him to say no.

But then Gladys had another thought, and her face grew warm. With such an impromptu invitation, Haydn might feel like they viewed him as a potential suitor.

But Haydn took the offer in stride. "Provided it's acceptable to Mr. Keller, I'll come over after church." Tipping his hat, he took the baskets outside, and Gladys followed him.

Haydn placed his baskets in the wagon then helped Gladys with hers. After they finished loading the wagon, and as she lifted her leg to get up, he slipped his arms around her and whisked her onto the passenger's seat. Never before had her spine tingled at the courteous gesture in all the times Pa had done the exact same thing.

By the time the momentary surprise had passed, Hayden had swung onto the driver's seat. "Are you ready?"

At her nod, he snapped the reins over the horse's head.

During the short ride to the mansion, Gladys glanced at Haydn's profile out of the corner of her eye. Brown hair streaked with lighter colors, strong, handsome, clean cut—a man who would look right at home in a city. She couldn't imagine him settling down in a small town the size of Calico.

Where had that thought come from? Haydn had no intention of staying in Calico. As soon as he finished his business with Mr. Keller, he would leave. She mustn't expect any romance from that corner.

Her spirits sank at that thought, but there was no reason she couldn't enjoy an afternoon in his company. He rushed, however. When she dawdled with every basket, he sped up, and they finished the project faster than Gladys thought possible.

Haydn dusted his hands on his Levis, flecks of snow melting on the denim. "After all that work, we've earned a warm beverage, don't you agree?" He opened the door and swept her inside before she could say no.

He settled her in the front parlor before heading to the kitchen. When she rose out of the chair to follow, he shook a finger at her. "You are not to help me. This kitchen is a man's domain." He smiled his devastating smile and disappeared.

Gladys took advantage of the reprieve to explore. Tinkling noises confirmed Haydn's presence in the kitchen, and she scooted out of her chair. The personality of the parlor should reveal something about its owner. She almost hoped Mr. Keller would wake up so they could visit some more. Their verbal sparring had given her pleasure, and she suspected Mr. Keller enjoyed it as well. Besides, he was the man God called her to reach with His love, not his more-than-amiable guest.

The room was considerably warmer than it had been on her

last visit, thanks to the cheery fire in the grate. Mr. Keller's wife had probably provided the homey touches. Two samplers took pride of place on one wall. In addition to a wedding design, a birth sampler included a verse about the blessing of a quiver full of children. Maybe they had hoped for a large family. As far as Gladys knew, the Kellers only had the one child. And he had moved away before his mother had died. No wonder Mr. Keller seemed so sad, angry even.

More surprising than the samplers was the collection of whittled creatures on the mantel. Birds and rabbits, a train car or two. She ran her hands over the smooth wood, thinking how much her little brother would enjoy them.

"I used to play with those when I was little." Haydn had returned with a tea tray.

Gladys swiveled, embarrassed at being caught snooping. "You were here as a child?" She wondered about the exact nature of the business between the two families. The question was hovering on the tip of her tongue when one of the rabbits fell on the floor with a clattering sound. Swooping down to pick it up, she discovered a tiny piece of his ear was broken off.

"So it's you back here, bothering my peace and quiet."

Mr. Keller stood at the bottom of the stairs, one hand on the railing, the other on a sturdy walnut walking cane. In his brown-eyed glare, humor gleamed. But Gladys couldn't return his banter. She felt like a naughty child, holding the mutilated rabbit behind her back.

"Caught!" Smiling, Haydn reached for the creature she was holding. "Are you worried about that little broken place?

I did that when I was a boy."

"That he did," Mr. Keller grumbled. "He threw those things every which way and that. I made a bunch more of them, but those are the sturdy ones that survived a boy's hard play." He crossed the room, his cane tapping the floor. He took the rabbit from Haydn and examined it before setting it back in its place on the shelf. "Silly thing for me to spend my time on."

After that brief glimpse into a happier time, Mr. Keller sat down. As he pulled a blanket over his lap, a cough seized him, knocking the cover to the floor. Gladys and Haydn sprang forward at the same time, their hands brushing. Haydn draped the blanket over the older man's shoulders while Gladys poured a cup of tea and added enough cream to cool it. She held it to Mr. Keller's lips. "Drink this. It should help."

He slowly drained the cup, and the coughing subsided. She glanced at Haydn, worry written on her features.

"Mr. Keller, you really need to see a doctor."

Haydn read the signs of the coming explosion even as his grandfather coughed into his handkerchief. "Nonsense. Just because my—Mr. Johnson—has brought you into my house, doesn't give you the right to tell me what to do."

"She's right, you know." Later, when the Old Man had settled down, Haydn would slip out and ask a doctor's advice. For now, all he could do was sit and watch. And pray.

Gladys fixed a second cup of tea. "Did you add any honey? It always helps me when my throat hurts." When Haydn shook his head, Gladys held the cup for Mr. Keller to drink.

The Old Man brushed it away. "I'm not so helpless that I can't feed myself. Why don't you leave a man alone to enjoy his privacy?"

"You know better than to treat a lady that way," Haydn said. Every unkind word Grandfather spoke diminished his chances of seeing Gladys again. Even if Haydn met someone he might marry and he chose to remain in Calico, who would want to stay around a man who could change his mood at the drop of a hat?

Grandfather rose out of his chair, shaking his cane at Gladys. "And don't bother coming back."

With a final desperate look at Haydn, Gladys stumbled toward the door.

Haydn dashed across the floor in two giant steps and held her cloak for her. Leaning close enough to whisper, he said, "I would still like to join you for Sunday dinner. If that is acceptable after today. I'll bring the dishes Aunt Kate sent over. You might not believe it, but he ate every bite of the stew."

She nodded. "Get him to see a doctor if you can, will you?"

He opened the door for her. "I'll let you know on Sunday. I'm so sorry things turned out this way today." He helped her in the wagon and watched her drive away, disappearing down the street. Her departure leached some of the color from the brightly colored baskets hanging on the porch.

"Shut the door, boy, before you let all the heat out."

All the warmth had fled the room with Grandfather's

outburst, but Haydn did as requested. He crossed the room and climbed the stairs.

When Grandfather coughed this time, it sounded forced, a plea for sympathy. Haydn made himself turn around and return to the living room. Grandfather picked up his teacup. "Get me some honey, will you? You'll find it behind the jams on the shelf underneath the counter at the back of the pantry."

Haydn smelled the chicken soup he had left steaming on the stove. Bless Aunt Kate. This was perfect for Grandfather. Deciding to risk his anger, Haydn dished out a deep bowl and brought it out on a tray along with the honey.

"Here's the honey. And something extra you don't deserve, not after the way you treated Gladys today." He opened the jar of honey and poured a bit into Grandfather's tea.

"Tea with milk tastes like child's pabulum." In spite of his complaint, Grandfather drank it. "I suppose Kate sent over the soup. She seems to think she can cure every ill in the world with some chicken soup."

"A lot of women agree with her. Including my mother." Haydn itched to get away, to go upstairs, but he made himself wait. This was a time to prove Paul's statement that "love is patient, love is kind" and to continue helping when everything in him wanted to run.

The heated red of Grandfather's cheeks subsided, and he didn't cough again while he downed the bowl of soup. Neither one of them spoke until he finished.

Now that the immediate danger had passed, Haydn spoke his mind. "I'm ashamed of you, for the way you treated Gladys.

All she's done is offer friendship, and you attacked her."

Grandfather threw back his head and laughed. "That's the spirit."

Haydn stared.

"I was waiting for you to show some backbone, something to light your fire about that young thing. I guess I did it, didn't I?"

It was Haydn's turn to frown. "You frightened her so bad, she may never return."

"No worry about that." Grandfather chased a final chunk of chicken around his bowl. "She's too much like Kate to give up easy." He placed the bowl back on the tray. "When are you seeing her again?"

"Sunday. Her mother invited me to join them for dinner."

"Excellent." Grandfather rubbed his hands together. "Time to meet the family."

❧

The remainder of the week passed quietly enough. Occasionally Grandfather's coughing woke both of them up in the middle of the night. Haydn had taken to leaving a mug of tea with milk and honey on Grandfather's dressing table when he went to bed. Downstairs, hot water simmered in a teapot over low heat for the night, in case he needed more. If he needed help, he had a bell he could ring to call Haydn. He didn't get any worse, and although he didn't get any better either, Haydn decided the doctor could wait for now.

Grandfather shooed him away earlier than usual on Saturday night. "Stop fussing over me like an old mother hen. I've got my bell here if I need help." He picked it up and shook it. "If you want to make a good impression on Gladys's father, you'll put on your best suit to go along with your fresh haircut. If you want to get her mother on your side, you'll praise her cooking, even if it's charred, and her wonderful children, even if they run on top of the tables."

Haydn had to smile at that. He'd never cared enough about a woman to worry about what impression he made on her family. But Gladys, she just might be different.

Haydn didn't know how Grandfather had guessed about his trip to the barbershop. His mustache was trimmed about a quarter of an inch, the hair at the back of his neck shaved, the irksome cowlick at the top of head cut short and tamed with pomade. Would it be obvious to Gladys as well? He shook the thought away. No need to dwell on it. Every man got his hair cut sooner or later.

The season kept Haydn from taking flowers to offer his hostess, so instead he'd stopped by Finnegan's Mercantile and asked the owner for any candies he carried. As he paid for the candy, he spotted a silver hair comb that had ruby-colored stones set in the handle. On an impulse, he added that to the purchase. He could imagine it holding Gladys's dark curls in place.

Sticking the items in his pocket the next morning as he prepared for church, Haydn debated the wisdom of giving Gladys the comb. He might as well ask her father for permission to court his daughter if he gave her such a personal gift. Despite Grandfather's conditional promise to fund the newspaper, or maybe because of it, Haydn wasn't ready to commit to courtship.

When he saw Gladys enter the sanctuary in the company of Ruth and two other women he hadn't met before, her hair sparkled in the light. He wanted to rush over and give the comb to her right then and there. The girls disappeared into the cloakroom before he caught up with them, and he caught himself. He waited, ready to greet Gladys as they came out.

"—since he's so rich."

Haydn thought it was the blond who said that. "Oh, Mr. Keller is rich enough to buy himself ten carriages if he wanted to," Gladys said.

The words hit Haydn like a slab of ice, and he stumbled away. Maybe Gladys Polson was nothing but a money-hungry schemer after all.

Chapter 6

Gladys wasn't sure what she had said about Haydn that got her brothers so excited.

The youngest, Georgie, in his first year at school, couldn't wait to play trains with their guest. On Sunday morning he was pushing two small blocks of wood across the floor. "Choo-choo, chugga, chugga. Do you think Mr. Johnson will bring his caboose with him?" He had latched onto Gladys's mention of the carved toys.

"I don't think so. They belong to Mr. Keller, not Mr. Johnson."

Georgie shrugged. "I bet he'll play with me. I'll ask."

Whether he would or wouldn't, Gladys didn't know. "Maybe. Now put those away and stand up before you get your Sunday clothes dirty."

"He won't want to play trains with you," Glenda, the youngest girl in the family, huffed. "He's going to come outside and throw snowballs with us."

Gordon, Glenda's twin, told Georgie, "You can play with us if you want to."

"Why do you all think he's going to play with you?" Gladys asked. "Maybe Ma invited him so she and Pa could visit with him."

"They're all excited about meeting him because you haven't stopped talking about him." Grace, closest to Gladys in age at fifteen, grinned. "You start every other sentence with 'Haydn.' 'Haydn caught me when I fell off the ladder,' and 'Haydn helped me hang the baskets.' Ma only invited him so you could see him again."

After that too-close-to-home statement, Gladys didn't ask any more questions. When she'd left the Keller mansion a few days ago, she could have sworn Haydn was every bit as upset as she was at Mr. Keller's outburst. The way he asked if he was still welcome in their house had warmed her heart. His question hinted that he was eager to see her again, even to spend time with her family.

If she'd thought her family was bad, the sewing circle was even worse. Annie wormed the story of Gladys's last visit out of her in less than fifteen minutes.

"He's sounds mean as an ogre. I wouldn't go back." Annie shook her pretty blond curls.

"That's what I thought at first." Gladys struggled to put her thoughts into words.

"But God called you to love Mr. Keller, even when he's grouchy and mean?" Ruth guessed.

Gladys squirmed uncomfortably and stopped stitching for a moment. "Something like that. Only I don't know what to do next."

"Ask Mr. Johnson if Mr. Keller ate the soup you brought to him. Maybe you can bring more over," Ruth said. "Isn't there a verse in the Bible that talks about heaping coals of fire on your enemy's head? Not that Mr. Keller is your enemy."

"That's a good idea. I'll ask Haydn tomorrow."

That statement started the speculation all over again.

Gladys hoped her friends had worked the teasing out of their systems at their Saturday meeting. But on Sunday, when they all arrived at church about the same time, Annie started in again.

"It's a pity that Mr. Keller is so unhappy, since he's so rich."

"Oh, Mr. Keller is rich enough to buy himself ten carriages if he wanted to." Gladys fingered the lace on her collar and wondered why she had gone to so much trouble. "But money hasn't made him happy."

When they left the cloakroom, Gladys spotted Haydn across the sanctuary, and a smile leaped to her face. She lifted her hand to wave, but he didn't acknowledge her presence in any way. She wondered if he had forgotten about the invitation.

Ma came up beside her. "Don't worry, Gladys."

How mothers sensed these things was beyond Gladys.

"I'll remind Mr. Johnson of our invitation." Ma made her way through the crowd like a cat weaving its way through a maze of feet. Gladys couldn't see over the tops of heads well enough to see what happened, but he joined them at their house after the service.

But something was wrong. The ease that had fueled conversation between the two of them disappeared, and their words fell into uncomfortable gaps at the dinner table.

Haydn covered it well. He talked with Georgie about all

kinds of train cars, from engines to hoppers to the little red caboose.

"Can you whittle one for me, Mr. Johnson?"

"Not me." Haydn smiled. "Mr. Keller made those for me. I'm not any good at it."

"Then you can come outside and throw snowballs with us." Gordon sounded like Haydn's visit was for his special benefit.

"I will if your mother doesn't mind." The two of them discussed strategy, whether to use loose or hard-packed snow to throw.

Grace didn't say much to their guest, blushing whenever he glanced in her direction.

With Pa, Haydn discussed the finer points of Pastor Fairfield's sermon, taken from the love chapter in 1 Corinthians. "I try to love my wife like that. The way Christ loved the church." Pa pointed a fork at Haydn. "That's what I will expect from the men who marry my daughters."

Gladys could have sunk through the floor at that statement. What would Haydn think?

Haydn gave her a passing smile. "I don't blame you, sir." He didn't say anything to suggest he had any intentions toward Gladys at all.

The boys more than made up for Haydn's lack of interest in her, monopolizing his time from the moment they finished eating.

"Go ahead and talk with our guest." Ma tried to shoo Gladys out of the kitchen.

"I can't." Gladys pointed out the window. "He's out there playing with the boys already." Touching her collar again, she thought of the extra minutes she had spent on dressing this morning. Waste of time, as it turned out.

About the time Georgie tired of the game and stomped his boots at the door to shake off the snow, Pa met Haydn at the door and led him to the barn. Gladys took her time drying the dishes, her glance darting to the window more times than she wanted to admit.

When the two men exited the barn, Haydn headed down the street without returning to say good-bye to Gladys or her mother. Gladys stayed rooted to the spot until Pa came in.

At a single shake of his head, Gladys ran up to her room, holding back her tears until she could sob into her pillows.

✒

When Haydn first overheard Gladys's comment, he decided to excuse himself from his visit to the Polson house. But faced with Mrs. Polson's friendly insistence and Gladys's hopeful face, he'd felt helpless to refuse. Maybe he had heard Gladys's words out of context.

Unwilling to risk his heart, he sat as far as possible from Gladys at the dinner table. He spoke to her only when he had to. He never expected her to be money hungry, but Grandfather's warning had turned out to be prophetic.

In spite of his resolution to keep his distance, Haydn couldn't help being drawn to the family. Who could resist little Georgie, who clung to his arm and sent snowballs across the yard with great abandon and bad aim? Or young Gordon, eager to prove his coming manhood? Even the two girls, Grace and Glenda, had charmed him with their blushes and giggles. They were the kind of younger sisters Haydn wished he had.

Not a one of them seemed curious about how much money he had or didn't have. As Haydn whisked the boys back into the house to dry off before they got too cold, Mr. Polson appeared. "Care to join me, Mr. Johnson?"

Although phrased as a question, the gleam in Gladys's father's eye told Haydn he'd better not refuse. Inside the barn, Haydn's horse neighed a greeting, and Haydn stroked its nose.

After Mr. Polson's comments about loving his wife as much as Christ had loved the church, Haydn could guess what was coming. What timing. The first time a father took him aside to ask, "What are your intentions toward my daughter?" happened within days after Grandfather laid down the stipulation that Haydn marry before year's end.

Gladys's father took his time getting around to the point. At last he took a seat on a bale of hay and gestured for Haydn to join him. "When I was courting my wife, I was a bundle of nerves. I never imagined what it was like for her father. Now I think it's even worse." He smiled. "Gladys is our eldest, my firstborn. I love all my children, but for three years, until Grace was born, we poured all our love and energy into Gladys. So if anyone were to hurt her in any way. . ." He left the sentence dangling.

Haydn gulped. What had Gladys said to give her father reason to think he was courting her? All he had felt was a passing interest, a curiosity, no more, a feeling born of proximity and new surroundings and his grandfather's impossible demand.

Mr. Polson continued. "I also want to be sure my daughter and any children she may have will be taken care of. What kind of business are you in, Johnson? Do you have the means to support a family?"

Money, again. Haydn's heart dropped. Even if it didn't matter to Gladys, it did to her father. Maybe she felt compelled to marry money.

"I'm afraid there's been a misunderstanding, sir." Haydn used all the skills he had picked up in elocution class at the university. "Gladys is a fine woman, but all that lies between us is a joint interest in making life better for Mr. Keller."

Mr. Polson frowned. "I had the impression, from what my wife said. . . More than that, I've seen the way Gladys looks when she mentions your name. I've never seen her like that, and there have been several young men who've come calling."

The conversation had taken an awkward turn. Haydn offered an olive branch. "I have, however, enjoyed working with Miss Polson to get Mr. Keller involved with the community again. He has shut himself away from people for too long." He paused, wondering how much he could say without revealing too much. "I don't know how much your daughter has told you about her last visit. After she left, Mr. Keller expressed regret over his harsh words." That wasn't exactly true, but Grandfather hoped for something to develop between Haydn and Gladys. "Please tell her that she is welcome at the house anytime."

Mr. Polson stood, brushing off his pants, his back straight, as if relieved of a heavy burden. "You may stay and tell her yourself." His eyes were at peace again. Did the man think Haydn was courting Gladys after all? Wasn't he listening?

Haydn didn't want to talk with Gladys privately where she could read the doubt in his eyes. "Mr. Keller is awaiting me. In fact, I told him I expected to return before this. Please tell Mrs. Polson how much I appreciated the wonderful meal."

When Mr. Polson opened the barn door, only gray light greeted them. "It looks like it's going to snow," he said.

The temperature had plummeted, turning the afternoon much colder than the morning. The first flakes of snow fell as Haydn returned home. His mind sped across the contents of their pantry. Even without more of Aunt Kate's food, they had plenty to last for several days.

At the house, Grandfather was chopping wood. What was he thinking? Haydn hustled down the side path, but Grandfather disappeared before he reached the woodpile. He filled his arms with logs and headed for the house. During the short walk home, the fury of the snowfall had increased. Haydn shivered inside his thick coat.

Grandfather reappeared with a wheelbarrow. "What are you carrying all that wood for? Put it in here with the rest of what I chopped." He grabbed the top logs from Haydn's arms and dropped them in the wheelbarrow, glaring at Haydn.

"I'll get them inside. You go on in before you get cold." Haydn glared back.

"I'll have you know I've been cutting my own wood since before you were a speck in your father's eye." Grandfather's chin jutted out. He tossed two more logs onto the wheelbarrow before he grabbed his arm in pain. As he doubled over, his breath wheezing, he began coughing. Haydn dropped the wood he was holding into the wheelbarrow and put his arm around Grandfather's shoulders, helping him into the house.

Chapter 7

On Tuesday morning Gladys awakened to a white world with a shining blue sky. Snow covered the limbs of trees and the ground, in spite of Pa's attempts to keep the path to the barn clear.

With the blizzard's onslaught coming on the heels of Haydn's Sunday visit, Gladys hadn't had a moment's peace to herself to think about her conversation with Pa on Sunday night.

He had evaded Gladys after Haydn left until the children went to bed. In the quiet, she sought him out in his refuge, his study. Standing in front of his desk, she asked, "What did you and Haydn talk about for so long out in the barn?"

"Now, Gladys, don't jump to any conclusions."

A quiet knock on the door interrupted them, and Ma came in.

"I'd like to hear what you have to say." She took a seat. "And Gladys. Pull up a chair and talk like a sensible young woman." Once everyone was situated to her satisfaction, she settled back in her chair. "Now, Herbert."

"Did you ask him what his intentions toward me are?" Gladys spoke crisply.

"Not in so many words." Pa squirmed a bit. "I think he felt threatened when I warned him not to do anything to hurt you. And I asked him if he had enough money to support a family."

Taken aback, Gladys almost laughed. Of course Haydn had work. He had come to Calico to conduct business with Mr. Keller.

"Gladys," Ma said. "You've wandered away from us."

Blinking, Gladys brought her thoughts back to the conversation. "What was Haydn's answer?"

Pa cleared his throat. "I don't want to disappoint you."

"Stop beating about the bush." Ma's voice held firm, but her hand cushioned Gladys's in its grip.

"He said he had no interest in you in that way. That what brings the two of you together is your desire to bring Mr. Keller out of his solitude."

Gladys had come to the same conclusion about their relationship. So why did it hurt to hear the truth come from her father's lips? "He's right, you know." She squeezed Ma's hand.

Ma's gaze pinned Gladys, daring her to speak the truth. "If you say so, Gladys. I will confess"—she cast one of "those" looks at Pa, the kind that always reassured Gladys that her parents loved each other and everything was all right with the world—"the way you look at Haydn when you think no one is watching reminds me of the way I used to look at your Pa when we were courting."

Shame flamed heat into Gladys's cheeks. "You're the ones

who taught me there's a difference between wishing and the truth." Not wanting to say any more on that topic, she added, "But I do believe God has more for me to do with Mr. Keller."

"Then all is well." Pa looked as relieved as a dog who escaped a scolding after licking his master's face. "That is exactly what Mr. Johnson proposed: that the two of you continue to partner in your work with Mr. Keller."

As always, Ma knew all was not well with Gladys. She kept the younger children out of her way as much as she could with the seven of them housebound. Gladys didn't know if she could take another day inside. Now, with the storm ended, she determined to get to the diner, even if she had to shovel the path herself. She donned several layers before she walked to the kitchen. Ma was already there, stirring up eggs and oatmeal. "You'd better eat a hot breakfast before you go out in this cold."

At least Ma didn't argue with Gladys about heading to work today. Even though Gladys's insides felt like burning fire, she wouldn't refuse the food. She added a bit of butter and milk and honey and cinnamon to the oatmeal and took a spoonful. Delicious, soothing, especially with the light-as-air eggs that were even better than the ones Aunt Kate cooked at the diner. The warm coffee finished the job. "Thank you, Ma. For everything." She threw her arms around her mother and hugged her. "You knew I'd head to work today." She buttoned up her coat.

"Of course." Ma grinned. "You have to get more soup for Mr. Keller."

Haydn hadn't slept much since Saturday night. After Grandfather's foolish hours spent chopping wood outside, he had turned really and truly sick. Haydn had never experienced a storm quite like this. Wind and snow blew so hard, a person could get lost walking from his house to the barn and back. With Grandfather so ill, Haydn did what he could and prayed for the best until the storm ended.

Dozing in the chair beside his grandfather's bed, Haydn woke with a start in the middle of the night. Peering through the snow crystals on the window, he saw that the storm had stopped. Grandfather's breathing had eased. As long as he was resting, Haydn would take advantage of the opportunity to clear a path to the street. Grandfather needed a doctor, although Haydn felt uncomfortable leaving him alone in the house for the time it would take to fetch one.

Haydn grabbed a shovel from the mudroom and opened the front door. The snow had drifted higher on the porch than he expected, in spite of the protection of the overhang. He stayed in the doorway only long enough to clear a place to stand then he shut the door behind him, trapping the heat inside. Soon enough the effort he expended left him warm, and he worked with a will.

When he left the porch, the snow reached Haydn's knees, and moonshine sparkled on the diamondlike surface. He continued until the first rays of the sun reminded him of the passage of time. As much as he wanted to finish the job, he needed to check on his grandfather. He tramped up the steps and opened the door, carrying his boots and snow-soaked garments to the adjacent mudroom.

Haydn added another log to the fire. The extra wood Grandfather had chopped had come in handy after all. Upstairs, the Old Man slept so peacefully that Haydn put his head to his chest to make sure he was still breathing. Pioneers lived like this all the time, with no medical help available except what they could do for themselves, locked up in a single-room hovel with no way to reach the outside world.

Haydn's experience hadn't prepared him for this kind of isolation. He didn't mind taking care of Grandfather or clearing the path, but he couldn't do both at once. Padding down the stairs to the kitchen, he scraped the last of Aunt Kate's chicken soup into a bowl. They'd reached the end of the food she had provided. He'd have to cook their next meal, maybe sausage gravy and biscuits.

Grandfather managed to eat the small amount of soup and drink a few sips of tea before he slipped back into sleep. His breathing rasped, and he felt hot to the touch. Thrashing, he threw his quilts on the floor. Every time Haydn replaced them, he flung them down again.

Haydn didn't know if he should keep Grandfather covered or allow him to cool down, without the quilts. The front parlor seemed like a good solution. With the fire, Grandfather would stay warm even if he kicked off every cover. Haydn placed one arm under the Old Man's neck and another under his knees. Amazing how insubstantial his grandfather felt in his arms, his body emaciated by illness. He picked his way down the stairs and laid Grandfather on the couch. Plumping the pillow under his head and covering him with a quilt, Haydn looked into his face. Seen like this, the man inspired pity and even love. He had lived and loved and survived.

If Haydn wanted to please his oldest living relative, he was supposed to find a wife within the next two months. So far the only women of marriageable age he had met in Calico were all members of Gladys's sewing circle. The ones who gossiped about Grandfather's money. "Lord, what am I supposed to do? Are you going to send a bride my way by special delivery on a train?"

Grandfather grunted at that, and Haydn rushed to his side. "What is it?"

Grandfather opened those dark eyes, clear for the first time since his collapse. "God will provide." His eyes drifted shut, and Haydn almost thought he had imagined those few words.

❧

Because of checking on Grandfather so often, Haydn scorched his oatmeal. Bringing a big bowl out to the parlor, he ate it quickly and set it to one side. The family Bible sat on a nearby shelf, and he reached for it. With interest, he read the family record: his grandparents' marriage, his father's birth, the birth and death of a younger sister, his parents' marriage, his own birth as well as his younger brother's.

Of his grandmother's death, no record had been made. Looking at the flowing script, Haydn wondered if she had kept the records up to that point. He found no mention of his youngest brother, born twelve years ago. Haydn found writing materials in the study. No one else was available to bring the family record up to date. He added Grandmother's name but laid down the pen when he couldn't recall the exact date of her death. Maybe he could find it on her gravestone. After adding his brother's birth date, his eyes drifted to the page set apart to record marriages. With only two entries, the blank lines called to him. Whose name would be joined with his?

Haydn turned to the gospel of Mark, hoping Mark's active writing style, rather like the way he wrote for the newspaper, would hold his interest. But before he could even finish the account of John the Baptist preaching in the wilderness, the Bible dropped into his lap and he fell asleep.

Loud knocking awakened Haydn, and a familiar voice called, "Mr. Keller? Haydn?"

Gladys. How had she made her way to his doorstep through the snow?

❦

Gladys held Aunt Kate's basket on her arm. The unrelenting freeze continued even without wind-whipped snow driving icy pellets into her face. Pastor Fairfield was with her. He had rallied the men who made it to the diner to sweep through the town, stopping at every house not yet dug out from the storm. Gladys came with him as far as the Keller mansion, wanting to deliver food.

"Just a minute." Haydn called to them through the door. A light wind had scattered a thin blanket of snow over the porch boards she assumed Haydn had shoveled. She shivered and hoped he had convinced Mr. Keller to keep the front room warm. The doorknob rattled, and the door swung open with a welcome whoosh of warm air. "Gladys, Pastor Fairfield. Come in. What brings you out on such a cold day?"

"We're checking all the houses that haven't dug out from the snow yet," Pastor Fairfield said. "I see you started but didn't have a chance to finish."

"And I brought you some soup." Gladys pointed to the basket on her arm. She glanced into the parlor, where she could see Mr. Keller stretched out under a quilt. "Is Mr. Keller ill?"

"Yes." Haydn conveyed a lot of emotion with that one word. "What about the doctor? Is he available?"

Pastor Fairfield nodded. "He was one of the men at the diner whom we recruited to go door-to-door. I'll hunt him down and tell him he's needed over here." He patted the top of his hat. "I'll move on, then. Are you able to see yourself home, Miss Polson?" He shook Haydn's hand. "I'll ask my wife to come by later to see if you need any additional help."

Gladys nodded. "I'll go back to the diner. That's the first place people head when they get out of the house. Aunt Kate will need my help."

"Come in and sit a spell, if you care to." Haydn acted pleased to see her, as if they had parted on the best of terms. He helped her out of her coat and took her basket. "You're an angel sent by God Himself. We were down to my biscuits and gravy for supper, and I'll warn you, that's not too good."

Gladys smiled politely. She walked closer and stood over Mr. Keller, assessing his condition. His cheeks were flushed, and his breathing was raspy.

A quilt molded into the shape of a man filled the chair next to the sofa. Haydn drew another chair close to the sofa and held it for her.

"How long has Mr. Keller been sick?" Gladys settled into the roomy chair. She could barely touch the floor with her toes.

"When I got home on Sunday, the foolish man was outside chopping wood. He got very sick not long after that."

"And you've been by his side ever since?" She shook her head. "You can't do that night and day."

"It hasn't been so bad." The droop to Haydn's eyes suggested otherwise. "I've slept in snatches."

"And you stayed awake long enough to start clearing that path."

"I was trying to figure out how I could finish the path, get to the doctor, and keep an eye on Mr. Keller all at the same time." He leaned forward and tugged the quilt over the older man's shoulders. "I don't know what I would have done if Pastor Fairfield hadn't stopped by and offered to get the doctor."

Haydn was one special man, taking such good care of a business associate who could be as grouchy as a mama bear with cubs when roused. Gladys made a snap decision. "I'll stay here with him. If we need extra help, I'll ask the sewing circle. Mrs. Fairfield, too. You can't stay in Calico forever, not with business back home to attend to."

Haydn fell back against his chair, disappointment stamped on his face.

Chapter 8

Haydn's eyes strayed to the family Bible, which had fallen open to the page for recording family marriages. A couple of times recently, when his heart tried to cast Gladys in that role, he'd remembered what she said about Grandfather's riches. He still didn't know how important money was to her or what to expect if she learned about his relationship with his grandfather.

He realized his brief silence had distressed her. "My family's association with Mr. Keller is of long standing. They would not want me to return as long as he is ill." He stopped short of reminding her that his business concerns weren't any of her concern. That would be rude, when all she had done was offer to help.

The clouds in her eyes cleared, and she smiled. "The offer to help still stands. You can't continue to take care of him twenty-four hours a day. Let me at least help with that." She leaned forward, brushing his grandfather's hair back from his temples. "He has lovely, thick hair. Sleeping like that, he doesn't look sick. Like he could jump off that sofa and stomp down the walk and join us at the diner. I know Aunt Kate would like to see him."

When Gladys acted as solicitous as a granddaughter

might, Haydn didn't know what to think.

Someone knocked at the door, sparing him. He opened the door to a welcome figure carrying a black bag

Gladys sprang to her feet. "Dr. Devereux! I'm so glad Pastor Fairfield found you."

The doctor knocked snow off his boots. "I would have been here sooner except I had to go back to the diner for my bag. Now, what seems to be the problem?"

Haydn described the past few days while the doctor examined his patient. "There's not much to do beyond what you are already doing. Medicine has made some remarkable discoveries, but we still don't have a cure for the common cold. Let me see how bad he is." Dr. Devereux placed his stethoscope against Grandfather's chest.

"Get that thing off me. It's cold enough to freeze my skin." Grandfather pushed away the instrument and glared at Devereux. "I don't like doctors. All you do is say a bunch of words and charge a lot of money."

The doctor continued checking him. "I don't like the sound of his lungs. If he gets too restless, you can give him some of this laudanum." He poured a small amount into a bottle. "Only a teaspoon, and only if he really needs it."

"Dr. Devereux, should we use a cold compress? Or do they do more harm than good?" Gladys asked.

"I'm not sure what the scientists say. But I figure remedies folks have used for years must have some value. Otherwise, people would stop using them. Steam, too, can help clear his sinuses."

Gladys nodded. Haydn would ask for an explanation about a cold compress later. "One more thing I can recommend. Mr. Keller has a strong constitution, and I expect him to get better. But in case this takes a turn for the worse, perhaps you should inform his family of his condition. I've heard him mention a son. Do you know whom to contact, young man?"

Haydn stammered a bit. "Yes, I believe so." *Me.* "I'll send a letter to his son as soon as I find out if the postal service is working." He'd do that, too. His father would want to know.

"Good." Dr. Devereux shifted his bag into his left hand. "Unfortunately, family business demands that I leave town as soon as possible. My daughter is expecting a difficult, um, confinement. There is an excellent physician over in Langtry. He'll be here next week, but if you need a doctor before then, you can contact him and see if he can come."

The doctor must have seen the terror that Haydn felt at his words. "As I've said, most of the time these illnesses work themselves through the system. Mr. Keller is a strong individual, and I expect him to rebound. I'll keep you both in my prayers."

Haydn asked, "How much do we owe you for the visit?"

"I'm not going to pay that charlatan a single penny," Grandfather rasped.

"Don't worry about that now. You just focus on getting him better." The doctor disappeared through the door.

"I'll go home and gather my things before I return." Gladys stared at Haydn, as if daring him to disagree. "I'll let my parents know where I'm going to be, and I need to get word to Aunt Kate not to expect me. I'll set up a schedule with Mrs. Fairfield." As she ticked off the things she would do, Haydn alternated between wanting to hug her and to shoo her away.

By the time she came back, Haydn had started on biscuits to eat with Aunt Kate's soup. Gladys carried a small valise with her. "Where can I leave my things?" She headed up the stairs as if she planned to stay awhile.

"There's a room to the left of the stairs," he called after her. "Do you want to eat?"

"Yes." She peered down the stairs. "Let me finish those biscuits for you. Give me a minute." She returned a few minutes later, her feet encased in warm slippers. "You go out there and stay with Mr. Keller while I finish up cooking."

Haydn wished they could linger over the table, enjoying bowls of soup and biscuits slathered in butter. But that defeated the purpose of watching over Grandfather.

Pulling his chair away from the fire, where the warmth tempted him to slumber, Haydn opened his Bible to Mark's gospel again. What would Jesus do if He showed up in Calico today? Would He have stilled the snowstorm that cut Grandfather off from a doctor's help when he needed it? Would He accept an invitation to supper and heal Grandfather as long as He was in the house? Sometimes the Jesus of the Gospels seemed remote from life almost nineteen hundred years later.

Except for someone like Gladys, who loved people the way Jesus loved them. She brought out a tray with three bowls and a platter of biscuits. "I have an apple cobbler and whipping cream for dessert. Mr. Keller might not be able to eat it, but we can enjoy it."

Haydn spared a thought to wonder who had canned the jars in the pantry. Aunt Kate was probably behind the food. Gladys didn't touch her bowl; instead, she woke up Mr. Keller and fed him vegetable broth one spoonful at a time. She didn't stop until he emptied the bowl. "I bet a glass of milk would taste good, but I wonder if it would curdle in his stomach when he's sick like this." She lifted his head so he could drink from a glass of water.

Mr. Keller opened his eyes and roused enough to look around. "Minnie, is that you?" Lifting a shaky finger, he pointed it at Haydn. "Young man, you take good care of my Minnie, now." Refusing Gladys's offer of more water, he closed his eyes again.

"Minnie was his wife." Gladys's voice shook a little. "That was sweet." She exchanged the empty bowl for a full one.

"Do you want me to heat that for you?" His own empty bowl made him embarrassed. He hadn't waited on Grandfather; he hadn't even said a silent word of grace.

"This is fine." She gestured with her spoon. "Feel free to get yourself some more soup, or if you're ready, bring out the cobbler."

"If you don't mind, I'll take a second bowl of soup." He had given Grandfather the rest of the chicken soup yesterday. For himself, he hadn't eaten more than that bowl of charred oatmeal since then.

"Good. Then we can eat together."

After they finished the meal in companionable silence, Gladys insisted she would stay up that night with Mr. Keller. "You need to get some rest yourself, before you come down with whatever he has."

When she volunteered to share his burden like that, it was hard not to think of her as a potential partner in more than taking care of his sick grandfather.

⁊❧

On Wednesday night, Mr. Keller was restless enough to need laudanum. "I think it's gone into his chest," Gladys told Haydn.

"Do we need to go get that other doctor?" Haydn asked.

"Stop talking about me as if I'm not here." Coughing broke up Mr. Keller's words. That last bout of chest-racking coughs had awakened him. For the past twenty-four hours, he hadn't been able to sleep more than half an hour at a time. "I told you. No doctors. I hauled Minnie all the way to Topeka to see a doctor, and he didn't do her any good."

Gladys couldn't combat that argument, even when Haydn looked at her so pleadingly for an answer. "You heard what Dr. Devereux said. There's not much more the doctor could do." Taking Mr. Keller's hand, she made him look at her. "Mrs. Fairfield promised to ask Ma to bring over our medical book the last time she was here. It'll have some ideas we haven't tried yet."

She didn't add that she had asked Ma to also bring the small box where she kept her savings from work. She'd intended to use it for setting up her own house when she married, but she would willingly spend every penny if it would help Mr. Keller get better. Of course he had plenty of money, but she didn't know where he kept it. And she wouldn't feel right if she took it without asking him, even if it was to pay for his own supplies.

Someone knocked. "There she is now." Gladys hurried to the door.

Ma entered. "Mr. Johnson." She nodded at Haydn. Walking closer, she sat by Mr. Keller. "And Mr. Keller. It's good to see you again, although I wish it was under different circumstances."

"Is that Gladys your gal?"

Ma nodded, and Mr. Keller nodded with satisfaction. "She's a good one. I've told Haydn to hold on to her." He coughed and sank back against the pillows.

Ma handed Gladys the medical book. "I've marked a few remedies I've found work best. Go on, both of you, and look them over, while I visit with Mr. Keller."

Hugging the tome to her chest, Gladys walked into the kitchen, Haydn following behind. Neither one of them mentioned Mr. Keller's continued references to a match between the two of them. Keeping her tone brisk, Gladys turned to the first marker. "Here the author's talking about tea. Tea with honey—we're already doing that—and lemon." Her nose wrinkled. Lemons in February were as rare as fourteen hours of daylight. "Also peppermint is a good flavor for the tea. Maybe we can melt peppermint candy in hot tea.

I wonder if that would work the same way. Maybe lemon drops, too." They'd be easier to find than an actual lemon.

Haydn nodded. "Those sound too simple."

"There's more." She turned to the next section that described what to feed their patient. "It does recommend chicken soup. But listen to this. It says to cook it with cayenne pepper. And even to add hot peppers with the vegetables." She hadn't cared for green peppers the one time she'd tried them. "I might be able to get hold of some green peppers."

Haydn shook his head. "Green peppers aren't hot. It's talking about chili peppers or something like that. I had some once when I went to Texas. They burned my mouth. Maybe it's supposed to burn away whatever is troubling his chest."

"I'll ask Ma." Flipping to the last marker, she found the section on steam treatments and scanned the article. "It says oils can make steam more effective, eucalyptus and lavender in particular." Now, those things Mr. Finnegan probably carried. Some women used oils to add scent to bath soap or to make perfumes.

Gladys made a list of things to look for at the mercantile. She grabbed a pencil to figure out an estimated cost. She should have enough, although it might cut her savings in half.

"I haven't been able to find Mr. Keller's money," Haydn said. "And I didn't bring that much with me. Will Mr. Finnegan put it on account?"

Gladys covered the total with her hand. "You don't have to worry about the cost. It's something I want to do."

"You really mean that, don't you?" Surprise stamped

Haydn's face as he sat back. "You're willing to spend that much money on a man who's done nothing but yell at you?"

And say you should marry me. Gladys didn't point that out. "He's my brother in Christ. He's someone God loved enough to die for. I figure it's the least I can do."

She stomped out of the room before he could rile her even more by refusing her money.

Chapter 9

While Haydn waited, he heard Mrs. Polson say good-bye. He whirled on his heels and left the kitchen. Time after time, Gladys tore down his defenses with a simple act or gesture. He had seen the total for the supplies the medical book recommended. He didn't know where she could get her hands on that kind of money. Add to that all the money she lost by taking off the week to spend with Grandfather.

It was time he accepted her for who she was: a beautiful young woman who loved the Lord and for some reason known only to her and God, loved Grandfather no matter how he acted.

Haydn tossed his suitcase onto the bed and dug out his slim wallet. After his extended stay in Calico, he had spent most of the money he had brought with him. Paying for the last delivery of wood, a delivery Grandfather had insisted they didn't need, had nearly wiped him out. But what he had left, he would give to Gladys. It was *his* grandfather who was sick. He counted out the money, not nearly enough, and went back downstairs.

He pushed the money at Gladys. "Take this."

"You don't need to do that. I told you—I want to pay for this." She didn't touch the money.

"And so do I." He held out his hand, willing her to accept the money in spite of her earlier rejection.

"Why—so your business with Mr. Keller doesn't suffer?" He had hurt her.

The words hung between them. Haydn considered telling her the truth—*because he's my grandfather*—but his reasons were more complex than that. "Because I love him, too. I've grown up thinking of him as a loveless Ebenezer Scrooge of a man. But because of you, I've learned to love him, too." He pressed the money into Gladys's palm. "Take this from me. Please. Let me have a part in getting him well."

Gladys chewed her lip. "When you put it like that, what can I say?" A grin replaced her worried look. "And if there's any extra money, I'll get more food. Some of your supplies are running low."

Haydn glanced at the sleeping figure on the sofa. "Can you carry everything by yourself?" He wished he could go down to the mercantile with her, to enjoy a few hours of her company away from the sick man's bedside.

"I can." Gladys reached into her pocket and pulled out a change purse. "But why don't you go ahead? You haven't been out of this house for days."

The prospect sorely tempted Haydn, but he decided against it. "You need to do the shopping. You send me for eucalyptus oil and I might come back with castor oil instead."

"I'll be back before you know it."

Gladys didn't know if it was the steam treatments, the vegetable broth spicy enough to strip green from copper, or the dried-up lemon Mr. Finnegan found for her. But by Sunday Mr. Keller had improved to the point where she and Haydn could leave him alone and go to church together.

She rejoiced that it was Palm Sunday, the beginning of Passion Week. Ruth led her schoolchildren in a reenactment of Jesus' triumphal entry, waving pine branches instead of palms, and Jesus riding a pony instead of a donkey. Ruth had recruited Gladys's brother Gordon to hold cue cards for the congregation.

With Gordon's encouragement, the rafters of the church rang with shouts. "Hallelujah! Blessed is he who comes in the name of the Lord." Heart lifted in praise and worship, Gladys could hardly believe the same crowd had cried, "Crucify Him!" less than a week later.

On Monday morning, the doctor from Langtry pronounced Mr. Keller well enough to get up if he wanted to. Speaking with Gladys and Haydn in the front parlor, he said, "You've done an excellent job, both of you."

"It was all Miss Polson's doing." Haydn reflected the credit back to her.

"All I did was follow the suggestions in my mother's medical book." Telltale heat raced into Gladys's cheeks.

The doctor nodded. "Since I'm not needed here, I'll go check on a couple of Dr. Devereux's other patients."

Gladys's valise waited under her cloak by the front door.

"I'll say good-bye to Mr. Keller before I leave." She headed up to his room, where they had moved him earlier when he improved enough to climb the stairs. Knocking on the door, she called, "Mr. Keller?"

"That you, Gladys? Come on in." Mr. Keller sat up in bed, a pillow at his back. "It's about time I said thank you for all you've done. That young doctor said you had a lot to do with me getting better."

Gladys sat beside him, hands crossed in her lap. "It was God. I was only His instrument."

"You healed more than my body, young lady. You healed my heart. This next Sunday is Easter, isn't it?"

Gladys nodded. "My favorite time of year. I love Christmas, but Jesus' resurrection completes the story."

"You may be right." Mr. Keller patted her hands. "I plan on going to church with Haydn next week. We'll be looking for you."

"You will?" Joy spread through Gladys's body from the inside out. "That's the best news I've had since the first time I came to visit."

✲

Gladys called the sewing circle together to finish one final project for Mr. Keller. Late Saturday night, she knotted the final stitch on the surprise and wrapped it in plain brown paper with string.

Early Sunday morning, about the same time the women headed to Jesus' tomb, Gladys put the package in the bottom of a basket and added several of her mother's hot cross buns in a towel. Ma hugged her. "Have I told you lately how proud I am of you?"

"Too many times." She returned her mother's hug. "I'll see you at church if not before."

"If they invite you to stay for breakfast, go ahead and eat with them."

As Gladys headed out the door, her mother said, "He is risen!"

"He is risen indeed!" Gladys returned the greeting then picked her way down the street, a muddy morass from the melted snow. She knocked boldly on Mr. Keller's front door, none of the fear that had troubled her on her first visit stopping her this time.

She was about to knock a second time when Haydn opened the door, surprise evident on his face. "Gladys! What are you doing here so early?"

She followed him into the parlor. "I come bearing gifts. Ma sent boiled eggs and hot cross buns for your breakfast."

"That wasn't necessary."

"We wanted to." She continued into the kitchen, where Mr. Keller sat at the table. "Happy Easter, Mr. Keller." She removed the food from the basket and then lifted the package from the bottom. Feeling suddenly shy, she laid it in front of the old man. "This is for you."

Mr. Keller smiled. He *smiled*. "I got a present, and it isn't even Christmas. Get me some scissors, Haydn, so I can cut the strings. They're in the drawer next to the silverware."

He stripped the strings away and unwrapped the brown

paper. "It's a quilt of some kind. That's a lot of work."

"A small one. My friends helped me finish it." Gladys tugged the two top corners and stretched the quilt out, revealing a log cabin design in shades of blue. "You can use it as a lap rug. That way you can always be cozy and warm. I thought you might like it, going out today."

Haydn bent over it, studying the stitches. "You do amazing work." He had set the table with three plates. "You will join us for breakfast, won't you?"

"Gladly."

Before Gladys could sit, Haydn blocked her chair. "Will you join me in the parlor for a few moments?"

Did he have a gift for her? Gladys's heart beat faster. She hadn't brought a gift for him.

Once in the middle of the room, Haydn dropped to one knee. After stumbling back a step, Gladys steadied herself, and Haydn caught hold of her fingertips. "Gladys Polson, you opened my eyes to a love I had never known. How could I help but fall in love with the woman who showed me the love of the Lord every day since I've met her? Although I'm not worthy of you, I still dare bare my soul to you. Will you marry me? Be my wife and share my life and my love?"

"Yes. I'll even follow you back to Topeka, if that is where God leads you."

The tap of a walking cane announced Mr. Keller, carrying his new quilt. "That won't be necessary."

Gladys wondered why Mr. Keller was interrupting this private moment, but she decided she didn't mind. They waited until he joined them and placed his hands on their arms. "Haydn won't be going anywhere. He'll be staying right here and starting a newspaper." He settled in his chair, and Gladys darted forward to tuck the new quilt around him. "Gladys, I'd like to introduce you to my grandson, Haydn Norman Keller."

Haydn grinned somewhat sheepishly. "You don't object to being a Keller and living here with my grandfather?"

Gladys looked from one man to the other, comparing those identical sparkling brown eyes. How had she missed it?

"Gladly. Tomorrow and for the rest of my life."

"Kiss her, boy."

And Haydn did.

MISS BLISS
AND
THE BEAR

A soft answer turneth away wrath;
but grievous words stir up anger.

PROVERBS 15:1

Chapter 1

Annie Bliss hesitated as Fort Blunt, located about five miles from the town of Calico, came into view. Reaching behind her, she touched the bundle of socks, scarves, and mittens she had knitted for the soldiers stationed there. The idea shimmered like a leaf after the rain when it first occurred to her, but now each clop of her horse's hooves on the hard ground brought a smidgeon of doubt. *Lord, please let them accept this offering in Your name.*

Gladys Polson rode with her. After their sewing circle decided to take on local mission projects, Gladys acted first. Her bravery in reaching out to the town's curmudgeonly rich hermit encouraged Annie to think of young men serving their country far from home.

"They're just boys like my brothers. Nothing to it." Annie spoke the words as if hearing them out loud would bolster her courage.

Gladys darted a glance in Annie's direction before returning her attention to the road ahead. "You'll be fine."

A man's voice boomed through the thick fortress wall, loud enough for them to catch words here and there. "Poorly laundered. . .wouldn't pass inspection by a blind general. . ."

Annie took a deep breath. Although the man's anger frightened her, it also gave her impetus to go ahead. Perhaps God would use her gifts to remind angry soldiers like this one of His goodness.

The stockade gate swung open and a petite woman came out, her shoulders hunched over with more than the basket full of uniforms. She glanced at the two women on horseback with a wan smile. "Good day."

A burly figure lumbered away from the gate, each footfall echoing his words to the trembling woman in front of them.

Even if the woman was a poor laundress, she didn't deserve the soldier's anger. Annie said, "Maybe he just woke up on the wrong side of the bed this morning."

"I don't think his bed has a right side, at least when it comes to women." The laundress shifted the basket to her other hip. "I hope your visit doesn't involve the Bear."

"Bear" described the man's gait perfectly, and Annie smothered a giggle. "Thanks for the warning. Can we help you carry that laundry somewhere?"

"It's just around the corner, but thanks for the offer." Nodding her farewell, the laundress headed in the direction of a stand of trees on the south side of the fort.

"Ready?" Gladys asked.

For answer, Annie urged her horse through the open gate. Around the flagpole, a platoon drilled under the careful watch of their lieutenant. The cantankerous man had disappeared.

The lieutenant called one of the soldiers to take over the drill and walked through the ranks toward the women. Young and handsome, his features suggested someone who didn't take life too seriously. "Lieutenant Chaswell at your service." He swept his cap from his head and bowed. "How can I assist two such fair ladies today?"

Annie smiled at the flattery. "We're hoping to speak with Captain Peate, or if he is unavailable, with his wife."

"Certainly." Chaswell lifted his arms, and Gladys accepted his help in dismounting from her horse. Annie followed suit, her hand brushing against the bundle of knitted items, reminding her of her purpose. Any chance to slip in and take care of their business unnoticed disappeared with the men drilling. As they walked to the captain's lodgings, every pair of eyes tracked their progress. Out of the corner of her eye, Annie spotted the Bear making his way to a building with a cross on top, probably the fort's chapel. At least he was heading in the right direction for a man with a troubled spirit.

Jeremiah Arnold hadn't missed the arrival of the two women, nor the way Chaswell had jumped at the opportunity to greet them. Although he kept his gaze averted, he hadn't missed the way the sunshine bounced off golden hair cascading below a green cap, and it disturbed him more than the laundress ever had with the poor quality of her work. Had he been too hard on her? *No.* Women had to be as tough as men to survive in this harsh environment, perhaps even more so.

The visitors reminded him of his reasons for joining the army. He shook his head to dislodge the memories that threatened to pour over him like molten lava if awakened. No wonder the soldiers called him Bear. Years of trying to make restitution for past sins often left him as grumpy as a bear awakened out of hibernation.

In the absence of assigned duties, he headed to the chapel. Once he crossed the threshold, peace welcomed him. The chapel wasn't much, a wooden structure that barely rose above freezing in the winter and baked them in the summer. But on this fair day in late April, spring had arrived and the atmosphere was perfect, the temperature matching the uniform like a glove on a lady's hand.

Thinking about women again, are you? With a growl worthy of his nickname, Jeremiah jumped to his feet and walked the perimeter of the pews. The captain sat in the first row week by week unless away on business, his wife at his side. Jeremiah hurried through his prayers on their behalf, not wanting to dwell on Mrs. Peate's visit with the two guests.

On to the second row. Chaswell attended every week, along with a handful of young recruits who struggled more than most with army life. Although Jeremiah hoped to have a similar impact on the men placed under his care as Chaswell seemed to have, very few of the younger men sought him out during their free time. Fighting against jealousy, Jeremiah thanked God for Chaswell's faith.

Jeremiah continued down the rows, lifting up specific prayers as he passed each man's usual seat. Seats in the pews were tightly regimented, by the men's own choice.

At last he arrived at the back row, the refuge of the five

men who drifted in and out of the services. Their names were branded on Jeremiah's brain. Who needed military discipline the most often? Any one of these five. Which recruits might desert their post? One of them already had, his replacement arriving with the same rebellious attitude.

Which men spent their paydays at the saloon in town, taking advantage of all the entertainment the place had to offer?

The thought confirmed Jeremiah's sermon topic for tomorrow: a warning against strange women, drawn from several passages in Proverbs. Sometimes Captain Peate chided Jeremiah for preaching too often on the same subject, but each and every time he felt God's leading.

The front door squeaked open, and Jeremiah opened his eyes. The young man in front of him snapped a salute. "Lieutenant Arnold, sir!"

"At ease, soldier."

The lad dropped the salute. "Mrs. Peate wishes to see you in her quarters, sir."

"I will be there promptly." Jeremiah remained behind while the private left, breathing in the quiet before heading outside. A light breeze stirred the air, heady with gentle rains and thunderstorms, new tree leaves and blooming flowers. A perfect day for a ride if he had time later.

With a longing glance at the stables, Jeremiah headed for the captain's quarters. Whatever Mrs. Peate wanted with the chaplain involved the morning's visitors—unwelcome, intruding females.

"I think it's a marvelous idea. Even the roughest of the men will welcome the homey touch." Mrs. Peate filled the coffee cups.

After a single sip, Annie reached for cream and sugar. Even so, she could barely swallow the strong brew. Gladys set down her cup after a single taste.

"Over the years I've become fond of army coffee." Mrs. Peate lifted her shoulders in apology. "But I know it's not to everyone's taste. I have cool water if you prefer."

At nods from both guests, she bustled into the kitchen. She reappeared a few minutes later carrying a tray with a pitcher, glasses, and a plate of cookies. "Please help me eat these. The cook doesn't like me baking for the men, and I can't eat them all myself." A wistful look raced across her face, replaced by her pleasant smile. "I apologize for keeping you waiting. Lieutenant Arnold should be here shortly. As chaplain, he is in the best position to know who will appreciate the scarf sets the most."

Gladys patted Annie's hand in silent support. Ever since Haydn Keller, the grandson of Calico's richest citizen, had asked for Gladys's hand in marriage, she believed anything was possible. If only God had led Annie to assist a family instead of a fort filled with strange men.

Not men, she reminded herself, but lads like her brother. A touch of home might keep them on the straight and narrow. Her thoughts strayed to the grumpy man she had observed yelling at the laundress. Now that man could benefit from kindness.

Someone knocked on the door, and Annie straightened her back. Why waste energy worrying? The chaplain would make an excellent ally.

"Here he is." Mrs. Peate walked to the door and opened it. "Thank you for coming so quickly, Lieutenant. We have guests who are eager to meet you."

A booted foot with a heavy gait. . .stocky body and scowling expression. Surely God wouldn't expect her to. . .

The Bear was the chaplain?

Chapter 2

Annie's knees shook a teensy bit as she stood and faced the chaplain while Mrs. Peate introduced them. Lieutenant Jeremiah Arnold looked ordinary enough, average height, with a build more like a boxer than a man of the cloth. His resemblance to a bear came mostly from his attitude, exuding a barely controlled strength. Gray streaked a thick, reddish-brown beard, and dust coated his blue uniform. Annie thought she could sense him struggling to hide his impatience.

He bent at the waist. "Pleased to make your acquaintance, Miss Bliss. Miss Polson." His deep tones came out as a growl.

Annie opened her mouth to respond but didn't know what to say. Before the silence stretched too long, he said, "I'm at your service. Can I assist you in some way?"

In contrast to his appearance, not to mention the anger he had directed at the laundress, a hint of interest flickered in his dark brown eyes. Was it interest. . .or a challenge to give him a reason for him to help her?

Have not I commanded thee? Be strong and of a good courage; be not afraid, neither be thou dismayed: for the LORD thy God is with thee whithersoever thou goest. The verse Annie and her friends had chosen as their motto came to mind. If David could kill a real bear in battle, she could face down her Bear as well. Annie might wield knitting needles and yarn instead of a slingshot, and she certainly wasn't looking to kill anyone. But she *was* battling for the souls of young men. "My brother is stationed at Fort Laramie. Sometimes he gets lonely and longs for a reminder of home. His letters gave me an idea for a mission project, and Fort Blunt came to mind."

She's pretty when she blushes.

Where did that thought come from? Jeremiah had eschewed the comforts of hearth and home after his personal dance with the devil years ago. He hadn't allowed anyone or anything to come between him and his vow of chastity in all the years since. Flattening his features, he kept his voice level. "Mission? Are you handing out free Bibles? We already take care of that."

"Nothing like that." Miss Bliss opened a burlap sack and dumped the contents on the table for his inspection.

Bliss. . .what an appropriate name for such a stunning example of prairie beauty, with her halo of golden hair and rosy cheeks. Jeremiah had expected the young woman to have a chocolate cake or maybe dried apple pie in her sack. Instead, she presented him with a woolen cap, mittens, and scarf, all of a durable navy blue that matched his uniform. Next she handed him a pair of thick brown woolen socks. Every soldier could use such practical items. "I could also knit sweaters if they would be of any use."

103

Jeremiah picked up the socks and examined the stitches while Mrs. Peate did the same thing with a mitten. A brief nod informed him of her approval. But Jeremiah had other concerns. "Where did this 'mission project' idea come from?" *Are we going to be inundated by a lot of do-gooders hoping for a glimpse of the soldiers?*

Miss Bliss opened her mouth, but Mrs. Peate spoke first. "I'm sure you have a lot to talk over. Lieutenant, why don't you escort our guests back to Calico and discuss your questions along the way? My husband mentioned you had no official duties today."

Although Mrs. Peate phrased it as a suggestion, Jeremiah knew better than to disagree. If he felt responsible for the souls of the men at the fort, the captain's wife felt the same way about Jeremiah.

He swallowed a chuckle as he remembered his earlier desire for a ride in the open. God's sense of humor was at work once again, answering Jeremiah's unspoken request with the unwelcome company of two women. Accepting the inevitable, he brought his heels together and bowed slightly. "Certainly, Mrs. Peate. Miss Bliss, Miss Polson, I will return in a few moments with my horse."

Jeremiah considered the two women as he fetched his horse. Why did he find himself drawn to Miss Bliss? *Stay away. Focus on things more important than a pretty face, like country and duty and family.* The advice he doled out to straying men did little to change the direction of his thoughts. Staying away was easier said than done, since Mrs. Peate had practically ordered him to accompany the women. He prayed for an extra helping of the self-control he had needed since his fiancée's death.

When he returned, the sack in Miss Bliss's hands was empty, and she was prepared to leave. He nodded his appreciation at her readiness.

"I look forward to seeing you again, Annie. And Gladys, feel free to return as well. I'm thrilled to hear how God is working through your projects." Mrs. Peate hugged each of them in turn.

Jeremiah dismounted to help both ladies into their saddles. Mrs. Peate waved good-bye as they headed toward the gate. She would expect a report on what he learned when he returned.

"Let's go. The men won't see you if we leave now, since they're heading for the mess hall."

The women simply nodded, and he was thankful for their sensible response. After the gate shut behind them, the sun came out from behind a cloud and poured its glory into Jeremiah's soul.

Stick to business, Lieutenant. Don't let a pretty face lead you astray.

✑❤

The ride back to town stretched out. Gladys was probably thinking about her beau, Haydn Keller. Of course he knew all about the sewing circle's mission projects—he had to, since his grandfather was the first person to benefit from the love shown in Christ's name. Annie hoped Gladys wouldn't reveal her secret project to help the soldiers to anyone else.

Lieutenant Arnold relaxed in his saddle, looking slightly more human on horseback, but he didn't speak. If she mentioned her plans to him, she suspected he would scowl at her. Even so, she wanted to communicate her mission to the man tasked with the soldiers' spiritual well-being. She spurred her horse to come alongside the lieutenant.

"Lieutenant Arnold."

"Miss Bliss." He didn't offer any indication that he wished to speak to her.

Annie chewed her lip while considering what to do next. She decided on a risky move. "My prayer that God will comfort young men so far from home will only succeed with your help. I want us to be friends." She drew a deep breath. "So please, call me Annie. My friend's name is Gladys." Out of the corner of her eye, she saw Gladys's nod. "And what may I call you?"

"Bear" ran through her mind. She couldn't guess which of them would be more embarrassed if she used it.

His back straightened and the muscles around his eyes tightened, as if trying to recall his Christian name. "You may call me Jeremiah."

If he was named after the weeping prophet, they shared more than the vocation of preaching. The lieutenant seemed to carry a heavy weight. But she would make the syllables sing on her tongue. "Thank you, Jeremiah. What would you like to know about my project?"

He slowed his horse down. "I only saw a few knit items.

Well executed, no doubt."

The compliment brought a faint smile to Annie's lips.

"What kind of help do you need? Why do you need my help?" He stopped, as if realizing how rude he sounded. "Start at the beginning."

"Gladys came up with the idea in the first place."

Gladys took over the explanation. "Last Christmas, a missionary to China came to speak at our church. The Ladies Sewing Circle decided to support them." She gestured for Annie to continue.

"I've always done better when I can see what I'm doing." Heat tickled Annie's cheeks. "They sent us a picture of the children in their orphanage. They were all so skinny. The first thing that came out of my mouth was—"

"—they look like the Smith children." The two women spoke as one, and Annie laughed. A grin flickered around the Bear's—*Jeremiah's*—mouth. He looked much nicer when he smiled.

Gladys picked up the story thread. "Then Ruth—the schoolteacher, Miss Fairfield—mentioned that every year there's always at least one family that's dirt poor. So we decided we wanted to help them, too. When we got to thinking about it, we knew there were several people in town who needed a demonstration of God's love. So all four of us prayed about what God wanted us to do."

Jeremiah pounced on the mention of a fourth woman. "And who is the last member of your quartet?"

Annie schooled her features not to show the inward

wince. How to explain Birdie's inclusion in the group?

Gladys came to her rescue. "It's our local seamstress, Birdie Landry. She does exquisite work."

Jeremiah narrowed his eyes, as if he knew of Birdie's reputation. Annie rushed in before he could make the connection. "Gladys knew what she wanted to do right away—it's a lovely story. . ."

A scowl reappeared on Jeremiah's face, and Annie hastened on. "But that's a story for another time. I couldn't make up my mind on my project until I received a letter from my brother. He doesn't ever complain, but this time he mentioned how much he missed us at Christmastime. Then I read an article about Fort Blunt in the newspaper"—a wide grin lit up Gladys's face at the mention of Calico's first newspaper—"and I knew what I wanted to do. Everyone at the fort is someone's brother or son or sweetheart, and many of them would welcome a touch of home." She shrugged. "I'm good with knitting needles."

"And so she came up with this marvelous idea." Gladys beamed.

"I had a sweetheart once." Jeremiah seemed surprised that he had spoken aloud. His horse stopped moving altogether at the lack of direction, and the man's torso twisted, as if he was surprised.

Annie reached out a tentative hand then pulled it back, biting her lower lip. "What happened?"

"She died—in a gunfight." He clamped his mouth shut and offered no further explanation.

"How awful," Annie said. The thought that Jeremiah Arnold's bear persona owed its existence to such a sad occasion made him seem almost human.

Maybe God intended for Annie to tame the Bear.

She'd rather face down a firing squad.

Chapter 3

A silent Jeremiah wrestled his memories back into the lockbox where he stored them. The women kept quiet while he brooded, a minor miracle. One of the playful memories of his father surfaced. *I have it on good authority that there will be no women in heaven.*

And why is that, Mr. Arnold? Mother knew the answer, of course, but she played along.

Because the apostle John says after the seventh seal was opened, "There was silence in heaven about half an hour." And I never knew a woman who could keep quiet that long.

Jeremiah didn't blame men for wanting the kind of marriage his parents had had. But women like his mother were as rare as a snowstorm in July. His one foray into romance had proved that. Fannie might have died in the gunfight, but their relationship was doomed long before that happened.

The magnetism in Annie's face drew his eyes. Curiosity played across her features, maybe wondering what caused his smile a moment ago.

But she didn't say a word, not until they passed the nearest farm to the center of town. "Mrs. Peate said you could provide me with information about the number of men in your regiment, but I need pencil and paper ready when you tell me. Why don't you come ahead to my house? You can rest while I write it all down before you go back to the fort."

But I'm not tired. Jeremiah didn't say the words aloud. Instead, he said, "I don't want to create additional work for your mother."

A smile played around Annie's lips. "Between my mother and Aunt Kate—she's not actually my aunt, but we all call her auntie anyhow—they would feed the whole state every day if people would only come by. We always have plenty."

"As long as I'm back before taps." Mrs. Peate would expect him to stay a bit, but also a part of him—a small part, but something he recognized nonetheless—wanted to spend more time with Miss Bliss. *Annie.*

They rode into the town proper and passed a large house with baskets of ferns and flowers dangling from the eaves of the porch. The two women grinned like children with a lollipop.

Annie slowed down the pace of her horse. "Gladys is too modest to tell you herself, but she's the one who hung all those flowers on Mr. Keller's house. God surprised us all by sending her to the richest man in town." She sighed. "I hope God blesses my endeavors with the soldiers as much as He blessed Gladys's with Mr. Keller."

A story lay behind those short sentences. Jeremiah started to ask for more information, like what could a rich man need from this young woman? But before he could voice his curiosity, they reached a corner and Gladys paused her horse.

"My house lies down this street. It's been my pleasure to meet you, Lieutenant Arnold. I'm praying for God to bring revival to the fort." She said good-bye to Annie and turned her horse down the crossroad.

Jeremiah found himself alone on the street with Annie, subject to scrutiny by any passersby. They had reached the main street. At any moment, someone might appear and start rumors about him or, even worse, about Annie. "Is your house nearby?"

Annie pointed across Main Street. "Straight ahead a couple of blocks." She flicked a glance down the street before urging her horse forward. Her horse picked up the pace as if he knew home was only a short distance away. Jeremiah's mount followed. On the way back to the fort, he would give her free rein to stretch her legs in a long, loping gait. He did some of his best thinking while on horseback, and he had plenty to talk over with the Lord after the events of this day.

They came to a stop in front of a house painted a cheerful yellow that reminded him of Annie's hair as well as her personality. Even the tulips blooming around the front of the house were yellow. Yeasty aromas floated through the open window, teasing his taste buds. Jeremiah followed Annie to the barn, where they settled their horses. Back outside, he hurried forward to open the door for her.

Annie flashed a grin at him and called through the doorway. "Mama, I'm home, and I brought company."

"Come on in."

Jeremiah followed Annie through the door and spotted a

woman who must be her mother. Aside from the silver mixed in among her golden strands, they shared the same wide smile and merry blue eyes. Her gaze took in his uniform. "Lieutenant, welcome to our house."

At her word, his shoulders straightened and his back stiffened as if at attention. His one vanity was the success he had made in the army. It was one of the reasons he kept reenlisting, although that decision was looming again before the end of the summer. He was impressed that Mrs. Bliss could differentiate the various ranks in the cavalry. Maybe her son's service had prompted her recognition of his insignia.

"Mrs. Bliss, it is my pleasure."

Annie bustled around the kitchen. Without any verbal communication, he found himself at the table with two thick slabs of bread and butter and fresh-brewed coffee. Better than anything Shorty the cook had served in the canteen anytime recently. Mrs. Bliss added both sugar and milk to her coffee, took a sip, then turned her pleasant face in his direction. "So what do you think of Annie's idea? Do the men need socks and mittens and such?"

Jeremiah wished he could say no. That would alleviate the problems presented by Annie and her winsome ways. Half the young men in the regiment would vie for her attention, and the other half would wish they could.

But every winter he heard grumbling among the men about the bone-crunching cold of Kansas winters. More than that, Jeremiah saw God's hand in Annie's mission. He wouldn't say no to God, not even when a woman was involved.

"The men will welcome the knitted items. Even now, in April, we get an occasional cold spell. My greatest concern is for your daughter's safety."

"I can't think of a safer place for my daughter than among the men sworn to protect our country." Mrs. Bliss smiled.

As if wondering where the food had gone, he stared at the empty plate before him. Annie whisked it away and returned with a slice of dried apple pie with a wedge of cheese, as well as the coffeepot. She topped off his cup before sitting again, this time with paper and pencil in hand. She looked at him expectantly. "How many soldiers are at the fort?"

Jeremiah calculated the answer. The number varied on a monthly, if not weekly, basis. "The number of officers is fairly stable. In addition to Captain Peate and myself, there's one more lieutenant and eight sergeants. A couple of them are married." If he could limit her mission to the officers, perhaps no harm would result from her interference.

"I discussed that with Mrs. Peate. She suggested I make sets for everyone—maybe even for the wives themselves. I need an exact number of the soldiers and their wives."

Cornered, Jeremiah gave her the total.

Annie jotted the numbers down. "Mr. Finnegan—the owner of the mercantile—has ordered extra yarn." She turned her hand over, palm up, and studied it. "The men's hands will be larger than mine, of course. Is anyone an unusual size? Any six-fingered hands?" She grinned at her own joke.

The conversation continued in much the same vein, her questions stretching Jeremiah's knowledge of the men under his care. By the time the interview ended, Mrs. Bliss had refilled his plate twice more, once with a ham sandwich, and again with a bowl of bacon-flavored green beans. When she gave him corn bread fresh from the oven, he raised his hand in protest. He was already full enough that he would battle drowsiness during his evening duties.

Annie frowned at her notepaper. She made a few more calculations and set the pencil down. "I have all the information I need. I should have a good start within ten days. When would you like for me to return to the fort?"

"That's not wise." Jeremiah knew his refusal sounded harsh, but he would not tempt his men, nor would he put Annie in harm's way. "It would be best if someone from the fort comes here to get them." Like the next time Mrs. Peate came to town for her shopping.

"Lovely." Mrs. Bliss answered instead of Annie. "Plan on taking your lunch with us on Tuesday next."

Not me again. But to refuse the invitation would be rude. "I, uh, will of course let you know if anything comes up to prevent my return." He would prefer a gunfight to facing down two such charming ladies. History had proven his weakness when it came to women.

From her spot at the window, Annie watched Jeremiah's back until horse and rider disappeared from view. He confused her more than any man she had ever met. At times he was as grouchy as a bear intent on finding food. Other times she glimpsed a cuddly cub that was hurting and wanted his mother.

Children ran and skipped down the street. Where had the day fled that school had already dismissed? With a sigh, she turned back in her mother's direction. "Do you need help with supper?"

"No, go ahead and get started on your knitting." Her mother shooed her out of the kitchen.

Annie took a skein of navy blue yarn and cast stitches onto the needles. Three rows later she realized she had miscounted the first row, and she unraveled everything back to the first knot.

Her mother joined her in the parlor and pinned her with one of those looks. "So. . .tell me."

Annie tucked her tongue in her cheek while she finished counting the row. Once again she had miscalculated the number of stitches. She pulled them off the needle with a savage yank. The story about the conversation between the laundress and the "Bear" poured out of her. "I can't decide whether he's a bear waking up from his winter's nap or a bear cub that's, well. . ." Heat rushed to her face.

"As cute as a baby kitten?" Mama's voice held a hint of laughter. "He's probably both. No one is all good or bad all the time."

"Not even Pa?" Annie dared to ask.

A faraway look swept across her mother's face. "You wouldn't know it to see him now, but he was as rough as a man can be who has spent most of his life only among other men." Mama picked up one of the boys' trousers for mending. "And we've both heard how grouchy Norman Keller was the first time Gladys visited. Now he's showing up at Aunt Kate's diner several times a week." She winked. "There are a few of us who would love to see the two of them find love the second time around."

Annie harrumphed. Perhaps some woman could picture Lieutenant Bear Arnold as a nice man, but not her. "He's helping me only because Mrs. Peate asked him to. How can my plan work if he opposes it?"

Mama stuck her needle in the trouser leg. "Annie Abigail Bliss, you're giving one man too much power. If God is for it. . ."

". . .who can be against it?" Annie rubbed her forehead. "You're right, of course." She forced a smile. "But you have to admit it would be easier if he was as excited about it as I am." She cut off the end of the yarn that she had twisted too much to use. She shifted to green, to remind her of spring, and dug in her basket for larger knitting needles. This time her first row came out evenly spaced and with the right number of stitches. "Thanks for reminding me."

"Easier, perhaps—but not as much fun." Mama's laughter resounded in Annie's ears, and she made short work of the mitten's cuff.

Chapter 4

A loud cry awoke Jeremiah in the night. He battled his blankets and sat up straight in bed, his Colt in his right hand. His head swung around, but no one moved in the shadows. Chaswell, the only other officer in the bachelor's quarters, snored, his sleep uninterrupted.

No enemy threatened Jeremiah or the regiment's safety; only his own painful nightmares troubled him, the same ones he'd suffered after Fannie's death followed on the heels of his parents' deaths. Those dreams had ended years ago until Annie Bliss and her knitting project had disturbed his peace.

The women Jeremiah had dealings with as chaplain fell into two categories. He offered officers' wives the same respect he afforded their husbands. As far as camp followers and other such women in every station and town in the west, he warned his soldiers to keep out of their way and took care to follow his own advice.

He had minimized his contact with pretty young things like Annie Bliss. Chaswell likened his behavior to a horse with blinders. But Annie had burst on the scene, tearing the blinders from his eyes and forcing him to see the spirited, godly young woman with a mission from God.

The sky had lightened to a predawn gray, and he saw no point in seeking slumber again, "perchance to dream," as Hamlet despaired. After he scrubbed his face, he grabbed his Bible and headed for the stable. He had enough time to ride to his favorite place to greet dawn, about a five-minute ride from the fort.

He had spent more time on horseback in the past ten days than he had in the past ten months, and today he would add more miles to that total. He had to ride into town for his second meeting with the self-proclaimed missionary to the military.

Inside the stable, familiar odors greeted Jeremiah, and his horse's soft nicker welcomed him. He rubbed her nose while feeding her a bit of carrot. "I'm spoiling you." She stood quietly while he saddled up and led her outside before closing the door and climbing on her back.

The guard at the gate called, "Morning, Chaplain." Waving back, Jeremiah headed into the cool spring Kansas morning. Winter snow had disappeared only a week ago. God knew Jeremiah needed a place to escape and think things over.

Once he reached his spot and settled his mare, he reached for a blade of new spring grass. He tried whistling down the shaft, without success, before he stuck it between his teeth. David might have done the same thing when he was a shepherd. The habit lingered from Jeremiah's boyhood.

The mare matched Jeremiah well, but she was getting up in years. If he chose to reenlist, he would need a new horse. She deserved to end her years in peace, but where could he find her a home?

Annie's horse was well cared for, as was everything he noticed about her home.

Annie, again. Jeremiah jerked at the blade of grass and spat it on the ground. What did it take to get the girl out of his mind? This spot near the fort had become sacred ground as he spent time here, bringing the faces of his departed loved ones to mind. Over this past winter, their faces had lost focus, smudged by a mental eraser. The lack of fidelity to their memories, not to mention his disastrous dalliance with a saloon girl, made him feel unclean, unworthy. He had dreamed of being Hosea to her Gomer, only she dragged him down to her level and then died in a drunken gunfight at the saloon. He had fled into the army for escape six years ago next month.

Had all his years ministering to the men under his care counted for nothing? Sunshine rippled over his open Bible. "Lord, You promised me perfect peace if I keep my mind stayed on You. I'm trying, Lord. But I'm not at peace. I want to head in the direction You're leading me, whether to remain in the army or leave it for something new."

No answer came, at least not one he could hear. Today he would cling to the promise of God's abiding presence when he came face-to-face with Miss Annie Bliss for their second meeting.

His mare nuzzled his neck, bringing him a small measure of comfort. He stood and scratched her nose. "If God gave you the gift of speech like Balaam's donkey, what would you say?" After he climbed on her back, he urged her to a gallop, one that cooled his skin and cleared the fuzziness of his brain for the morning ahead. If he couldn't resolve his feelings, he could at least ignore them for a few hours and complete his duties out of force of habit.

Upon his return to the fort, the young guard saluted him. "Lieutenant Arnold, Mrs. Peate has asked to see you after breakfast."

Jeremiah bit his lip. He wouldn't get the expected reprieve after all.

⁊❤

"Are you sure you don't need my help?" Annie hovered in the kitchen.

Her mother chuckled. "If you keep this up, I'll bring out my damask tablecloth and china."

Annie could just about imagine the horror on the Bear's face if they went to such lengths. "Don't do that!"

Mama laughed. "I have everything under control. Why don't you bring your basket in here to finish that last mitten, and we can visit while we work?"

Annie tilted her head sideways while she considered. She usually kept her projects away from the kitchen, where flour or water could destroy hours of needlework with a single fling of a spoon. But she could tuck the mitten and skein into a small sack that would protect them from most spills. "I'll do that."

In the living room, she glanced at the basket full of completed sets. She was working on the final pair. God Himself had sped her hands, and even the additional yarn had arrived at Finnegan's Mercantile two days earlier than expected.

She sat down at the table and cast the first row with blue yarn, which she would mix with bright yellow stripes. Like the last one she'd finished, she'd make it large, a good match for the strong, sturdy hands she had seen as the Bear handled the reins on his horse.

She shook her head, hoping to clear away renegade thoughts of the chaplain. "It's a good thing I finished these early."

Mama looked up briefly from the pudding she was stirring. "I confess, I was hoping for more opportunities to invite Lieutenant Arnold for a visit. He seemed so sad. You mentioned he lost his fiancée, but that was a long time ago."

Annie didn't know how to respond to that. The most serious romance in her short eighteen years consisted of a stolen kiss from Abe Pettigrew on the occasion of their graduation. He had wed Hannah Swenson last November, and Annie rejoiced.

"You feel sorry for *him*?" Annie doubted the laundress at the fort would agree. She had felt the scrape of the Bear's teeth first hand. She finished the cuff of the mitten and began work on the hand.

Her mother tested the pudding and took it off the fire. "Annie girl, don't you know that grumpy people usually have been hurt in some way? Don't you remember Mr. Keller's reputation as a scary hermit before Gladys braved him in his house and discovered a lonely old man?"

Were Mr. Keller and the Bear alike? "I guess if the Samaritan could love the man on the Jericho road, I can find a way to get along with the—" She stopped herself from saying "Bear" just in time. "Lieutenant."

"That's the spirit." Mama dished pudding into individual bowls and began whipping cream.

A short while later, Annie finished the last stitches before tying off the yarn inside the thumb. Outside the window a chestnut-colored mare appeared. Annie's heart sped and her dry mouth forced a cough from her throat. She tucked the finished mitten into the sack and stood.

"Why don't you go ahead and greet our guest while I set the table?" Mama grinned as if she knew every one of Annie's thoughts and desires.

Draping a shawl over her shoulders, Annie headed out the door. The lieutenant looked less like a bear today, more human, the way he was rubbing the mare's nose and talking to her.

"Good morning, Jeremiah."

He jumped at her words, the wary look returning to his face. "Annie."

She noticed the absence of any kind of gloves or mittens on his hands and hoped he would find her blue-and-gold creations useful.

Mama opened the back window. "Dinner is ready."

"We'd better hurry." Nervous laughter bubbled from Annie's mouth. "She's been cooking enough food to serve an army." A genuine chuckle followed that comment. "I mean. . ."

He smiled, and his features lightened, making him look like someone closer to her brother's age rather than an aging officer. Someone—almost attractive. She couldn't help noticing the shine of his boots, the crisp creases of his uniform.

With two steps, he reached the door first and opened it for her. He bowed and gestured her inside. "It smells heavenly in here."

"We're serving you breakfast. I hope you don't mind."

He looked at her, a question in his eyes. "I don't mind. I hope your mother didn't go to any extra trouble for me, though."

"She loves it. My brother—the one in the army, up in Wyoming, you know—he says he never gets a decent fried egg."

"Eggs scrambled with every ingredient on hand, but not fried, no."

The sadness sliding through his eyes reminded her that he had no one to cook his eggs to order for him. She wondered about his family. Mama's words about hidden hurt made a little more sense, especially as long as this softer, kinder bear cub stayed in charge.

They arrived in the kitchen before they could engage in further conversation.

Mama pulled a pan with toast from the oven and slid two slices onto Jeremiah's plate. "Lovely to see you again, Lieutenant. Tell me, how do you like your eggs?"

"Over easy." He settled into the indicated chair and studied the array of available jams.

Annie fixed Jeremiah's coffee the way he liked it. Mama filled the frying pan with four eggs, and Annie hid a smile.

When Mama joined them at the table, she invited Jeremiah to say the blessing.

Jeremiah folded his hands into a tent and bowed his head. "Thank You, Lord, for Your bounty and these kind folks who have served it. Please lead us to do Your will. In Jesus' name, amen."

The simple prayer caught Annie by surprise. He spoke like someone who talked with God like a friend, who used everyday language to battle everyday problems in the arena of prayer. Another layer she hadn't expected from the Bear. She breathed her own silent prayer. *Lord, let me see the lieutenant as You see him.*

When she opened her eyes, steady brown eyes studied her. He smiled as if he had heard her internal prayer then turned his attention to the food in front of him. Mama replaced his toast as soon as he finished his two slices. He ate every bite with relish before pushing back from the table. "Thank you for the delicious meal, Mrs. Bliss." His eyes sought out Annie, questioning whether she had helped.

"It wasn't anything hard. Annie's been working night and day on the hat and scarf sets."

Jeremiah lifted his eyebrows. Annie rose and reached for Mama's plate, but Mama shooed her away. "You go into the other room to discuss your project with the lieutenant. I'll take care of the dishes."

Jeremiah appeared behind Annie's chair in a second and then escorted her to the front room, treating her with all the courtliness of a born gentleman. So far today he had been politeness personified.

"From what your mother said, you've been working hard." Jeremiah gestured to the sack with bright colors peeking out of the top.

She nodded. "I finished the last set this morning. I wanted everyone to receive his at the same time. This sack here"—she handed the bag at her feet over to Jeremiah—"holds the special sizes. The rest are back in my room."

"Do you need any help?" Jeremiah asked.

She started to say no, but she had too many bags for a single trip. His suggestion only made common sense. She nodded and led him to the back room. While he gathered the bags, she reached for his special set. Her breath quickened, and she made herself count to five. After a deep breath, she straightened her shoulders and returned to the living room a step behind Jeremiah.

"Is there anything I should know before we distribute the scarf sets?"

His question kindled a fire in her stomach that spread up her neck and cheeks. Swallowing to moisten her dry throat, she held out the small paper sack. "I made these especially for you."

Chapter 5

*A*nnie made a set especially for me. Jeremiah reached down from his mare's back and touched the bulging saddlebag to reassure himself of the reality.

Vivid blues and almost-gold stripes. As smart as a dress uniform during a parade march. She had even added the correct insignia appropriate to his rank. As far as he knew, none of the other sets had anything so unique. The sky overhead and the bracing wind both predicted the same weather: a late-season cold snap, one that could range from hailstones to tornadoes or even a snowstorm. Jeremiah might have a use for Annie's gift sooner than expected.

The men might talk about the special touches added to Jeremiah's set, but he couldn't refuse Annie's gift any more than he could tell Mrs. Peate he had neglected to offer her invitation to tea. The gift had rattled him, and he escaped soon after that, forgetting the message from the captain's wife. He'd have to go back.

If he turned around now, he had time to offer the invitation before the dinner bell sounded at the fort and before bad weather set in. The hope of avoiding future trips to town exceeded his embarrassment about his oversight. Maybe this would be their last meeting and he wouldn't have to return after today. He turned around and headed back into town.

On the way back into town, he spotted Annie's friend Gladys with a young man. Funny, he hadn't lost a moment's sleep because of her. She had already completed her mission; Mrs. Peate would worm the entire story from Gladys the next time they met.

This young woman didn't frighten him nearly as much as Miss Annie Bliss. Jeremiah reined in his mare and approached the couple. The horse snorted, and they turned in his direction.

"Why, Lieutenant Arnold, how pleasant to see you again." Gladys looked up at him with a welcoming smile.

The man with her bowed in Jeremiah's direction. "Haydn Keller, at your service, Lieutenant."

"Pleased to make your acquaintance." Jeremiah nodded at young Keller. "Mrs. Peate asked me to extend an invitation for the four young ladies involved in your mission project to join her for tea on Saturday afternoon." He handed Gladys an official invitation.

Gladys held the letter where Keller could see while they both read it. "I would be delighted to accept. How thoughtful of her to have the tea at a time when Miss Fairfield can come. Please thank her for us." Her eyes swept over the sacks attached to the back of the mare. "I see you've already been to Annie's house. I trust she said yes, too?"

"No, actually"—the words came hesitantly to Jeremiah's mouth—"I forgot to ask her." He considered asking Gladys to deliver Annie's invitation, but Mrs. Peate would not approve.

Before Gladys could ask another question, he said good-bye and headed toward Main Street and beyond, to the house with the pretty yellow paint.

This time when he rode up to the house, no one poked her nose outside. He tied his mare to the stair rail leading to the front porch. After retrieving the remaining invitations from his saddlebag, he knocked on the front door. When Annie opened to his knock a minute later, her hair was messed, her eyes sparkled, and she looked as relaxed as Jeremiah had felt as long as he was riding in the direction of the fort.

"Why, Jeremiah, I didn't expect to see you again so soon. Please, come in." She opened the door to invite him in.

Jeremiah stepped inside the door. "Mrs. Peate asked me to deliver these invitations to you when I saw you, but I forgot. She is inviting everyone involved with your special mission projects to tea on Saturday." He cleared his throat. "I ran into Miss Polson with Mr. Keller on my way back. She has already accepted."

Annie clasped the envelope that Mrs. Peate had penned with such care close to her chest without opening it. "I shall of course come, and I will get the invitations to Miss Landry and Miss Fairfield as soon as possible. Tell her thank you for us." He remained in place one awkward moment too long, and Annie smiled. "Would you like some tea before you return to the fort? The air is getting nippy."

A warm drink, a cheerful kitchen, and a young lady's smile. . . He forced himself to remember such things were forbidden to the likes of him. "I am sorry, but I have already tarried too long." On impulse, he added, "I truly appreciate the items you made for me."

He clapped his hat on his head and skedaddled, her surprised face etching itself on his mind.

❧

"Mrs. Peate is very nice. I don't think I could have finished my project without her support." Annie dangled the sleeve for the sweater she had started in front of her. A couple more inches for length, she decided. She changed the colors of the stripes with every sweater to individualize them.

Birdie pinned together material for a dart. A skilled seamstress, she dressed perfectly modest yet managed to look the most stylish of the four of them. The dresses she made for herself could have been taken from the pages of *Godey's Lady's Book*. "I don't know if I should go." She kept her eyes focused on the sewing in her lap.

Ruth turned the invitation she had received over and examined it again. "Mrs. Peate invited all of us." She looped thread around her needle for a French knot and finished the stitch before looking up again. "Did you have any. . .business. . .with the soldiers in your former occupation?"

A pale pink spread across Birdie's face. "Yes." The word came out as a whisper.

All sewing ceased for the moment. Tears formed in Birdie's eyes. Annie handed her the handkerchief she had tucked into her sleeve.

Ruth, ever the pastor's daughter, revived first. "God has forgiven your past. You no longer have a reason to be ashamed."

Birdie shook her head, raising her wet face to the others. "But just seeing me might lead some of them to sin."

"You comport yourself very differently now. Besides, we'll be going straight to the captain's quarters, so we may not run into any soldiers." Annie scrambled for words to assuage Birdie's worries. "And you look so different now, they might not recognize you in any case."

Ruth nodded. "Your sunbonnet will hide your features."

"Please say you'll come." A frown formed on Annie's face. "You don't want to miss a chance to meet the Bear. If Mrs. Peate invited him." Even as Annie said the words, guilt assaulted her. Even though he had softened the last time they had met, he might condemn Birdie if he ever learned about her past. He was the kind of man who wouldn't tolerate less than perfection, or any immoral behavior. Or maybe he was one of the soldiers who. . . No. Even her worst suspicions about him hadn't entertained that picture. "Then again. . ." Annie almost regretted repeating the invitation.

Resolution animated Birdie's face once again. "Mrs. Fairfield keeps telling me I should venture more into the community and live the new life Jesus died to give me. I will go to the tea."

"That's the spirit." Gladys smiled. "Let's pray that yesterday's snowfall will melt before Saturday."

"I wonder if they distributed the scarf sets before the storm." Annie changed green yarn for blue. "I'm not wishing for more winter, but I'd like it if the soldiers can use them before next November."

The others laughed, and Ruth patted her hand. "They can at least use socks year round."

On Saturday they met for an early lunch, and then Annie drove them out to the fort in her father's wagon. Once they left town, they could see the new grass carpeting the countryside.

Annie flicked the reins over the horse's back, and he picked up speed. A figure on horseback flew down the road toward them, fast enough to deliver the message that Paul Revere carried on his important ride. The pace was so fast, in fact, that she didn't recognize Lieutenant Arnold until he slowed down to greet them.

The cool air dried the cobwebs from Annie's throat as she drew a deep breath. "Lieutenant, I wasn't expecting you to accompany us."

The Bear straightened in the saddle, transformed from a Pony Express rider back into a soldier. "We received word of a small renegade Indian band roaming the next county over. We wanted to ensure your safety on the road." In spite of his wooden appearance, his voice carried urgency.

Gasps came from behind Annie in the wagon. Gladys asked, "Is Calico threatened, then?"

"Not so long as you stay in town, Miss Polson. But the commander has expressed concern about travelers headed east."

"Thank you for joining us today." Annie brought her hand to her throat. She glanced at the horizon, empty except for the new grass and a stand of trees in the distance. "Shall we get moving?"

The lieutenant altered his speed to match the pace of the

wagon, traveling at their side and swiveling his head every few moments to spot any potential dangers. When they arrived at the fort, the gate was barred and every guard post manned with two soldiers.

So much for an unobtrusive entrance. Annie glanced back at Birdie, who was looking away from the fort and had bent her head and folded her hands as if in prayer. There had to be another way. "Lieutenant, we don't want to disturb the men on duty. Is there a back way to reach the captain's quarters?"

Jeremiah nodded as if in approval. "Of course. After we get through the gate, we'll take a sharp turn to the left."

In spite of their plan, the wagon trundled through the gate at the same moment a barked order of "about face" turned all the men in the regiment in their direction. Birdie's head dropped even lower.

Military discipline reigned, and the men remained at attention. However, Annie was certain the men would comment on their visit. According to her brother, any alteration to a soldier's schedule provided fodder for speculation. The arrival of visitors would be the centerpiece of dinner discussion in the mess hall.

"I apologize for the timing." Jeremiah didn't look at her, but the stubborn jut of his chin suggested how much the apology cost him.

"There is no need. Of course the men are training for the potential Indian threat." She trusted she was speaking for all of them. They arrived at the captain's quarters without further commotion.

His touch as he helped her off the driver's seat felt soft as he brushed her arms, at odds with his posture. This close, she felt his strength and the urge to provide and protect radiating from him. Qualities that made him a fine soldier also testified to his character, in spite of her initial impression.

Solid husband material. Annie rocked on her feet as the thought crashed into her mind.

Chapter 6

J eremiah glanced over his shoulder as he followed the ladies to the door. No one had followed them, but he was sure he would be teased, by Chaswell if no one else, about the bevy of women he accompanied that day.

For now, he focused on the task in front of him. Mrs. Peate insisted he remain with them for tea in case something regarding Annie's project came up. During the minutes he had spent taking care of the horses, the five women in the small parlor had seemed to multiply, the air filled with high voices, soft laughter, and a rainbow of colors rarely seen outside of flowers in a field. Mrs. Peate had promised her husband's attendance, but accompanied by two squads, he had left early in the morning to scout out the Indian threat. Jeremiah was on his own with the quintet of women. Shooting a glance at the ceiling, he sent a pleading look in God's direction. *Is this Your sense of humor at work? Because it doesn't make any sense to me.*

Visible evidence of Annie's mission hung on the coatrack—Mrs. Peate's scarf and mittens. They had already proven their worth during the late winter storm. Both personal and practical, the gifts had earned a big thank you on behalf of the company.

Why did God continue to arrange meetings with the first woman to catch his interest since his fiancée's death? After today he hoped to put her behind him. The course Jeremiah had chosen since his fall from grace hadn't changed even if he was less and less satisfied with the prospect of spending the rest of his life alone. Any one of these young women would turn the heads of every soldier in the fort; some of the men might even make good husbands.

"Come in, Lieutenant. Thank you for escorting our guests safely to the fort." Mrs. Peate motioned him forward. "Captain Peate is convinced the rumor is nothing more than that, a rumor. If he believed there was any substance to it, he would have insisted I cancel the tea."

Jeremiah nodded. He hadn't been sure if he preferred a postponement over getting the occasion done with. Keeping her voice low, Mrs. Peate admonished, "Come now, Lieutenant. Relax. You never know what will happen."

Jeremiah relaxed his shoulders and shook his hands by his side to release some of the tension from his body so he wouldn't crush a hand in a handshake. The four guests had taken spots around the parlor. He guessed that the one with her dark hair up in a bun must be Ruth Fairfield, the pastor's daughter and teacher. Gladys's hair was an ordinary brown. The other two crowns of hair sparkled in spite of the fading light outside the window—Annie's hair was pure gold, and the last woman had hair the shade of a rich cinnamon, almost red. Had Annie told him her name? If so, he had forgotten it.

Mrs. Peate introduced them to him, repeating each

one's name as if she had known them for weeks instead of a few minutes. He had correctly pegged the dark-haired lady as Ruth Fairfield, the schoolteacher. The redhead, Birdie Landry, made her living as a seamstress. Something about her stirred a memory, but he couldn't place it. "Of course you have already met Miss Polson, who helps out at Aunt Kate's diner, and Miss Bliss, who has worked so hard on behalf of the men here at the fort."

Annie's smile widened, implying a long acquaintance instead of their brief encounters. "Mrs. Peate was telling us that you have distributed all the sets I sent. The men who have them were grateful for them when the storm hit, and the rest are looking forward to receiving theirs."

Jeremiah thought of his own mittens and scarf, hidden beneath his great coat on the coat tree. After all her work, Miss Bliss deserved a better thanks. "I know I made good use of them myself. The men kept so warm, they had enough energy left over for a snowball fight when they were off duty."

The thankful smile on Annie's face gladdened his heart.

❧

Annie clapped her hands and laughed. "Wonderful!"

"In fact. . ." Mrs. Peate poured tea into a cup and handed it to Jeremiah before she addressed Annie. "Your gift went over so well that I wondered if you would be willing to expand on your original idea."

Annie clapped her hands together again then tented her fingers under her chin. Ruth laid a hand on her shoulder.

"I already started working on sweaters for the men,

although I don't know if they can use them before next fall. Here's the first one." Annie reached into the bag at her feet and pulled out her finished product, done in forest greens and sky blues. Form dictated she should give the first sample to the captain, even though she had pictured Jeremiah while she made it. "This one is for the captain." She handed it to Mrs. Peate.

Jeremiah followed the exchange with a flicker of interest in his eyes. Mrs. Peate ran her fingers over the yarn, making appreciative noises as she did so. "You do amazing work."

"It's nothing."

Ruth clucked her disapproval at Annie's less than gracious response. Annie hastened to add, "I enjoy working knitting needles more than a hook and eye. With three older brothers, I've had a lot of practice darning socks and making mittens."

Their hostess passed the sweater to Jeremiah, and he took up the conversation thread. He held up the sweater against his chest, and Annie pictured how he would look wearing it. "As long as it's this weight, it will fit under our uniforms." He nodded his approval, and a ridiculous happiness grew in Annie's heart.

Mrs. Peate refilled their cups of tea then took a sip of hers before leaning forward as if imparting a secret. "The sweaters are a good idea, but I was thinking of something more imminent. My husband and I feel that our young men would benefit from socializing with lovely young ladies such as yourselves."

Annie glanced at Jeremiah. His eyes were fixed on the fire, unreadable.

Mrs. Peate continued. "Are there any upcoming events that our men could attend? A parade, a barn dance, a box social?" Her smile seemed to dare him to disagree in spite of the scowl on his face.

Annie looked to Gladys and Ruth, the three of them communicating in silence the way they always did when a question arose. Birdie kept her eyes fastened on her lap. She might not welcome the arrival of a bunch of rowdy soldiers in town, especially if any of them might recognize her.

Then Birdie glanced up. "I think that's a good idea." She returned her gaze to her lap.

"I can think of a couple of events coming up where our soldier boys would be welcome. Gladys, perhaps Haydn knows of others." Annie looked at her friend.

"I can ask him if he's heard anything," Gladys said.

"Perhaps we could do more. I know several people in town who have family members in the army. Maybe they would like to adopt the young men so they can enjoy a taste of home." Annie's eyes misted as she thought of her brother "And of course, the visits might ease the longing the families feel for their boys."

Mrs. Peate's nod revealed her enthusiasm about the idea. "What a lovely idea. Don't you agree, Lieutenant?"

He agreed more readily than Annie expected, although she spotted a gleam of amusement akin to her brothers' before they planned a practical joke on their unsuspecting mother.

Or maybe Mama only pretended she didn't suspect anything. What had she said? *Behind every grown man lurked a small boy who wanted to come out and play.*

Jeremiah looked every bit the grown man when he said, "Of course we don't want to expose the fort or the town to danger as long as the Indians remain at large."

Indians. Annie repulsed a shudder at the thought. Calico had been peaceful for all the years she had lived there.

"Naturally we will wait until this threat is settled. Lieutenant Arnold, you are the logical person to serve as a liaison with the community. And Miss Bliss, will you represent the community?"

Ruth normally took the lead in situations like this, but the men at the fort were Annie's project, not Ruth's. Annie extended her hand to the man who resembled a bear less and less every time they met and more like an ordinary—perhaps even extraordinary—man.

⌇

For the first time in his life, Jeremiah almost hoped the soldiers might encounter signs of Indian activity. If the men were involved chasing a phantom enemy, they could delay exposure to womanly wiles.

Not every woman was like Fannie, of course. But his distaste for the task only increased after the women left and Mrs. Peate relayed a bit of essential information, gleaned in a few quick seconds from the woman herself. Redheaded Birdie Landry worked at the Betwixt 'n' Between Saloon before she came to know the Lord last year. Mrs. Peate promised Birdie was a new person in Christ, and he could trust her. But in case any of the soldiers had strayed with her. . .

Jeremiah ground his teeth at the thought. In principle, even prostitutes could be redeemed—consider Rahab and Mary Magdalene—but he found the account of Hosea's wife more believable.

Jeremiah brought his attention back to Mrs. Peate, who was still talking. "I know you think you are hard on the men, that they'd rather go to Sergeant Chaswell about their problems, but when it comes to serious questions, they come to you." She leaned forward. "That's why my husband recommended you as chaplain at this fort. He saw that men seek you out when they need someone to talk with. He only made it official by getting you assigned here."

Jeremiah had no response to that, but only stared down at his hands. Guilty hands, ones that had failed the woman he claimed to love twice. First, he used her in the same way other men had. And then he deserted her when she needed him, and she had paid with her life. Ever since then he had been unable to turn away anyone who came to him for help. He'd taken a vow of chastity—and sworn to keep others from repeating his mistakes. "I just listen, that's all. And pass on a few words of advice."

"And now you'll advise them about taking part in the community activities." Mrs. Peate patted his hand. "I'm trusting God for a quick and safe solution to the Indian problem. But you will hear of that before I will."

Her prayer must have flown to heaven on wings, because the captain returned the next evening and sought out his officers. He and the scouts had found a few Kaw Indians, doing nothing worse than trying to hunt the long-gone buffalo before returning to Indian territory. After determining they posed no threat to white settlements, the scouts escorted them to the border before returning to the fort with good news.

The captain kept Jeremiah back when the others left. "I see that Miss Bliss has been busy with her knitting needles again. That sweater she made for me is a work of art."

"Yes sir."

"I understand my wife has suggested the soldiers join the folks of Calico for community events."

Jeremiah nodded.

"And that since you and Miss Bliss have established such a good working relationship, that the pair of you should partner on this project as well."

"Yes." Jeremiah kept his answer as simple as possible, hoping his brevity might convey his distaste for the task.

"Perhaps you and Miss Bliss will partner in other ways as well, hmm, Lieutenant?"

Jeremiah's face pulled in a frown before he could stop it. The captain waited him out, forcing him to make some response. "I doubt that, sir."

"Lieutenant." The captain hesitated before he said, "Jeremiah. I have known you these many years. Perhaps the time has come for you to set aside the fears from the past and march into the future that the Lord has for you. God sent Miss Bliss to our fort to do more than distribute hats and scarves."

Jeremiah couldn't get the captain's words out of his mind as he went to bed that night.

Is it possible, Lord?

Chapter 7

I sn't God wonderful?" Annie knew she was carrying on like a schoolgirl, but she couldn't stop herself. Jeremiah was escorting her back home after making arrangements for "adopting" the soldiers. "You identified six young men who could benefit from a homey touch, and we found exactly that number of families willing to spend time with them."

"In that case, He supplied in excess of the need. I thought you intended to assign someone to your own family, because of your brother."

Annie stopped in midstride. Did the man not realize. . . ? "He supplied exactly the right amount. My mother and father believe God arranged for my family to take *you* in. As the spiritual leader of the others, you need a place you can cast those worries aside."

Annie had tried to convince Ruth to ask her father to take the chaplain under his wing. Ruth declined. "Why would God want that when He sent the lieutenant to you?"

Jeremiah drew in a deep breath. "Shall we walk a ways farther?" Instead of heading left toward her house, he pointed in the opposite direction, toward the Keller mansion and the Polson home. Annie could only agree.

They strolled—far from the lieutenant's normal pace, which was so fast Annie felt like she was drilling with the army—down the street without exchanging a word. Annie's senses expanded, taking in the smell of the new leaves forming on cedar trees, the beauty of sunflowers dancing in the breeze, the song of a sparrow, even the warming temperatures that defied comfort in either wool or cotton.

At the Keller mansion, Jeremiah paused to look at the baskets of flowers cascading across the fresh wood of the porch. Annie knew that the difference Gladys had made in the Keller family went far beyond house repairs. Mr. Keller hadn't missed church a Sunday since Easter, and he had even shown up at Aunt Kate's diner on a regular basis. Such a positive outcome for Annie's project remained unclear.

Annie opened her mouth, but God's still, small voice told her to hush.

"The more I've worked with you, the more I've seen God at work. So I will accept your invitation to join your family." He shrugged his shoulders, as if getting rid of a heavy weight.

"It's our pleasure." *It's my pleasure.* A warm feeling washed over Annie. The Bear was turning more and more into a cuddly cub every day, one who still mourned the loss of his fiancée. But she feared any mention of that would bring stony silence. She rushed to the next topic on her mind, to rid herself of the unexpected emotions flooding over her. "The first community event will be a box social, a week from Saturday. The money raised will go toward the charity the entire women's missionary society supports." She smiled at him. "The society has been very kind and supportive about our individual mission projects. It's time we returned the favor."

The bemused expression on the lieutenant's face suggested she should hurry. Mr. Keller came out to the porch and waved, reminding Annie how long they had lingered on the street. The lieutenant offered her his arm. "Shall we go back?"

Strong fingers cupped her elbow. Annie didn't know what to make of his touch, so she continued with the discussion of the box social. "We are hoping that the majority of soldiers at the fort can take part. Or we could bring the social to the fort—" She hurried on at the frown that crossed his face. "Or we could hold two box socials, so that everyone can attend one or the other."

Jeremiah blew out his breath. "Two separate days sounds like a good idea."

❧

"And the basket goes to Mack Jackson."

Annie stepped forward, a warm smile beckoning Private Jackson forward.

Jeremiah released a breath he didn't realize he was holding, fighting the feelings that swirled in him. When Mrs. Peate echoed Annie's request for Jeremiah to attend both socials, he hadn't anticipated this situation. Surely he couldn't—it was impossible—jealousy?

No. He pushed the thought away. In light of the speculation circulating about him and Annie, he should be happy that someone else had won her box. After he unknowingly bid on her box last week, he had made private arrangements with Pastor Fairfield to donate money this time instead of bidding.

But of all the men in the company who could have won Annie's basket, Jeremiah would have listed Jackson as the least desirable. He had spent time in the stockade more than once. He resisted even Chaswell's attempts to get to know him.

Jeremiah realized he was still scowling in Jackson's direction and hoped no one had seen him. All manner of good-natured ribbing would follow if they had.

Chaswell won the next box, and Jeremiah smiled as Ruth Fairfield stood. Haydn Keller had bid on Gladys's contribution—that must have been prearranged. Mrs. Peate approached him. "This next box should prove interesting." She smiled at the larger-than-usual box.

Jeremiah raised his eyebrows. "Why is that?"

"Kate, the lady from the diner, decided to contribute. She told me she had the right because she was unmarried, and some of the soldiers might prefer a more mature woman."

Jeremiah wondered how Mrs. Peate knew all this. He was amazed at the way women communicated—information reached the most remote home even faster than the Pony Express.

Ned Finnegan, the storekeeper acting as auctioneer, peered inside the box. "Lots of good food in here. Ham sandwiches thicker than a man's fist. Crispy fried chicken. Beans and potato salad, two pies, a wedge of watermelon. . ." He smiled. "I can't tell you the name of the lady who fixed this box, but we can all make a guess." He winked at the men remaining in the audience.

An older gentleman stood, leaning on a cane. Even before Gladys appeared at his side, Jeremiah guessed he was Mr. Keller. His surprisingly strong voice called out, "Is the auction open only to our soldier boys, or can anyone in the community bid?"

Finnegan glanced at Annie, whose eyes sought Jeremiah out, questioning him. He nodded his approval, and she whispered in Finnegan's ear.

Finnegan banged his gavel. "We have no objection. Let the bidding begin."

A couple of soldiers—one thinner than a stick no matter how much he ate and the other an older, stocky man with a hearty appetite and a body shape to prove it—combined their resources to bid on the box, but they couldn't keep up. When the bid reached fifty dollars, they dropped out. The entire group broke out in applause when a blushing Miss Kate accepted Mr. Keller's arm and retreated to a quiet spot on the church lawn. Jeremiah looked back at Annie. She was clapping, bouncing up and down, her skirt lifting enough to show an intriguing patch of stockinged leg. Jeremiah looked away. He was too old to be distracted by the glimpse of a lady's limb.

All around Jeremiah, couples separated from the group gathered in front of the auctioneer. Five soldiers remained, not counting himself or the captain, and five baskets remained for auction. Annie must have arranged that. Interesting to see that the fourth member of the younger women's circle hadn't sent a basket. At least he assumed she hadn't; he hadn't seen her at today's festivities at all. For someone with her background, she showed great discretion. From what he had observed of Birdie's involvement with Annie's group, she was proving her new life in Christ over and over again; but how could he say anything to her without causing offense? Instead, he offered thanks to God and revised his long-held opinions.

But one woman's change didn't mean every one would follow her example, any more than most prostitutes followed the example of Mary Magdalene in the Gospels, Jeremiah reminded himself. He was still right to warn the men under his care against the dangers of women, especially those who fell into sin.

When Mrs. Peate learned that Jeremiah didn't intend to bid on a box this week, she had insisted that he join her and the captain for the meal. As the auctioneer called "sold!" on the last basket—coupling a shy young lass with an equally shy soldier—he crossed the lawn to the spot near the front steps where the captain had spread their quilt. Jeremiah appreciated the central location, which allowed him to keep an eye on most of the young couples.

He surveyed the groupings, probing for potential trouble spots. Mrs. Peate leaned over and poked him gently in the arm. "At ease, Lieutenant. This is a social event, and the captain has commanded that everyone have fun."

"Even you, Jeremiah." The captain was one of the few people who called Jeremiah by his given name.

"Especially you," his wife added.

Jeremiah listened with half an ear while he sought for the one couple he cared about the most. Annie spread a quilt under a tree even as Mack gestured toward a spot farther back. She shook her head and continued working. When she turned her back to unpack the box, Jackson withdrew a flask from his coat pocket and poured something into the jar of lemonade Annie had already set out on the quilt.

Jeremiah sprang to his feet, Mrs. Peate looking up in alarm. "Come, now, you must relax and enjoy yourself today."

Jeremiah directed his response to the captain. "You may wish to join me." He stalked across the grass, soldiers and townsfolk alike looking up in alarm as he strode past.

✿

Annie busied herself smoothing out the wrinkles in the quilt as best she could. Even after Ruth informed her that the lieutenant wouldn't bid today, she knew she must set an example and entertain one of the soldiers. Now she prayed for grace to endure the meal. So far, Private Mack Jackson had set her teeth on edge with his abrasive actions and his attempts to lead her farther and farther away from the main group.

When she could avoid him no longer, she prayed for one last measure of grace and turned around with a smile on her face. He offered her a glass of lemonade. That was thoughtful of him. She told herself to give the young man a chance.

As she reached to accept the glass, someone knocked it out of Jackson's hand. Before she turned, she suspected who she would find. The Bear had returned.

Chapter 8

Jeremiah grabbed Private Jackson by his uniform collar, lifting him until his toes dragged the ground. They filled her view, two figures shadowed against the noon sun, locked in fight. If it could be called a fight—the private's arms flailed wildly without reaching their target.

Annie heard rather than saw people gathering around them. Mrs. Peate appeared silently and took Annie's arm, edging her away from the two men. Slowly, she tuned out Jeremiah's heavy breathing and the private's indignant protests.

Voices crowded in. She couldn't identify the speakers.

"Maybe he was getting fresh with her."

"I hear she's the one who made us the mittens."

Others chimed in, all talking over each other, too many to make out more than a word here or there. Mrs. Peate eased her backward through a sea of blue uniforms, and they reached the ring of watching townsfolk. At the opposite side of the circle, Annie saw Ruth talking quietly with Pastor Fairfield. As he shouldered his way to the center of the circle, Annie sent up a prayer for a peaceful resolution. Had all their prayers and hopes led to this? Why had Jeremiah attacked Private Jackson?

The pastor stood between Jeremiah and the private, arms

extended to keep them apart. Other men from the town joined the circle, but Annie couldn't distinguish their voices from those of the soldiers to know what they were saying. Captain Peate joined the preacher at the center, and Annie breathed a sigh of relief.

Pastor Fairfield dropped the hand holding Jackson back. The private lunged forward, swinging a right hook at Jeremiah. His fist connected with the lieutenant's nose with a bone-shattering thud.

A lad young enough to still be in school landed a punch on a soldier's arm. Three, four, five punches followed, as the ladies backed away in fright. Mrs. Peate tugged Annie in the direction of Ruth and her mother, who were part of a group of women who stood at a safe distance from the brawling men. "You are the pastor's wife?"

Mrs. Fairfield nodded.

"I am Mrs. Peate, the captain's wife. Let's gather the women together and pray." At Mrs. Fairfield's agreement, they called to the others, gathered in a circle, and Mrs. Fairfield voiced a quiet prayer.

In spite of the men's shouts, Annie was aware when more women joined the circle. A hand clasped hers, and she opened her eyes briefly to catch sight of Aunt Kate standing next to her. Annie then reached on her other side for Ruth.

As each woman added her prayers, the sounds of the fight intruded less and less. Gladys was pouring out her heart when the pastor's voice broke into their prayer meeting. "It's over, ladies."

Annie opened her eyes. At the spot where she had begun her lunch, Captain Peate had gathered the soldiers in rows. The men of the town circled the lawn, collecting baskets and quilts.

A grim-faced lieutenant marched toward the women. He kept his eyes trained on Mrs. Peate and Annie as he addressed the group. "I apologize for the disturbance today. I have the captain's word that everyone responsible for starting the fight will be sent to the stockade." He paused, and Annie noticed the swelling forming around his nose and left eye. "Including me." He looked at the ground then straightened his shoulders in determination. Thrusting his shoulders back, he looked determined to face the worst. "I saw the private adding liquor to Miss Bliss's pitcher of lemonade. Several other men brought liquor with them, against the captain's orders. They also will be punished."

Private Jackson had added liquor to her lemonade? Annie shivered at how close she had come to drinking alcohol. In that case, she was glad for the way the lieutenant had barged in and knocked it away. She nodded her understanding and appreciation.

The women disbanded, joining their husbands to clean the lawn. At the captain's command, the soldiers ran in formation around the perimeter of the lawn behind the church. Jeremiah nodded at the men running in rank. "He'll keep them at it until they're exhausted, and then he'll make them march double time all the way to the fort."

"Does your nose hurt?" The question blurted out of

153

Annie's mouth instead the words of reproach she had imagined earlier or the words of thanksgiving he had earned.

Touching the offending feature, he winced. "It's not broken. I've suffered worse." He dropped his hand back to his side, and he stared at the ground as if looking for encouragement. When at last he lifted his face, pain that had nothing to do with his nose showed in the lines wrinkling his forehead and tugging his mouth into a frown. "An apology can't begin to express my regret about what happened here today. Miss Bliss—Annie— we have failed you. I have failed you."

The man I've called the Bear just apologized? It was time to return that nickname to the cave where it belonged.

℘

Jeremiah looked to the back, where the men began to slow their pace. He belonged back there, accepting the discipline he deserved for starting the fight, for not preventing trouble in the first place. Instead, he stayed rooted to the spot, imprisoned by the kindness of the woman before him.

A soft hand floated against his nose, tracing the path of the broken skin. "Look at me."

He lifted his face and looked into her bluebell-colored eyes, tears rimming the bottom of her irises. "It is I who must offer thanks to you. If you hadn't knocked the glass down, I would have. . ." He followed the path of the swallow pushing down her throat. "I would have drunk it."

He opened his mouth to apologize again. If he had done his job, no one would have brought whiskey to the social.

Her feathery fingers fell against his lips. "Don't apologize.

I am thankful that you protected me, as well as anyone else at risk."

Jeremiah didn't agree. If he hadn't agreed to the risky idea of the soldiers mingling with townsfolk, she wouldn't have been in danger. But her faith, her passion, convinced him to try. Hadn't his experience taught him anything at all? Six years ago he thought he could change a woman's heart, and instead, she died in her sin. Perhaps he should be thanking the Lord that no one was seriously hurt today; but there was danger, and some promising young soldiers might lose heart for the military life. He took a step back, the spot where her fingers had touched his lips burning at the separation.

He forced backbone into his words. "Given what happened today, I need to reconsider whether we should continue with the planned activities or not." He turned on his heels before she could protest and crossed the grass to the ranks of soldiers at a pace as fast as their run.

❧

A week later, life at the fort had returned to normal. Jackson spent three nights in the stockade for his role in throwing the first punch; the other culprits spent a single night. The captain had questioned Jeremiah for his side of the events. When he explained about the whiskey flask, the captain relaxed.

The captain called him back today. Jeremiah remained at rigid attention. Although Captain Peate had not sent him to the stockade, Jeremiah still felt responsible for every man who ended up there. Against all his vows to avoid entanglements, he had allowed Miss Bliss—Annie—through his defenses.

And look what had happened. He kept his chin up and his back straight, ready to absorb whatever reprimand the captain threw his way.

"At ease, Lieutenant—Jeremiah." The captain sat down and motioned for Jeremiah to do the same. "You have my decision on the incident at the box social. I do not hold you responsible for the brawl. Sit down—I hate looking up at you." Jeremiah accepted the invitation but kept his back straight, only touching the chair at his shoulders.

"Now, concerning the continuing relationship with the community. That is a thornier issue." He glanced at the sheet of paper in front of him, lifted it between thumb and forefinger, and gestured with it to Jeremiah. "Pastor Fairfield has written a letter to me. He suggests postponing the planned events to give both parties a couple of weeks to simmer down. The folks of his church have graciously agreed to give our men a second chance, and I have promised him that the men responsible for the problem will be restricted to the fort. Miss Fairfield and Miss Bliss will be here shortly to discuss the details."

Jeremiah headed for the stable to put his horse away. He rubbed the mare's nose, trying to lasso his thoughts. Although he knew what he must do, he feared his best intentions would disappear the instant he caught a whiff of the smell of white jasmine in Annie's hair.

He was adding extra oats to his horse's feedbag when he heard the stable door open. Mack Jackson stood in the doorway. "Chaplain?"

Love your enemy. . . . This is hard, Lord. "Yes, Private?"

"I know Miss Bliss is here from the church."

Jeremiah stiffened, not wanting to hear whatever he had to say. "You'd best not go near her."

"Oh no, sir. I only wanted you to tell her how sorry I am for the way I behaved. I don't expect her to forgive me. I don't deserve that. But. . ." His voice trailed off, and he shrugged.

Jeremiah narrowed his eyes and stared at the young man through slits. "I will convey your words to Miss Bliss."

Jackson didn't move.

"You are dismissed, soldier!"

Jackson saluted and left.

Jeremiah slowly followed. No use wishing the women wouldn't come. One last look heavenward, and he walked with purpose to the captain's quarters.

The door opened as soon as his knuckles rapped on the door. Annie—Miss Bliss, he reminded himself—hovered in front of him, her face echoing his own uncertainty. Tears spilled out of her eyes, when she hadn't even cried on the day of the box social.

"Oh Lieutenant." She sniffed and dabbed at her eyes with a handkerchief. "How good of you to come."

At the signs of her distress, he wanted nothing more than to comfort her. He settled for holding the back of the chair for her.

On her right, Ruth tipped her teacup in his direction.

A burlap sack lay open at their feet, hues of dark blues and greens peeking at him. Annie had been busy with her knitting needles again. Catching the direction of his glance, she handed him the garment. "This is for you. I wanted you to have it, even if. . .I don't see you again." Her face crumpled, and she began crying again.

Had someone demanded the soldiers no longer go to town? Why hadn't he been informed? "What has happened, Annie?" Her name slipped out of his mouth.

"My brother—Samuel, the one in the army—has been in an accident. His captain contacted us, telling us that his wound is serious. Mama took the next train out. We haven't heard anything since then."

Jeremiah's memory flew back almost seven years, to the day he had arrived home to a house that reeked of death. He leaned forward until he was nose to nose with Annie and the other women faded into the background. "Oh Annie." His hand reached of its own accord, his thumb brushing away the tear hovering beneath her left eyelid.

At his touch, she shuddered briefly. She opened eyes so blue that the whole of the Atlantic Ocean could flow in tears to express her sorrow. "The person who wrote the letter said my brother might die. Lieutenant—Jeremiah—I'm so scared."

When she reached for him, it felt like the most natural thing in the world to take her in his arms and rest her head against his shoulder while her tears drenched his uniform. He wanted to keep her there forever.

Chapter 9

As soon as Gladys reached for the last cookie, Annie grabbed the empty plate and headed for the sink. Footsteps followed her into the kitchen.

Annie busied herself with refilling the plate before turning around. Ruth, as she'd expected. Ruth, who had witnessed the humiliating display she had made at Mrs. Peate's home. Annie drew a deep breath and steadied herself to face whatever her friend had to say.

"You can't avoid me forever." The smile that accompanied Ruth's words held no reproach. "Gladys tells us everything that happens with Haydn."

"But that's different." Annie bit her lip.

"How?" Ruth broke one of the ginger cookies in two and handed half to Annie. "Eat this. Maybe the sugar will help you calm down."

Obediently Annie bit into the sweetness, but her insides still churned. "Gladys always said how charming and kind Haydn was. And all I've done is worry about working with the Bear. I made a terrible mistake."

A rustle of skirts alerted Annie to the presence of the others. "Do you mind if we join you?" Gladys asked.

Ruth motioned them in, and Gladys gestured for Birdie to join them. Soon the four women were sitting around the kitchen table, their sewing projects abandoned in favor of a good visit.

"You can trust us, Annie." Birdie spoke first. Annie didn't doubt her. She spoke so little that she wouldn't give away any secrets. "Have you told your mother?"

Annie shook her head. "Not everything." In spite of the low mutter, her friends heard. Heat racing into her face, she met their concerned gazes one by one. "I should have known better. I'm not the right person to do missions. I'm too selfish, too flighty. . ."

"And I'm good enough?" Soft pink tinged Birdie's cheeks. "You all keep telling me I'm a new woman in Christ. I am not the person I used to be." Lifting her chin high, she looked pointedly at Annie. "It's time you listen to yourself. You don't have to be perfect, only forgiven." She hurried on before anyone else could barge in. "And the same is true for your Bear. You've never doubted his faith, only his abrupt ways."

"Have you ever considered that maybe he's the person God wanted you to help all along?" Ruth smiled at Birdie.

Annie dropped her head into her hands so she could hide her face. No one spoke until she looked up again, somewhat composed.

"Even if all of that is true—and you're right—I threw myself at him. No better than a. . ." With an apologetic glance at Birdie, she said, "Well, you know what I mean."

"I was there." Ruth spoke in even tones. "He initiated the

intimacy. And if there was anything inappropriate about it, Mrs. Peate would have put an end to it right away. You know that."

Gladys grinned. "From what Ruth has told us, he sounds like a man in love."

"Then why hasn't he contacted me?" Annie shut her eyes against fresh tears. "I'm afraid he's disgusted with me and never wants to see me again."

"You're not done with each other." Ruth grinned. "My father met with the church elders, and they are ready to plan the next social. We need you and the lieutenant to help us plan."

"Oh no, not again." Annie groaned.

"I can do all things. . . ." Birdie quoted Paul's words to the Philippians. "Stop worrying and let God work through you."

Annie looked at her friends, letting her gaze linger on each dear face. "You're not going to give up until I agree, are you?"

"No," Gladys said cheerfully.

"Then I'd better get back to knitting sweaters." She stood, and the others followed.

❧

A week later, Annie kept reminding herself of all the reasons why she had agreed to meet with Mrs. Peate and the lieutenant again. This time Gladys rode with her.

"You're quiet today." Gladys bounced on her horse. Annie knew she would have preferred a sturdy walk, but the fort was too far away. "You have a lot on your mind, between your brother's injury and the lieutenant."

Annie nodded. "I can't do anything for my brother, and I wonder if I'm doing the right thing with the soldiers. All I wanted to do was to make things for young men who were cold and lonely so far from home."

"If it matters, Mr. Keller and Haydn both like the idea very much." Gladys's face softened as it always did when she mentioned her beau. "Haydn says his mother would like to start a similar project at the closest fort. And my mother wonders why the ladies didn't think about doing it long ago. In spite of what happened." Gladys added the last under her breath.

Annie brought her thoughts back to the present. Gladys remained pleasantly quiet while they passed cottonwood trees, their leaves now green instead of white, the rush of winter runoff sounding over the stones in the brook. *He washed me white as snow.* Even here in the open fields green with new wheat, God reminded her of the gift of new life in Christ, the clean slate He gave those who believed.

A meadowlark swooped overhead, its cry raising praise to God, at peace in doing exactly what God had created it to do. After a week's soul searching, Annie knew what God wanted her to do. She just didn't know if she could do it. Even if she wanted to. *Lord, fix my "wants." I will obey You; make me a vessel of Your love.*

The yellow-bellied bird glided through the air and landed on a tree branch. Cocking its head, it chirped at Annie. Such a simple act reminded her of God's promise to love her more than the sparrows of the field.

"It will be all right." Gladys interrupted her thoughts. "You'll see. 'All things work together for good to them who love God.' You know what Paul says. Even when you work with a bear of a man." She chuckled. "Come to think of it, at the beginning Mr. Keller was a bit like a bear waking up from hibernation, hungry and growling."

That almost made Annie laugh. In the distance, she spotted the gates to the fort. "Good. We're almost there." She urged her horse to a slightly faster pace, and they arrived at the fort not much later. The guard was one she had met several times before. What was his name? Ruth would remember, along with a number of pertinent details. He tipped his cap at the two women. "Good morning, Miss Bliss. Lieutenant Arnold informed me you would be visiting Mrs. Peate today with a guest." He swung the gate open.

"Thank you, Private." She gave him her bravest smile and rode in.

"Thank *you*, ma'am, for the socks. They've been most welcome."

His kind words and the beam Gladys directed at Annie helped sugarcoat the fears rumbling through her stomach. This shouldn't be so hard. *I can do all things through Christ which strengtheneth me.*

Jeremiah appeared on the lawn in front of the captain's quarters as they neared. Annie knew the moment he spotted them. A smile spread across his face. He had shaved his chin so that he sported a goatee instead of a beard.

163

Jeremiah felt the smile forming on his lips. He wanted to call it back when he saw the answering look on Annie's face. Stricken, afraid—of him? His heart constricted in ways he hadn't felt since his fiancée's death.

Annie glanced at her friend and said something Jeremiah couldn't hear before she dismounted and walked with her horse in his direction. "Good afternoon, Lieutenant."

A small smile had taken the place of the frown.

Lieutenant again. How Jeremiah wanted to invite her to call him by his given name again, but he didn't dare ask. Not here, not like this. Instead, he nodded, removing his cap. "Miss Bliss."

Her mouth twisted, but she edged closer to him by a few inches. Her horse snorted, blowing warm air over Jeremiah's suddenly cold hands. He reached in his pocket for a bite of carrot he had set aside for his mare and held out his hand with the treat. While the horse munched, he faced Annie. "How are you today? Any news about your brother?"

"Nothing about Samuel yet." Annie sighed. "But I'm fine. I'm glad I met you out here."

Jeremiah's heart double-timed in his chest. "Is everything all right?" What a ridiculous question to put to the woman he had held in his arms. The hard shell that he had put so much effort into erecting around his heart had shattered, and every question pierced him like a fresh arrow.

Mrs. Peate stood in the doorway. After waving to her, Jeremiah offered Annie his elbow and led her away from the Captain's quarters, granting them as much privacy as was available at the fort. "What's troubling you? Have you changed your mind about helping with the outreach between the fort and the town?" He held his breath. "The men who acted inappropriately the last time will be confined to the fort."

She shook her head. "That's not it at all. I believe. . ." She kept her face toward the ground, where he couldn't read her expression. When at last she looked up, resolution shone in her eyes. "I believe God wants me to speak with Private Jackson. With a chaperone, of course." Her voice sped up. "God wants me to forgive him as He has forgiven me."

Jeremiah blinked against the sense of unreality flooding him. "You wish to speak with Private Jackson?" He repeated her question foolishly, as if he was slow of understanding.

Annie nodded. "And I would like you there as well."

Jeremiah had no answer to Annie's convictions. Not when God was prodding him to do the same. "You shame me, Miss Bliss. When do you want to see him?"

Annie's clear blue eyes searched his face. "Now, if he's available. I don't feel free to make further plans until I have settled this matter."

Jeremiah nodded. "He should be nearby. I'll let Mrs. Peate know we'll be back soon so she won't worry." He pressed her hand, spoke briefly to their hostess, and rejoined Annie. "Come with me." After they took care of the horses, he led Annie to the chapel. "I'll be back with Private Jackson. You should be safe enough here." He smiled ruefully. "Aside from

Sundays, I'm almost always alone in our house of worship."

Annie's gaze swept across the room, and she chose a seat on the front row. "I'll be praying."

On the way to find Jackson, Jeremiah wanted to slow his pace. Instead, the Holy Spirit urged him to speed. He spotted Jackson striding away from the barracks. "Private!" Jeremiah shrank at the edge in his voice.

Jackson stopped in his tracks, turned smartly on one heel, and faced Jeremiah. "I was coming to see you, Lieutenant."

That solved one problem, how to explain his sudden reason for seeking out the private. "Come with me to the chapel."

Jackson took a couple of steps away from the open windows of the barracks, where they could speak without fear of being overheard. "I know that Miss Bliss is here again today. I wish to speak with her." Before Jeremiah could form an answer, he rushed on. "To apologize for my behavior the last time we met."

Jeremiah nodded. "That's good, because she wants to see you as well. She is waiting for us in the chapel."

Chapter 10

When Jeremiah opened the door to the chapel, he saw no sign of Annie. Then, with a rustle of skirts, she stood to her feet by the front pew, a serene expression having overtaken the fear etched there earlier. She nodded her thanks to Jeremiah, but she looked directly at Private Jackson.

Rather than walking to the front, Jeremiah remained near the door, where he could see and hear what happened. "Go ahead." He nudged Jackson's back, praying that he was making the right decision.

Jackson walked the aisle with military precision. The uniform he wore today was clean; he had spent as much time on his appearance as he had back on that fateful Saturday. He cleared his throat. "My mama says ladies should go first, but I'm the one who did you wrong, so I figure I better speak up. The captain told us no alcohol would be allowed, but some of the boys. . ." He glanced back at Jeremiah and shrugged his shoulders. "Mainly me, I admit. I didn't see the harm in a small drink or two, and I thought it would help when I was speaking with a woman I never met before. We'd both be more relaxed, see. . ." His voice trailed off.

"If we were both drunk?" Annie's voice held a strong hint of vinegar.

Jackson hung his head. With shoulders hunched over, he lifted it again. "I'm sorry. I did wrong, and maybe I encouraged some of the others to do the same thing. You don't have any reason to forgive me, but I wanted to speak my piece."

At that, Annie smiled, a sweeter smile than anything she had ever sent Jeremiah's way, and jealousy tickled his nerves. Then she smiled at him as well, and his world turned right side up again. "That's why I wanted to speak with you, Private. God reminded me that I need to forgive you. I've already talked with God about it, but I needed to tell you in person. I have already forgiven you."

Jeremiah had shifted his place so that he could see both their faces. The enthusiastic nod of Jackson's head resonated like a great huzzah.

Annie lifted a finger. "But there is one more person you need to apologize to."

Confusion crossed Jackson's face. He nodded at Jeremiah. "The chaplain?"

Annie looked confused for a moment, then her expression cleared. "Perhaps. But I was speaking of God. Have your asked His forgiveness? For what you did at the picnic?" She drew a Bible from the back of the pew on her right. "Have you ever asked Him to forgive you for all the bad things you've done in your life?"

The wooden floor squeaked as Jackson shifted his feet. "Not exactly."

"Do you want to?"

When he nodded, Annie turned a pleading look to Jeremiah. "We have the right man here to help you do that. I can share what I know, but. . ."

"I guess that's all right."

Annie returned to the first row of seats and knelt. Jackson bent his knees and joined her on her left. Jeremiah joined them on the other side. "You don't need any fancy words, Mack." Calling him by rank or surname seemed inappropriate for a man seeking a relationship with the personal God. "You've already done the hardest part, admitting what you did was wrong. With God, you admit you have done wrong things— sins—many things." He went on, talking about Jesus' death on the cross and the forgiveness God offers to everyone who believes in Him.

Annie joined the conversation. "Do you have any questions?"

"No." Jackson shook his head. "I mean, I've heard you preach about this lots of times. I just never thought I needed to worry about it." He looked a long second into Jeremiah's eyes. "Until now."

"So is this something you want to do?" Jeremiah paused. He always felt he had to add this last bit. "I'm not asking you as Lieutenant Arnold. If you only say the prayer because your superior officer says it's a good idea, it won't go any higher than the ceiling. I'm asking you as your fellow man, another sinner who needs God's grace as much as any other man."

"Yes sir. I know this is what I want to do." Jackson looked

between Annie and Jeremiah. "So is this when I pray?"

Annie and Jeremiah nodded as one, and Jackson prayed a sinner's prayer, one more man brought into the family of God.

Tears tumbled from Annie's eyes, and only strict discipline kept Jeremiah's from brimming as well. All of his calling and Annie's mission to befriend soldiers had led to this moment in time.

*

The soldiers marched into Calico to cheering crowds in honor of Decoration Day. Annie scanned their ranks. Young Private Jackson wasn't among them, even though they had decided the wrongdoers could attend if they wanted to. If the rest of those soldiers were like Mack Jackson, they needed the reminder of God and family more than the others.

Children ran in circles behind the soldiers, boys on bicycles, girls waving streamers. Men who had served in the Civil War, regardless of which side they fought for, carried the stars and stripes. One of the youngest veterans, who would have been only a boy during the fighting, beat a slow drum as they marched, each man's face a study in hidden memories.

Their expressions reminded Annie of Jeremiah. She spotted him, his uniform emphasizing his broad shoulders, at the back of the line. Most of the soldiers under his care were too young to have fought during the civil conflict, but she imagined that chasing rampaging Indians and hunting for criminals also caused a measure of pain. Of course he would reenlist. He must. His calling didn't allow for the same things that other men enjoyed, things like family and a permanent home. A shadow fell across her heart.

Jeremiah had promised Annie two surprises today. She hoped he didn't plan on announcing his reenlistment plans. He had kept himself aloof from her today. She had no idea what his surprises would bring.

The parade reached the end of Main Street and halted at the town square. A few booths had been set up on the grass. Wanting to keep to their original purpose—to raise money for schoolbooks as well as to reach out to the soldiers—businesses around town had proposed several money-making schemes while leaving other things free of charge. Aunt Kate offered free weekly dinners for three months and one of her best lemon custard pies to the highest bidders, while serving free ham and beans to everyone at the fair.

The fort supplied the beverages. Annie joined the line in front of the booth and scanned the square for Jeremiah without success.

"What would you like to drink? Lemonade? Sweet tea? Water?"

Annie studied the sign on the booth. The first glass cost five cents, but the refills were free. "I'll take a glass of sweet tea, please." She dug a nickel out of her reticule and turned to hand it to the soldier behind the table.

She stared at Mack Jackson's face, eyes stone-cold sober. He was dressed in his heavy woolen uniform, and looking unbelievably happy in spite of a slight sheen of sweat on his forehead. "Miss Bliss!"

Annie felt herself answering his wide smile. "It's good to

see you again. You look like you're doing well."

"I am, thanks to you and the Lord. And Lieutenant Arnold of course." He glanced behind Annie. "I'd better take care of our guests."

"I'm happy for you." Annie leaned close for one last question. "Do you know where Lieutenant Arnold is? I didn't see where he headed after the parade."

Mack shook his head. "I'll tell him you're looking for him if he comes by here."

Annie thanked him and slipped through the crowd. An equally full crowd gathered in front of Aunt Kate's booth— where she knew Gladys was helping—so she decided to wait. A brief stop at each booth did not produce Jeremiah. His absence surprised her.

She crossed the square, mingling with the crowd, in the direction of the church. People spilled over into the street, and she thought she caught sight of Jeremiah's distinctive form heading toward her from the north, on the road leading out of town. She moved toward him, sliding through gaps in the crowd, until at last she reached the edge. She had a surprise in store for him as well.

Two people accompanied Jeremiah, a man and a woman. She recognized the woman instantly. *Mama. What is she doing back in Calico? With Jeremiah?*

The other man came out of Jeremiah's shadow. Walking with the aid of a crutch, the man dragged his left leg. His gaunt face haunted her memories. He looked like—it couldn't be—her brother Samuel.

She broke into an unladylike run and raced down the nearly empty street, into his waiting arms.

✺

In the past, Jeremiah had done his share of informing relatives of the death of a loved one.

This was the first time he'd taken part in reuniting a wounded soldier with his family. That must account for the warm feeling spreading through his limbs.

No, that wasn't the reason. Not if he was honest with himself. If he had learned anything in the last few days and weeks, he couldn't hide behind assumptions and half-truths. Happiness had sped his steps home, but he didn't start smiling until he saw Annie.

If only he could be certain she returned his feelings. She had marched into his life, challenging his faith and his ministry and turning his world upside down. Whether she saw him as a man worthy of love—her love—he didn't know.

Samuel stopped his forward progress and braced himself. Mrs. Bliss stood by his left side, offering her support. Jeremiah retreated behind them. Whatever Annie's feelings toward him, this moment belonged to the Bliss family.

Tears streamed freely from Annie's face as she flung herself into Samuel's arms.

Samuel's face twisted, and he blinked. Jeremiah guessed he was ready to cry, but that would embarrass a young man who already had lost so much. He stepped into the gap. "Captain Peate corresponded with your brother's commanding officer. I received word earlier this week that it was time for him to muster out, and Captain Peate agreed I could escort him and your mother home. So—here we are."

Mrs. Bliss placed her hand on Jeremiah's shoulder, embracing him as part of her family. "The lieutenant has been wonderful. We would have had a hard time making it back without his help." The look she directed in Samuel's direction spoke volumes of love and family. Love Jeremiah had once experienced and had doubted he would ever enjoy again this side of heaven, until he met Annie.

Annie glanced at Samuel's leg but immediately looked up at her brother's face again. "You can tell me about that later." She laid her head on her brother's chest. "I'm so happy you're home. I want to run home with you, but I'm responsible for the dance in the town square." She stepped back. "Everyone would love to see you, but I'm sure you're tired."

"We have a lot of time to catch up with each other. Go ahead and have fun." Samuel smiled at his sister. Annie took a reluctant step in the direction of the square.

"I'll see him safely home," Jeremiah promised.

"After that, promise me you'll come to the social." Annie sounded worried that he wouldn't make it. If only she knew. "I saw Private Jackson at the beverage booth, so I believe I have discovered both your surprises, but I have one of my own."

Jeremiah would have marched double time for a full day to receive another one of her dazzling smiles. "I'll come as soon as I can."

As they neared the Bliss home, Samuel's speed increased

to a jagged run, his left leg dragging behind him. He collapsed into the chair in the parlor that Mrs. Bliss readied for him. "Go ahead, Lieutenant. You have business to attend to with my sister."

Jeremiah resisted the temptation to study his reflection in the store window. Nothing he could do would make him worthy of Annie's beauty. In a deep blue calico dress, a red, white, and blue ribbon attached to her collar, she shone with a patriotic brilliance. He hurried his steps to join the jostling crowds, fiddle music replacing the chatter of the crowd.

However, first he had to attend to his duties as chaplain. He sought out Mack at the beverage stall, which was doing a brisk business. "Lieutenant!" The private grinned. "What would you like? It's on the house." Mack dropped a nickel into the coin jar.

"Lemonade, please. I'm glad to see you doing so well." Jeremiah scanned the crowd, not spotting Annie.

"Miss Bliss was here earlier, looking for you. But I haven't seen her since the dancing started."

"I'll look for her there, then."

He found her at the edge of the dance floor, her dress swaying slightly in time to the music. When she saw Jeremiah, she whispered in the fiddler's ear and walked in Jeremiah's direction.

Annie reached Jeremiah when the music ended. The fiddler addressed the crowd. "This next dance is lady's choice. Gentlemen, await your ladies."

A shy smile skipped across her face. "May I have this

dance, Jeremiah?" She extended her hands toward his, inviting him to swing her around in his embrace.

She picked me. "It would be my pleasure." Gathering her close, he led her onto the dance floor. Thanks to long-ago lessons, he slipped into the rhythm easily, and Annie felt natural in his arms. The music ended all too soon. "Can you escape for a moment, or do you have to stay here?"

"I can get away for a few minutes." She accepted his arm as he led her to the only semiprivate spot within reach, near the library. He wanted to pick one of the tulips planted there but left them for others to enjoy. All he had to offer Annie was himself. That would have to be enough.

"Miss Bliss. Annie." He had practiced what he would say at this moment, but now that the time had arrived, he couldn't find the words.

"Yes, Jeremiah?" Her blue eyes invited intimacy.

"The first day you showed up at the fort, you set an earthquake in motion in my life. I know I'm just a used-up soldier, ready to leave the army and see what God has next for me. But you've opened my eyes to what God can do with a willing heart. Do you have room in your heart for someone like me? I promise I will spend my life trying to honor you and love you in the way you deserve, every day, for the rest of your life."

Fresh tears glistened in her eyes. "Jeremiah. People told me you were a bear, but you're a cuddly cub, one who wants to be loved. I would be honored to be that woman—whether you stay in the army or whether God leads you somewhere else." She stepped into his embrace, raising her face to his.

Jeremiah slowly savored the taste of her lips. With God ahead of him and this woman beside him, he could move into the future, free of his past.

BUTTONS
FOR BIRDIE

If any man be in Christ, he is a new creature;
old things are passed away;
behold, all things are become new.
2 Corinthians 5:17

Chapter 1

Birdie Landry smoothed her gloved hand over the sign one of her sewing circle friends had made for her: FRESH EGGS CHEAPER BY THE DOZEN. She could picture it now, sitting inside the window of Finnegan's Mercantile, drawing customers in to buy her eggs from Ned.

I'm doing Ned Finnegan a favor. Gerard's, the other general store in town, didn't offer eggs. Birdie could have danced for joy when Miss Kate agreed that she could raise chickens on the property. She figured she would have enough eggs to pay for her room at the boardinghouse Miss Kate ran in addition to the diner, and then sell the extras for cash at the mercantile.

Those two and a half dozen hens represented the first step in bringing Birdie's dreams for her mission project to life. She hoped and prayed that Ned wouldn't hold her past against her.

No, Birdie told herself. Her friends—imagine, calling the daughter of a pastor a friend—kept reminding her that she was a child of the King. As in the fairy tales she had loved when she was a girl, that made her a princess. Unlike the stories, she didn't expect Prince Charming to ride up and save her.

Mr. Finnegan treated her with respect, like any other woman who frequented his store. Mr. Gerard had frequented the Betwixt 'n' Between on more than one occasion, although he had never requested Birdie's services.

Every day Birdie was reminded of her former occupation as she walked the streets of Calico. No matter what route she traveled from the boardinghouse, she passed one of her former clients' homes. Mrs. Fairfield, the pastor's wife, encouraged her to pray for the men and the families involved. She called it heaping coals of fire on their heads.

Like the pretty white house standing to her right. The bank president lived in that place. Birdie kept her eyes open as she prayed, hoping to imprint the image of new summer grass and children at play on the lawn over the sight of the man in his long underwear.

The door to the house opened, and Birdie crossed the street. She tugged her sunbonnet forward and kept her gaze focused on her feet. No one else appeared in her line of vision as she turned onto Main Street. Because of the early hour, earlier than most people came to the store, she hoped to catch Mr. Finnegan before he had any customers.

Spotting the deputy sheriff heading down the street, Birdie ducked into the doorway of the mercantile. Mr. Finnegan smiled at her as he unlocked the door. His slight build and kind face matched his occupation.

He opened the door wide and stood back so she could enter. "Good morning, Miss Landry! You're up and about early today."

He said that every time she came, although he must guess her reasons for the hour. She shifted the bag holding the sign from one arm to the other and prayed for courage.

"I see you have something in your bag already. Are you wanting to trade?" He walked to his register and leaned forward on his elbows.

With that unexpected opening, Birdie stammered a bit in her response. "No. I mean, yes, I hope to, in the future." She drew a breath.

"Sit a spell and tell me what you have in mind." He led her to a table at the back of the store underneath a sign that promised a fresh cup of coffee. Without asking, he poured some into a dainty china cup and then refilled his usual mug. "Did you bring some of Miss Kate's doughnuts, by any chance?"

Birdie spread out the extra pastries Miss Kate had sent with her. Mr. Finnegan took one, broke it in half, and dunked it in his coffee. "Delicious."

He turned the bag in Birdie's direction. "Go ahead and take one."

Birdie shook her head. "Thank you, but I already had some for breakfast."

Ned arranged the rest on a tray, fingers tapping on a sheet of paper as he counted up the total. "Tell her I'll add the credit to her account. People do love her doughnuts and cookies. But you didn't come here just to bring Miss Kate's doughnuts." He invited her proposition with a smile. "I always welcome a chance to examine new merchandise."

New merchandise. Birdie's mind fled to the day Nigel Owen had used those words to introduce her to a man he promised would be gentle with her. She shoved that thought out of her mind, reminding herself that to her knowledge, Ned Finnegan had never set foot in a saloon.

Ned waited for Birdie—he thought of her as Birdie, as pretty as a cardinal, with hair to match—but she seemed in no hurry to speak her mind. He sent up a quick prayer for wisdom.

Pulling something out of her bag, she laid it on her lap. He resisted the temptation to take a peek. She looked at him briefly before returning her attention to her coffee cup. "You already carry my ready-made dresses, so I have no right to ask anything more from you."

Ned's heart twisted. She acted like she didn't quite trust him, and why should she, after all she had endured at the hands of evil men? *"Give her time,"* God's still, small voice urged him. So he kept his voice to a strict, businesslike enthusiasm. "You have done me a service. I sold the first dress you brought in here in two days' time, and I've had several requests for more." He folded his hands on the table. "I would be happy to take anything you create with your needle."

Once again the sunbonnet lifted, and he caught sight of those vivid blue eyes, as wide and as innocent as the midday sky, in spite of everything she had gone through. "Thank you for that, and I plan on bringing you more soon. But I have another proposition for you. You see, I have the opportunity to buy some laying hens. . . ." She stalled.

"You're wondering if I would be interested in buying eggs." Ned's mind raced around possibilities. Gerard didn't carry eggs. He calculated he could charge three cents for two eggs. "What price did you have in mind?"

She looked at him again. "I was wondering if you would pay a dime for a half dozen?" She looked away, as if unwilling for him to examine her face.

He would need to adjust his prices, but he didn't hesitate. "Twenty cents a dozen, a penny apiece if you have more or less on a given day." He offered his hand, and she shyly shook it.

"Now can I see what you have in that bag?" He kept his voice light, but she had aroused his curiosity.

"I'm afraid I presumed upon your kindness." She placed the object in her lap on the table between them.

Reading the sign, Ned laughed. "I am honored that you would offer me this business opportunity. I'll put it in the window right away. When do you expect the hens to start laying?"

Birdie kept her eyes on Ned while she explained her timetable for setting up the henhouse, filling it with birds, and letting them settle into their new environment. "I'll check back with you in a week."

"Good. Until then. . .do you need any fabric? Thread? Feed?"

Birdie opened her mouth, closed it, then glanced away as she said, "I don't have the funds for more than the feed."

Tempted to respond with a "put it on account," Ned considered how to help her without offending her pride. Somehow God had smoothed Birdie's ruffled feathers enough to accept Aunt Kate's offer of a roof over her head and daily food. Kate's relationship to Gladys Polson, one of Birdie's friends, helped. Ned had experienced Birdie's prickly pride firsthand. But God's love compelled him to try again.

Something Ned had heard tickled his memory. He pulled out his account books and scanned the lines. When he couldn't make out the ragged words, he pulled his glasses from the top of his head to his eyes. He didn't like the way he looked wearing them, but no one as lovely as Birdie Landry would ever look twice at someone as homely as he was, whether he wore glasses or not.

He found the entry and turned the ledger so Birdie could see. "Several of my customers are eagerly awaiting your next ready-to-wear dresses. Mrs. Olson is so eager, in fact, that she paid in advance so we would hold the next dress for her. I can use your share of the money for the supplies you need." He held his breath, hoping she would agree.

"Mrs. Olson?" Birdie's eyebrows furrowed. "My regular dress pattern might not fit. I want to be sure she is pleased with the product. Besides—" Sighing, she rested her fingers on the counter where the sewing notions were kept. "It's not good business to accept pay before the work is done. That's what happens when farmers borrow money against their crops. They end up losing the land." Such a sad look came over her face that Ned wondered if she had experienced that herself. Maybe that had forced her away from home and into a place like the Betwixt 'n' Between. "I don't like to accept money before I've done the work."

Ned had an answer for that. "That's the way I usually do

my business. Get horseshoes on my Ellie, I pay the blacksmith before he starts. When I added a backroom to the store, I paid for expenses right up front."

"Get a meal at Miss Kate's, and you pay after you eat the meal," Birdie shot back. "I know the Bible says if a man doesn't work, he doesn't eat." Her back straightened. She had drawn her line in the sand, and she wouldn't cross over it.

Ned could quote half a dozen verses that talked about taking care of widows, orphans, and the poor, but Birdie would argue she didn't fit into any of those categories. Taking his glasses off the bridge of his nose, he scratched his head with an earpiece. "Tell you what. Do you have enough material and whatnots to make something for a baby? A quilt, a christening gown? My sister. . ." Heat crept into his face. He was uneasy discussing such an intimate matter. But he kept his voice steady. "She's in a delicate condition, and I've been thinking about what to give her. Anything you make would be a marvelous gift. You could probably fix that up quick, and then you'd have money for additional supplies." He kept his eyes locked on hers, willing her to agree.

Birdie returned his stare, her features not betraying her thoughts. She had a good face for poker. At last a rare smile burst out, bathing Ned with the first rays of sunrise. "I have some scraps that would be perfect for a baby quilt. When would you like it?"

Ned's niece or nephew wasn't due for six months, but Birdie didn't need to know that. "As soon as you can finish."

Birdie curled her fingers against her hands one by one, as

if she was calculating the hours. "I should be able to finish it by a week from this Saturday." Her smile faded like the last hint of color on the horizon at the end of the day. "Thank you for your business, Mr. Finnegan." With a final nod of her head, she left his store.

Most men would do almost anything to put another one of those smiles on Birdie's face.

With God's help, Ned hoped to be the one who did.

Chapter 2

These are all the scraps I have." Gladys handed a bag of fabric to Birdie. "I had set these aside to show to all of you before you told me about the baby quilt. If you find anything you can use, please take it off my hands. And here are the threads I pulled out from the seams, in case you can use them as well." She dropped a spool half full of thread into the bag of scraps without waiting for Birdie's answer.

Since Birdie and the others shared alike when they had extra bits of sewing materials, she didn't refuse the offer. The materials in the bag personified the adage her ma had branded on her mind: "Use it up, wear it out, make it do, or do without." But no matter how Ma scrimped, they never had enough. Pa drank money as soon as he got ahold of it.

Birdie reached for the spool and dropped it into her basket. Sorting through the scraps she had gathered, she decided on a pinwheel pattern in yellows, greens, and lavender. She had enough white fabric to mix with the others without purchasing anything else. "I've dealt with some stubborn men in my time, but I've never met anyone as bad as Mr. Finnegan. He wasn't going to let me go until he found a way to give me money."

The other women exchanged glances, and Annie laughed out loud. She examined a square Birdie had already finished. "He's not *giving* you anything. You've put a lot of hours into this quilt already. I couldn't make anything so fine in a month of Saturdays." She turned it over and examined the tiny knots on the back. "And to think you did this with leftover thread. You are a gifted seamstress."

Birdie's spirits lifted at the kind words. She had used those skills to repair dresses for the other girls at the Betwixt 'n' Between. Then there came a time when she didn't ever want to pick up a needle again. That changed after Mrs. Fairfield talked her into joining the Ladies Sewing Circle and she'd made friends with the women in this room. Ruth described the surprising turn of events as God turning something bad into something good.

"You're smiling." Gladys spoke like someone taking notes for class or a report to her newspaper editor fiancé, Haydn Keller.

"So spill the news." As usual, Annie was more straightforward. "You're smiling like Christmas Day."

Birdie cut one of Annie's scraps of fabric into two squares while she considered her answer. "It's something Ruth said about God making something good out of something bad."

"That comes from Romans," Ruth said. " 'And we know that all things work together for good to them that love God, to them who are the called according to his purpose.' "

"Or that verse in Isaiah about beauty for ashes." Gladys nodded.

Birdie looked at each woman, seeing the love in their eyes. When she first ran to the parsonage after fleeing the Betwixt 'n' Between, she half expected the pastor, or his wife, to throw her out. At the time, she was desperate enough to try anything. "I never imagined myself in a place like this, making something for a baby, working among friends." Tears she bottled up while at the saloon clung to her eyelashes, as they often did these days. "God is *so* good."

Annie laid aside her knitting needles long enough to pat her arm. "Yes He is. Even my Bear has learned that much."

Strange how these mission projects had led to love for Gladys and then for Annie. Birdie held no such illusions for her own future. Men wanted purity in a wife, and she had given that up a long time ago. Even Christians had to live with the consequences of earlier bad choices.

The four of them bent their heads over their sewing and knitting. "Who are you making those for, Annie?" Gladys asked. "Seems like you've made enough socks to keep everyone in that fort in socks for a whole week."

"Not quite." Annie laughed. "They get holes in them, or they get lost in the laundry, or a new soldier comes. Jeremiah lets me know, and I don't mind at all. And what about you? You're making yourself another wedding quilt and not allowing us to work on it with you."

Ruth stitched endless arrays of diapers, sheets, and other items to give to people who came to the church in need of help. Guilt tickled Birdie's conscience, and Ruth tilted her head. "Now what's bothering you?" Her gray eyes softened.

"You're all working on your mission projects for free. And Ned is going to pay me for this." Birdie lifted the corner of the quilt.

Annie and Gladys exchanged a look. At Gladys's nod, Annie said, "You ask too much of yourself, Birdie. The three of us are blessed to live with our parents. You pay for your lodging—"

"No I don't. I help Miss Kate, that's all."

"If you didn't live there, she would pay you for your help. She pays me when I help out at the diner," Gladys said.

That fact was the only reason Birdie accepted the room. She felt better now that she had the laying hens and could offer as many eggs as Miss Kate needed for the diner.

Ruth said, "You won't accept help in getting your supplies, so you have to make money somehow to start on the clothes you want to give to your friends."

When Birdie sighed this time, peace lifted her heart like a feather on the wind. "I always feel so much better after we get together."

"That's why God tells us not to forget about gathering together. It's easier to wander away from Him when we're alone." Ruth finished stitching the sheet she was working on and turned down the top, starting a floral embroidery along the edge. "How is your mission project going?"

"So-so." When they first discussed projects in January, Birdie knew exactly what she wanted to do: help other girls stuck at the Betwixt 'n' Between. But doing that required so many things she didn't have yet. A small house they could share together. Proper clothing. Work. Safety. All of that took money. Ever since childhood, money had been the problem. God had provided for all her needs, just as He promised. Was she wrong to want more so that she could help others?

Ruth worked a leaf pattern on the sheet. "It will all work out in God's time. But it can be hard to wait." She pulled her needle and thread through the fabric. "I keep telling myself the same thing, while I wonder when God will show me what He wants me to do."

Ruth already did plenty by helping her parents with the church ministries. But she wanted something more personal, a specific person or situation.

Annie tied off a finished sock and stuck her needles through the remainder of the ball of yarn. "I'm done for the day. I need to leave soon to meet up with the Peates. Before I go, do we have any more prayer requests?"

Birdie enjoyed this part of their meetings the most, although she was still too shy to pray in front of the others. "We should pray for Mr. Finnegan's sister, and the baby."

"And Jeremiah told me one of the new soldiers is having a hard time adapting. Jeremiah is afraid he might desert." Annie never gave the names of the soldiers she asked prayer for, and she didn't this time.

Gladys slipped her needle into the fabric of the quilt top. "Haydn says the snowstorm damaged a few soddies. We should pray for those families."

They had discussed their personal prayer concerns many times. Today they had touched on Mr. Keller's health (improving), beaus for Ruth and Birdie (in spite of their objections), Ruth's hopes for the upcoming school year, and salvation and so much more for Birdie's friends.

Ruth finished the leaf she was working on and put the sheet away. "I'll start." They put away their projects and closed their eyes in prayer.

Prayer. Birdie had seen too many answers in the short months she had been a Christian to doubt its power. As each woman prayed for Birdie's friends by name, she could believe good things would happen. God would make something good out of something bad.

If only her faith remained as solid during the middle of the night.

☙

Ned prided himself on not revealing his emotions on his face. A successful store owner couldn't afford to offend potential customers. But Birdie's question today left him speechless. He recovered quickly. "You want red flannel? To make long johns?"

"I can make them for less money than they spend buying them from the catalog. Better quality, too." If Birdie was a store owner like Gerard, she would be rubbing her hands in anticipation of potential sales. "What I want to know is if you'll carry them in your store." Her smile indicated she expected an automatic yes answer.

Of course Birdie had seen men's undergarments, although Ned had shut his mind to that part of her past. But this venture would drag her back to the past and not the future she planned. Wouldn't it?

The light went out in her eyes, and Ned realized he had waited too long with his answer. "Never mind. I'll make money other ways." She handed him the day's basket of eggs. As she had promised, two dozen good-sized eggs each day.

He gave her forty cents. "This is enough for a couple of lengths of flannel." His voice sounded strangled to his ears as he lifted the bolt onto the cutting table. The scissors lay in the table drawer, and he busied himself with sharpening the blades while he waited for her instructions. After he marshaled his features into agreement, he lifted his face. "You're right, they would sell well."

When she didn't object, he nipped the edge of the material and cut in a straight line. "Do you need thread?"

Birdie shook her head and asked, "Do you think it's a bad idea?"

Her eyes told him she wanted a serious answer. He took his time slipping the scissors back into the drawer. When he looked at her again, the folded fabric lay between them like an exhibit ready to convict her in court. "I believe it's fine as long as no one knows who's making them. I haven't told anyone who's making the ready-made dresses, but I don't know if it's a secret. Some people might add four and four and make ten."

Ned's spirits flagged as Birdie's shoulders slumped, hunched over as if in defeat. She wouldn't look at him. The moment stretched like taffy, until Ned feared the fragile bond of trust between them would stretch too far and break. *What do I say, Lord?*

"Wait."

Ned put together the additional supplies Birdie needed for the long johns, offering his support in spite of his reservations. Once finished, he set the materials on the counter between them and waited. One moment she was slumped over, staring at the floor. In an instant, she changed. Straightening her back so that her shoulders made a proud line, she lifted her chin and looked him face on. "Pastor Fairfield and his missus tell me that I have to avoid even the appearance of evil, because people will assume the worst. They also warned me that I might be tempted to return to my old ways. Tell me, Mr. Finnegan, is making long underwear for soldiers the kind of behavior they meant?"

His mouth suddenly dry, Ned could only nod. Popping a lemon drop into his mouth, he worked up enough saliva to speak. In the few seconds that took, he could see the tremble in Birdie's shoulders as she maintained her composure, trying to appear as if his answer didn't matter one way or the other.

"I'm sorry, Miss Landry. But it seems that way to me." Ned had to find some way to ease the defeat he'd read in her earlier posture. The smile that he had practiced on grouchy customers came in handy. "Annie Bliss is part of your sewing circle, right?"

Birdie nodded.

"She's made connections with the commander's wife at the fort. Together they might come up with a way to keep your role anonymous. Maybe she could even pretend she's the one making the underwear."

The starch left Birdie, and her nod wasn't forced. "I'll do

that. I'll also ask Mrs. Fairfield for her suggestions." Her face returned to its usual placid expression, and she turned to exit the door.

"Don't you want the fabric?" Ned called to her departing back.

In the doorway, she turned. "I will once I have my answer."

That woman had enough pride and determination to build Rome in a day. Spunk, people would call that quality in someone else. She had used it to survive her past, and it gave her the courage to start over again now.

She was everything Ned was not, and he liked her all the more for it.

Chapter 3

Thank you for agreeing to meet with me in town." In spite of wearing her most modest dress, a deep blue that buttoned up the neck and at her wrists, the hem only far enough off the floor to avoid dragging in the dirt, Birdie felt stripped as Mrs. Peate fixed steady eyes on her.

"I am honored that you would ask me to help with another one of your missions. God has done some amazing things through our friend Annie." She nodded across the table where Annie and Gladys were seated. Mrs. Fairfield had joined them this morning as well.

"Here is some fresh coffee." Miss Kate bustled out of the diner kitchen.

Finding a place to meet had proved problematical. They all agreed from the beginning that the meeting should not take place at the fort. Annie had said, "They figured out I was making their mittens, hats, and scarves because they saw me at the fort. That, and the fact I was spending so much time with Jeremiah." A small giggle testified to her present happiness.

If they met at Miss Kate's boardinghouse, another resident might see Mrs. Peate there and make the very connection they wanted to avoid. Miss Kate had suggested an alternative: they could meet at the diner an hour before opening. If someone happened to see them sitting quietly in the corner, they would assume the women were Gladys's or Miss Kate's guests.

Birdie's stomach twisted like a pretzel as she wondered whether the business opportunity she had conceived was of the Lord or of the devil.

Once all five ladies had settled at the table, sipping coffee and eating hot biscuits, they turned their eyes on Birdie. She spooned sugar into her coffee and stirred it, stalling for time. Ever since Ned questioned the wisdom of her enterprise, she had suffered a torrential rain of doubt.

Miss Kate appeared at the door again. "Just go ahead and tell them, dearie."

"That's my Aunt Kate," Gladys grimaced. "She loves getting into our business. All with the kindest of motives, of course. She practically forced Haydn on me."

"And look how that turned out." Annie grinned. "So unfortunate that you discovered the man God wants you to marry."

Birdie decided to speak before they got sidetracked with matrimonial pursuits. "That doesn't matter, since there is no man involved in this matter." Her thoughts ran guiltily to Ned, his kindness and the way he championed her to the community. "At least, there is no man in particular."

"Stop speaking in puzzles." Mrs. Fairfield took her first sip of coffee. "My dear Mr. Fairfield always tells me to begin at the beginning."

Birdie could do that. "Ever since I became a Christian, I've dreamed of helping other girls get away from that place. When I was invited to join the sewing circle, I believed God had given me a sign. One of the first things the women need is modest clothing."

"What a lovely thought." Mrs. Peate nodded approvingly. "The captain often says a man feels the most like a soldier when he's wearing his dress uniform. Changing the look of the outside helps to change how you feel on the inside, even though the Lord values what's inside a man."

Bacon sizzled in the kitchen, and Birdie's stomach growled. She placed a light hand on her midsection as if that would stop the sound.

Miss Kate brought a tray with steaming bowls of oatmeal. "I'll have bacon and eggs for you in a minute."

"We didn't intend to make you work." Birdie's stomach didn't agree.

"Nonsense. Since it's already cooked, go ahead and eat."

Mrs. Peate ate a few bites of oatmeal. "That woman is a genius with food." She dabbed her mouth with a napkin. "I love your idea, but I don't understand how the men of the fort are involved."

Now came the hard part. Birdie didn't want to complain, but. . . "I've made money sewing since I became a Christian. God has provided for all my needs, but it takes everything I make to pay for my living expenses and supplies. Recently Miss Kate agreed to let me keep laying hens to make money a little faster."

Mrs. Peate ate a few more mouthfuls before Birdie started up again.

"I had another idea to increase my earnings. I thought about all those single men at the fort and wondered where they get their long underwear. If they would buy their long underwear from me, I could use the extra money. When I asked Mr. Finnegan for red flannel, he acted like it was a bad idea."

Mrs. Fairfield sighed, and Birdie froze, wondering what it meant.

When she didn't speak, Birdie continued. She turned to Annie and said, "I did wonder if *you* wanted to take on this business, since you already know the men. You could make a little extra money." She struggled to keep her expression neutral. If their secret was discovered, people wouldn't question Annie as much as they would someone with Birdie's past.

Miss Kate brought in bacon and eggs, and Annie turned her attention to her plate, her face a delicate pink. She speared a bite of eggs before she answered. "I'll stick to making things with my knitting needles."

The others nodded, and Birdie had a sinking sensation in her heart. The thought of a man's underwear made Annie uncomfortable. Birdie couldn't remember the last time she'd experienced embarrassment. No wonder Ned talked about the appearance of evil.

Mrs. Fairfield looked at Birdie with so much compassion that tears jumped to Birdie's eyes. "It's a bad idea. I shouldn't have asked," she said.

Mrs. Peate set her slice of bacon aside. "It's an admirable idea. From what I've seen of the men's laundry, they could use some new things. Why don't I think about the situation and see what we can do?"

"In the meantime, start sewing, so you can sell them as soon as we've figured it out," Annie said.

Birdie shook her head. If she bought supplies before she knew she had a buyer, she might waste money. Even though she hoped to speed up the process of making extra money, she needed to wait for God's timing.

"If the work makes you uncomfortable, you shouldn't pursue it. God will give you what you need," Mrs. Fairfield said. She reached out and squeezed Birdie's hand. "But the plan is a sound one, if that is what you feel led to do. Just remember, you're not on your own."

But Birdie had a hard time believing that. She had been on her own, all her life.

*

Ned kept the red flannel hidden on the shelf beneath the cash register, waiting for Birdie to ask for it. Morning after morning, she walked into the store, dropped off her eggs, and took her money without asking for the flannel.

The bell over the door jangled. Birdie swung into the room and set the basket by the cash register with renewed light shining in her eyes. "Four of my hens dropped an extra egg today. I have enough money to buy what I need to make a dress."

Ned headed for the shelf of calicoes. "What do you have

in mind?" How would the town respond to a pair of ex-saloon girls trying to make an honest living? Saloon supporters would object to the loss of "talent," and the Pharisees in town would object to their presence in church. If Ned was honest with himself, he'd admit he had reservations also.

Birdie followed him and hesitated by some of the fancier fabrics, a pretty beige silk that would look wonderful with her red hair, a fine wool on sale for a good price because it didn't sell well during the heat of summer. If he thought she would agree, he would offer it to her for the same price as the calico.

Next she passed behind Ned and studied the solid-colored cotton, the least expensive fabric. A frown creased her face, and she surveyed the calicoes, choosing a brown with white flowers, the plainest calico he had. She took the admonition to dress modestly very seriously, but even ugly fabric couldn't hide her beauty. "I'll take two lengths of this, with half a length of the brown." She pointed to a bolt of cotton.

Ned set out the box with sewing notions for her to examine, and she choose thread and a handful of buttons. "This is wonderful. Michal has indicated she's ready to leave as soon as I have a dress ready."

Another customer came in, and Ned left Birdie for a few minutes to measure out potatoes and flour. After the lady left, Birdie brought the supplies to the counter. "How much is it?"

"I'm glad you can do this at last." Ned told her the total and made change for her. He glanced at the shelf below the register, his hand touching the bundle of flannel still waiting for her. He picked it up and set it down next to the calico.

"I would like for you to take this. A bonus for being a good supplier and customer. Since I already cut the flannel, I can't sell it to someone else."

The light in Birdie's eyes dimmed. "Thank you, but no. I decided against doing that. I'll pay you for the flannel, of course."

"Nonsense." Ned shook his head. "You never bought it."

"While we're talking. . . ," Birdie started.

Another customer entered and Birdie cuddled the fabric against her chest. He expected her to disappear with the same quiet stealth that dictated most of her movements. But she waited for the new customer to finish her business and leave the store before she addressed Ned again.

"You've had a busy morning."

"Business has been good lately." Although Ned welcomed the trade, he knew Birdie felt uncomfortable unless the store was empty.

"I've noticed that. Do you need additional help?" She tugged the fabric against her side and stared at her fingers before looking up again. "You're already doing so much for me that I feel guilty for asking."

"You can ask me anything." Ned's heart sped a little at the thought of what Birdie might ask of him.

"It's my friend. She'll need a job, and I wondered if you could use an assistant."

Ned scratched his head. "So far I've kept up with the extra business. I can't really afford to pay anyone."

Birdie's face fell, and she turned away. He should never have mentioned money.

"Of course. I should have realized. . . Never mind. God will provide. That's what Mrs. Fairfield always says." With that, she scooted out the door.

Birdie slumped at the street corner, away from the window where Ned could see her. *I can't stay here long. I can't start crying my eyes out while I'm in public, where anyone can see.* She called on the iron backbone that had seen her through so many difficult times. After a minute, she raised her face, free of tears, and walked down the street as if she had a right to be there. Once in the boardinghouse, she raced up the stairs to her room and flung herself across the bed and allowed the sobs to shake her body.

I'm worthless, no matter what Pastor Fairfield says. No one believes in my dream. Why should they?

She had thought Ned was different, but he didn't want anything to do with a dirty saloon girl any more than anyone else did. God and Pastor Fairfield might see Birdie with new eyes, but no one else did. She allowed herself to hope that the members of the sewing circle liked her as well as their friendship suggested. "But not Ned." With that final thought, she burrowed her head into the pillow, allowing her tears to soak the fabric.

Get up. We don't allow any bawling in here. Customers come for a pretty face, not one all puffy from tears. The voice of Nigel Owen from the Betwixt 'n' Between intruded in Birdie's thoughts, as loud as if he were in the room with her.

Here, take some of this. It will take the edge off. Nigel had offered Birdie whiskey after her first customer humiliated her and bruised her in places she had scarcely known existed. She drank it that one time but then felt even worse. Never again. After that, she hid her true feelings, smiling on the outside while crying on the inside.

The new Birdie had no problem crying, but she held on until she could escape to a private place before she let go. Unable to put any more into words, she repeated the same three names—Annie, Gladys, Ruth—over and over. At last the tears stopped and she sat up.

The Bible on her nightstand opened to the eighth chapter of Romans, one Mrs. Fairfield said offered her great encouragement when she got discouraged. Birdie had read the chapter so often she almost had it memorized. She especially liked the verses about the Holy Ghost lifting up her heart "with groanings which cannot be uttered" and how neither height nor depth nor life nor death could separate her from the love of God. She reread the familiar words and clasped her Bible to her chest. She still couldn't believe the God of all the universe loved her like that.

A single tear dropped, and Birdie wiped it away. Exchanging the Bible for a brush, she ran it through her nearly waist-length hair, a hundred strokes. After she had calmed somewhat, she splashed water on her face until she had cooled, and looked into the mirror. Fiery hair framed her face, paler than usual except around the eyes, which were puffy and red. The puffy eyes didn't matter to her, and she knew they didn't matter to God, but Miss Kate would cluck over her. Birdie might skip lunch altogether. Why eat? She wasn't hungry. Instead, she took her Bible and sat in a chair by the window, sipping from a glass of water and reading first one psalm then another, soaking in the promises and expressing the outrage the psalmist felt.

After a while, Birdie heard Miss Kate's heavy tread on the stairs. Her landlady's voice followed a light knock on the door. "I brought you some soup, dearie. Please open your door."

Birdie closed her Bible and stood, deciding she could tell Miss Kate about what happened. She had shown an amazing amount of discretion. Crossing the room, Birdie opened the door. "Come in."

Miss Kate surveyed the room, dwelling on the soaked pillow and Birdie's face. "Dearie, what has upset you so much?"

Chapter 4

Haydn Keller held the latest edition of the *Calico Chronicle* where Ned could see it through the window. A glance at the clock told Ned he had about a quarter of an hour before his first customers would arrive. *Perfect.* He unlocked the door, and Haydn rushed in.

"I still can't get used to Calico having a newspaper of our own." Ned had advertised in the paper from the first edition two months ago, and the decision had more than paid for itself the first week. But this week's paper held some special information.

The headline above the fold on the front page grabbed Ned's attention first. LOCAL ENTREPRENEUR TO JOIN BUSINESS INTERESTS WITH RESTAURATEUR. The article promised upcoming nuptials between Haydn's grandfather and Miss Kate Polson before the end of the year. Haydn's smile made Ned laugh.

"If I can't feature my own grandfather when he announces his plans to get married, when can I?" Haydn clapped Ned on his back.

Ned perused the article. Gladys's outreach had helped the childhood sweethearts to reconnect. If Haydn's description of

Gladys made her sound a little prettier, a tad more talented, who could blame him? "When are you going to announce your own wedding?"

"All in good time, all in good time." Haydn rubbed his hands together, and Ned caught the glimmer in his eyes.

Ned continued perusing the article. "You don't mention the sewing circle." He looked at Haydn for an explanation.

He shrugged. "Both Annie and Birdie have reasons to keep their projects quiet, and as far as I know, Ruth hasn't chosen hers yet. Gladys said they preferred to keep their names out of it."

So Haydn didn't print all the news all the time, instead showing sensitivity. Ned found his ad on the bottom right-hand corner of the center page. COMING SOON: READY-MADE CLOTHING FOR EVERY NEED FOR BOTH MEN AND WOMEN. Pictures of men's long johns appeared in the ad, as well as of ladies' dresses.

Ned had thought long and hard about how to promote ready-made long johns without drawing attention to Birdie. The idea of advertising in the paper wouldn't let go. He could gauge interest and, hopefully, assuage Birdie's fears. "Perfect. Is this my copy?"

Haydn nodded. "Good luck. We're praying that you get a good response." He looked at the clock. "Well, I'd better get going and deliver the rest of the papers." He headed for the door.

Haydn timed his paper to print on Friday, for customers who came to town to shop on Saturday. The challenge of anticipating his customers' needs intrigued Ned. In some ways, he faced the same dilemmas Birdie did. Maybe he could teach her how to plot a profit-and-loss sheet.

As the customers lined up outside his door, Ned remembered Birdie's suggestion to hire one of the saloon girls. That move would probably attract the wrong kind of customer.

God's advice to Samuel to look at the inside of a man whispered in Ned's mind, but he pushed it aside as he helped first one customer then another. The biggest crowd passed through after the diner closed for the day. Soldiers had come to town in anticipation of another social event, similar to the ones held earlier in the spring. Several headed in his direction. Did he dare hope they would express interest in men's underwear?

Lieutenant Arnold, who was in the store with Annie Bliss by his side examining dish patterns, noticed them as well. "Let me know if any of that lot gives you trouble."

Ned scratched his head. "I'll keep that in mind. Thanks." Peering out the door, he spotted Birdie, her hair covered with a sunbonnet, hiding in the alley beside the diner. Ned couldn't be sure, but he thought she was reading the paper. He hoped the advertisement would come as a welcome surprise.

She glanced up long enough for him to see the scowl on her face. When she saw the soldiers headed for the store, she disappeared from view before he crossed the room. Sighing, he let the men enter. "I'm fixing to close up shop pretty soon."

The soldiers were uniformly youthful, perhaps as young as

sixteen, full of liquor and looking for a fight. Ned recognized a couple of them from the beer-infused brawl at the box lunch social a few months ago. Had they learned nothing?

Always professional, Ned forced himself to serve them with a smile. He didn't carry any items that would shame the buyer or the seller. As the men browsed, he asked, "May I help you find something?"

"Do you have any sarsaparilla?"

Ned nodded. "I do. Let me get it for you. How many of you want some?" He began pouring drinks from his soda fountain as fast as he could. "Could I interest you in large pickles?" He pointed to the barrel, hoping they would make their purchases and leave before Birdie decided to come another time.

Like children set loose in the store, the soldiers bought a variety of penny candies. One hesitated, torn between licorice and lemon drops, while the rest waited at the window. One of them, the oldest, if the extra creases in his trousers suggested years of use, whistled. "Well, looky there." He pointed across the street. "I didn't know them ladies came out in the daytime."

Ned's heart sank, but he stayed his distance, not wanting to draw extra attention to the object of the soldier's whistle.

The soldier who had requested sarsaparilla glanced at Birdie and shook his head. "Don't get your hopes up. They say the lady is out of business."

Birdie hastened down the street, out of Ned's line of vision. He couldn't imagine how she felt, all those men watching her walk down the street.

"Gentlemen, are you finished?" Ned asked, desperate to

draw their attention away from Birdie.

"Sure." The last soldier asked for lemon drops but kept his head craned, looking over his shoulder for a final glimpse of Birdie.

Ned had change ready even before the soldier handed over his silver dollar. "If you hurry, you'll get to the town square in time for the horseshoe pitch."

"I'll beat you there," a blond-haired lad said.

Relief flooded Ned as they headed in the opposite direction from Birdie, but he felt bad about what had happened. Once again, she had removed herself from a social event rather than draw attention to herself or the hosts. *Not this time*. She had headed in the direction of the boardinghouse. Ned had never approached her there, but maybe now was the time.

After Ned locked the day's earnings in his cash box, he dashed out the back door and hurried along the fastest route to Aunt Kate's house. Birdie entered the house while he was still halfway down the street.

To his surprise, Aunt Kate came up behind him. "Oh dear. I had to return for my second basket of cookies, and I saw Birdie race up the steps like a scared rabbit. Do you know what happened?"

"If I had to guess, I would say she saw someone from her past."

"Oh, the poor thing. When will people accept who she is now and stop worrying about her old life?" Miss Kate shook her head as she opened the door for the two of them.

Ned peeked in the front parlor before following Miss

Kate down the hall, glancing into any room that had an open door. They ended in the kitchen at the back, determining they were the only people on the first floor. A piece of newspaper stuck out from the oven. Ned opened the door and saw that the page with the ad was already charred around the edges, although the front page remained intact. "I understand congratulations are in order."

"Thank you." Miss Kate flushed a becoming pink before noticing the charred pages. "That's strange." She raised questioning eyes in Ned's direction.

Sighing, Ned snatched the paper from the fire. "I expect you'll want several copies. Too bad this one is burned. Do you mind if I go upstairs and see if Birdie will come down and talk with me?"

"Go on with you. You can use the front parlor. I'll be sending up prayers that you can get through to her."

Birdie heard the firm tread of Ned's step as he climbed the stairs and reached the second floor. She knew it was Ned, because she'd overheard his conversation with Miss Kate. But did she want to speak with him? The assurance God gave Joshua when he was faced with a frightening situation jumped into her mind. *Don't be afraid, for I am with you.*

Uncertain, she waited midway between the settee by the window and the door. The knock came, followed by Ned's voice. "It's me, Ned. Ned Finnegan."

Her feet walked in that direction as if God Himself moved them, and she opened the door a couple of inches.

"How can I help you?"

"Please come downstairs so we can talk. The house is empty except for Aunt Kate. We can sit in the front parlor without worry of anyone overhearing us."

Anyone passing by might catch sight of them talking and link their names together, anyone not at the town square, that was. "You should be at the fair."

His smile slipped at her nonresponsive answer. He shrugged as if it didn't matter, and she joined him in the hall. Wordlessly, she passed him and started down the stairs. Instead of the front room, she went to the sewing room at the back of the house. An unusual setting for a visit, but she couldn't think of another community room besides the parlor and the kitchen. She entered, pushing aside boxes of fabric and adding a couple of pins to her pin cushion before she took her favorite spot. Sunshine streamed through the window and illuminated her work space for most hours of the day.

Ned shifted a bag of scraps from the only other chair in the room and sat across from her. His arms hung loosely by his sides, and he tapped his leg with the newspaper without speaking. A faint sheen of sweat dotted his forehead, as if he had rushed to follow her to the boardinghouse. At last he spoke, his voice cool, as if he came calling every day. "Miss Landry, I know this is the last minute, but would you do me the honor of accompanying me to the fair today?"

Surprised by the question, Birdie blurted out, "No, I couldn't. I can't."

His eyes blinked closed, but when they opened again, his steady blue eyes studied her. "Do you object to my company, or do you want to avoid the people of this town?"

Embarrassment that didn't trouble Birdie when thinking about men's underwear flushed through her body, heating her cheeks.

"I saw you when the soldiers came into the store. The leader was one of the troublemakers at the first box social. Don't let him steal the joy of the day from you. He's a fool who doesn't know any better." Ned lifted an arm, as if to reach out and comfort her, but then dropped it to his lap.

Birdie surveyed the room, seeking an answer. She could plead work; she had almost finished the first dress for her friend Michal. But the man addressing her deserved better than that.

Ned opened the newspaper, folded so she could see the inside pages. "I'm sorry I was so harsh about your plans for the red flannel. I wanted you to see this." He handed her the paper.

She read every word of the advertisement for Finnegan's Mercantile again, including the offer for ready-made clothes "for every need." Heat refused to leave her face, but she forced herself to meet Ned's eyes, the unspoken question trembling on her lips.

He met her gaze head on, a small smile lifting the corners of his mouth. "I couldn't get your idea out of my mind. You have a good head for business; I've noticed that before." He held the paper in the empty space halfway between their chairs. "And you are the best seamstress I know. Please forgive me? I do need your help, and I welcome your company at the picnic."

Surprise, pleasure, and frustration warred in Birdie without a clear winner. Ned waited her out, not pressing her for an answer. "I still don't have enough money to pay for the supplies." She fell back on her original objection to accepting payment before completing the work.

"That's the beauty of doing it this way. For now, and later as well, if you prefer, I am hiring you as my seamstress. Imagine you lived in a city and I hired you to work at my garment factory. It's the same principle, only you will do a much better job. We can talk about changing the terms later if you prefer."

"You want me to be your employee. Except I'll be working at home." What a kind, *sensible* thing to do, even if she resisted the idea of working for a man ever again. This was different. Ned wanted her to work for him using a skill she had acquired as a young girl, unlike the last man who offered her a job. The problem of delivery remained, however. If she brought long johns to the store, people would talk. The swirl of pleasure she felt in the offer melted away. "I would have to deliver them to you. People would guess."

"Aunt Kate can bring them in, or even Mrs. Fairfield. No one will question either one of them." He inched forward in his chair, halving the distance between them, stopping short of making her uncomfortable. His whisper was intimate enough to carry over the inches between them. "And I am looking forward to the day that you can walk down the street with your head held high."

He had handed her innermost dreams to her on a plate. She could only nod her head. As soon as her chin dipped a quarter of an inch, he slipped the flannel package onto her worktable and extended his hand. "You can start practicing that today if you will come with me."

Chapter 5

Mesmerized by Ned's blue eyes, Birdie let him lead her to the kitchen. "May we escort Calico's newest affianced lady to the picnic?" Ned bowed as he said the words.

A blush danced across Miss Kate's face, smoothing and adding wrinkles in equal measure. "I didn't know you had such a way with words, Ned. But I hear my ride approach." She raced across the floor and peeked between the curtains. Birdie caught a glimpse of a four-wheeled brougham. Her landlady clapped her hands together. "Norman must have rented it from the livery. I told him to bring a wagon so I could carry baskets to the picnic. But he went all fancy on me."

"You are one blessed woman." Miss Kate's newfound happiness gladdened Birdie. She rejoiced with Gladys and Annie as well. She had no one but herself to blame for the choices that made marital bliss an impossibility for her. She squeezed her eyes shut. *Lord, shut my ears as well, to the harmful things people may say about me or Ned today. He is too nice a gentleman for rumors to dirty his reputation.*

Birdie rummaged up a smile. "Let's go."

Nodding his head in satisfaction, Ned swept Birdie out

the door as Mr. Keller climbed the steps to greet his fiancée. From Gladys's description, Birdie had pictured Mr. Keller as a frail, elderly man in poor health. Love had restored so much vim and vigor, he could almost have passed for Haydn's father.

He tipped his hat in her direction, as if she was a lady deserving his respect. "Good afternoon. Miss Landry, isn't it?"

If everyone in town treated her like Mr. Keller did, Birdie might enjoy herself today. With a lighter heart than she thought possible when she raced home, her heart skipped ahead of them as Ned led her to the town square. He used the shortest path, the one Birdie avoided at all costs.

Birdie's steps slowed then came to a paralyzed stop in front of the Betwixt 'n' Between, with the fear of a prisoner approaching her jail cell. How many hours had she spent imagining herself anywhere but the room she occupied above the saloon?

"Keep on walking," Ned urged. "Don't give them the satisfaction of thinking they have any more power over you." He increased the pressure on her elbow until she moved in step with him.

A few feet farther, she hesitated again. A slender, pale figure loitered in the shadowed corner of the saloon, young Michal Clanahan. When Michal saw Birdie, her eyes widened, and she beckoned for her attention.

Ned hadn't seen the exchange. His attention was focused ahead of them, where the sounds of a lively fair beckoned. Birdie wanted to enjoy the company of the good man at her side, but she had to help Michal. "*She is the first one of many.*"

God's voice sounded clear in her heart, and she came to a complete stop.

"Mr. Finnegan. . ."

"I'd be honored if you called me Ned." He took another step but stopped when she planted her feet. "We're almost there."

"Michal, the girl I told you about, is waiting over there." Birdie looked at him, willing him to understand. "I'm not certain, but I think she's asking for help."

❦

Ned had taken the route past the saloon on purpose. Birdie needed help to shake free of her past, and he hoped God had given him the job. But he hadn't expected to be made a partner in Birdie's desire to rescue soiled doves.

Before he could formulate a response, Birdie's hand slipped from his grasp. "I've got to find out what's wrong." With a furtive glance around, she raced along the side of the building that held the bar. It was without windows; no one could see her.

Ned hesitated, uncertain. Should he follow? Should he go on ahead? Instinct told him to move away from the front of the saloon, where he might attract unwanted attention. As he was turning away, the saloon doors swung open and a barrel-chested man sauntered outside. Nigel Owen, the saloon owner. Ned's guts twisted. At all costs, he had to divert Owen's attention from the back of the saloon.

The saloon owner gulped a mouthful of fresh air before he clipped a cigar and stuffed it in his mouth. "Finnegan, isn't it?"

Ned nodded. Did Owen know anything about his association with Birdie? "Are you talking to me?"

"I sure am." Owen gestured for Ned to join him in the shadows on the porch. "Come on over here so's we can speak like civil people."

Birdie disappeared behind the next building, her friend in tow. Ned forced his difficult-customer smile on his face. "You must be Mr. Owen." He took a couple of short steps, stopping a considerable distance from the saloon. Standing that close to the establishment made him uncomfortable. *This is for Birdie.*

"How's your business doing these days?" Owen lit the cigar and puffed on it, and Ned changed positions so the smoke wouldn't blow in his face. "They've been dragging a little bit at the Betwixt 'n' Between, I have to tell you. Us businessmen have to stick together."

Us businessmen? Ned didn't have anything in common with the saloon owner. "I have no complaints." *Maybe God is getting ahold of the people of Calico and leading them away from the debauchery you represent.*

Owen frowned, brushing ash from his vest. "I saw your advertisement for long johns."

Ned stared at him, not wanting this man to read anything in his expression. "Would you like to order some?"

Owen laughed at that. "Not a'tall, but I wondered if you know who I can ask to sew up some pretty dresses for my girls."

He must have guessed. "I would not ask that of anyone I know."

"That's too bad. I lost my best girl recently, and I don't have anybody who can make things like she did." Owen puffed on the cigar again and waved it in Ned's direction. "I expect to get some extra customers tonight, with all the soldiers in town today."

Ned's stomach soured, but Owen's face remained pleasant. "I'd best get back inside and see if any trouble's brewing. Next time you head my way, first drink's on the house." Wiggling the cigar, he disappeared inside, the doors swishing behind him.

Patting his pockets as if searching for something, Ned forced himself to stay put until Owen was no longer visible. Shrugging his shoulders as if giving up, he spun around and headed to the town square. This new business might keep Birdie occupied for the rest of the day, and he wouldn't hunt her down. She had needed months to accept him as an ally; there was no telling how the new girl would react to the sight of him.

Nevertheless, Ned stayed alert for any sign of Birdie. Because of the fair, not many places remained open. He sauntered around the perimeter of the square, looking for someone he could join without them asking what he had been doing. Why he was late. On one side, the livery remained open, renting vehicles like the brougham and offering free pony rides. Gerard's General Store also kept its doors open. Ned walked by without stopping to chat.

City Hall and the jail occupied the third side of the town square, leaving only the fourth side, where the church was located. Ned's boots scuffed the dirt, and he wondered if he could find Pastor Fairfield. He spotted Ruth wrestling with a water barrel near the church. She raised her hand in greeting. "Mr. Finnegan! So good to see you."

"Let me carry that for you." Ned grabbed the barrel from her. While he set it up next to the water pump outside the parsonage, he scanned the area for any sign of Birdie. The church seemed like the most logical place for her to seek sanctuary for Michal.

Ruth placed her hands on the pump. "It's clear something is bothering you. Can I help, or do you want me to get my father for you?"

He waited for water to splash into the barrel to cover their conversation.

"Over here." Birdie's gentle voice broke through the silence. She crouched at the back corner of the parsonage, waving them over. Ned saw no sign of the girl who had called to her.

The summons caused no change in Ruth's expression. She stopped pumping and headed for the kitchen door, and Ned followed.

"A friend of mine needs help," Birdie began without preamble when they reached her. "Since your parents helped me last time, I didn't think they would mind." She nodded at Ned. "Thank you for keeping that man away from us. We didn't know how we would get away."

Ruth opened the door, and Ned held it while the two women went inside. A pale-faced girl who looked young enough to still be in the classroom waited for them in the windowless pantry. Her tawdry dress and sad eyes told a different story.

Ned shut the door, and Ruth closed the curtains over the sink. "We're safe. No one can see inside."

The girl shuffled forward, her eyes on Ned.

"You don't have to worry about Mr. Finnegan. He's never been to that place." Birdie gestured Michal forward and held the chair for her at the table. "These are true friends, Michal."

Michal risked a glance at each of them before her eyes sought her lap again.

Ruth looked at Birdie, inviting an explanation.

"Michal met me outside of that place today." Birdie swallowed, as if finding it difficult to continue.

Ruth took over. "Are you involved in Birdie's former line of work?" How she asked such a question in quiet, even tones, escaped Ned. He wouldn't be able to put his mouth around it without sputtering.

The girl lifted her head at the question, looking at them with eyes as wide and blue as a newborn baby's. "Oh no, ma'am." Red slapped her face as she lowered it again. "At least not yet."

Birdie put her arm around Michal's shoulders, but she kept her gaze steady on the other two. "Up until tonight, that man has only asked Michal to sing." She patted her back. "She has the voice of an angel. But today he received a special request for someone new."

"And he said. . .he said"—the words seeped out from the cave Michal had made with her shoulders and head—"that tonight I would have to start earning my keep." At that she lifted her head. "I had to get away. I ran outside, not knowing where I could go, and then I saw Miss Birdie. . .and I knew I was meant to go to her."

"And I brought her here." Birdie leaned over, pulling Michal's head against her shoulder as the younger girl shook with unheard tears.

"And I'm so glad you did. First thing, let's get you over to the church. Even Mr. Owen respects the church as a sanctuary. Or the sheriff does. He refused to fetch Birdie, and he won't trouble Michal either." Suiting action to her words, Ruth draped a cape over Michal's shoulders before they hurried between buildings.

Birdie slipped her hand through the crook of Ned's elbow and smiled up at him as if they were like any other couple enjoying a quiet moment at the fair. They strolled through the front door of the church, which was left unlocked during the day in case someone came in need of solitude and spiritual refreshment.

As he and Birdie stepped into the cool darkness of the sanctuary, Ned's eyes needed a moment to adjust. The door to a back room, where mothers could retire with their infants during the service, stood open, and Ruth gestured them forward.

The furnishings of the room interested Ned. The presence of rocking chairs didn't surprise him, but he hadn't expected a mattress.

Birdie must have followed the direction of his surprised

look. "When I first came to the church, Mrs. Fairfield brought me here. She told me that from time to time strangers in need of a quiet place to stay come to their door, and I was far from the first person to take advantage of their hospitality."

Ruth straightened from adding a blanket and pillow to the mattress. "I hate to leave you here, Michal, but if I stay away much longer, people may wonder what happened to me. I'll come back later, with my parents, if that's all right with you."

"I can't thank you enough," Michal said.

Ruth exited the church the same way she came in, through a back door. Birdie sat on a rocker. "I'd like to stay." She looked at Ned. "I'll go out with you, in case anyone saw us come in together. Then I'll return through the back door." She smiled at Michal. Fear fought with courage in the look the girl sent Ned's way.

"I'll leave you alone to get settled while I wait in the sanctuary." Ned took a seat at the front, leaning his elbows on his knees and folding his hands in prayer. God had led him deeper into Birdie's plans than he ever intended to go. His questions felt trapped by the roof, unable to make it to heaven. He reached in the hymn rack for a Bible and leafed through a few psalms, stopping at Psalm 27: "Wait on the LORD: be of good courage, and he shall strengthen thine heart; wait, I say, on the LORD."

He'd been waiting all summer, but God didn't say how long he had to wait. His human mind wanted a limit, but maybe waiting was like forgiving a man seventy times seven: no limits given. All right.

As he leaned forward to put the Bible back in place, the front door swept open, letting in a blinding ribbon of daylight and revealing a barrel-chested man.

Chapter 6

Owen's body cast a long shadow down the center aisle. "Finnegan." The oily tone of his voice made him sound suspicious. "What are you doing here by yourself?"

A hundred different responses ran through Ned's mind. He rose to his feet and dusted off his trousers in a habit picked up in cleaning his store. "Mr. Owen. I don't believe I've seen you in church before."

Owen scowled, and Ned clamped his mouth shut before he antagonized the man. "But of course you are welcome. I come in here from to time to have a quiet conversation with the Lord."

"Talking with God ain't what's on my mind." Owen rotated, taking in the side windows, the lectern, and piano up front. "Who plays the piano for your meetings?"

"Mrs. Fairfield is quite accomplished. We are blessed."

"Preacher's wife." Owen made it sound like a cursed profession as he walked down the aisle to the piano. "My Ruby's never played a church song in her life. She knows all the popular songs though. She only needs to hear it once and she can play it right away." He plunked on a single key.

The note rang in crystal clarity in the almost-empty room, sounding an alarm as clearly as a bell steeple.

Owen glanced at the door to the left of the lectern and headed in that direction. Did the man intend to take a tour of the church?

"If you're looking for the preacher, he's at the fair. I spotted him on the square while I was coming here," Ned said.

"He's not the one I'm after. I'm looking for one of the mares from my stable."

Of all the euphemisms for the world's oldest profession, "stable" was one of the worst, implying that women were animals and not men's helpmates nor created in the image of God.

Ned's face must have reflected his distaste, because Owen laughed. "I know you don't take advantage of my girls, but I treat 'em good. One of them got her dander up, that's all. I'm going to talk her back, gentle-like." Cold, calculating blue eyes raked Ned from head to toe. "Maybe you seen her. A pretty little thing, bouncing brown curls and bright blue eyes, stands about yea tall?"

Even though Michal had looked anything but bright and bouncy, the description fit her well enough. What to do? Lie outright? Claim sanctuary?

The side door that led to the parsonage swung open, and Pastor Fairfield came in. "Mr. Owen, I saw you come in and wondered if you needed my help."

Owen's eyes narrowed. "The same as last time. I'm looking for one of my girls."

Genuine surprise appeared on the pastor's face. "Any one of them is welcome here, but none has come recently."

Ned kept his shoulders down, willing himself not to betray the two women only a few feet away from them.

"I repeat, the women are welcome to come and go here as they please. You have no business here. I must ask you to leave." In spite of the pastor's mild expression, his presence provided as solid a barrier to Owen's intrusion as any of the soldiers at the fair.

Owen took a step back. "I can't prove it. Not today." He planted his feet on the polished wooden floor. Pointing his finger the way a marksman would look down the scope of his rifle, first he singled out the pastor, then Ned. "Your preaching is interfering with a legitimate business. It can't continue. No sir. I won't stand for it."

"You're not fighting us, Mr. Owen. You're fighting God," Pastor Fairfield said.

Ned moved to the pastor's side, shoulder to shoulder at the forefront of the battle lines. He breathed in the pastor's bravery. "You must realize you can't win this battle. Go out the way you came in."

Owen shifted his gaze to Ned. "Your God may reign supreme here, but there's other times and places. You can't keep an eye on your store every minute of every day."

With that final volley, Owen turned on his heels and marched out the door, sunshine once again flooding the church as his back disappeared from view.

The pastor looked outside. "He's gone." Shutting the door,

he walked slowly down the center aisle. "Now, tell me what's going on."

❧

Birdie listened to the confrontation between the men. Ruth had returned to warn them of Owen's approach. Once the saloon owner left, Birdie straightened from the frozen posture she had taken at the keyhole. "He's left."

"Praise the Lord," Ruth murmured. Releasing the arm that she had around Michal's shoulders, she gestured for Birdie to come over. "You stay here while I catch my father up on what's happening."

The two women traded places, and Ruth left. Birdie flashed back to the day she had arrived at the church, as scared as Michal was right now. She put an arm around the girl's shoulders and pulled her close. "You'll be all right." Later she would tell Michal how she had escaped, how faithful God was in providing for every need she had, how God had made her over anew. Right now Michal only wanted to avoid returning to the Betwixt 'n' Between before morning. "The Fairfields are good folks. You'll be safe as long as you're here."

Ned was guarding them. Birdie treasured that thought close to her heart. Pastor Fairfield had recently preached about the honor roll of Bible heroes. She would add Ned to the list—an ordinary man who did extraordinary things because they were the right things to do.

Ruth slipped into the room. "I hate to leave you again, but people are expecting to see me at the fair. If I don't go back, they might ask uncomfortable questions."

"I'll stay." Even as the words jumped out of Birdie's mouth, an unspoken disappointment tugged at her heart, guilt traipsing along behind. When Ned invited her to the fair, she had dared hope for something. . .more.

What kind of Christian was she? God had given her the very thing she longed for, the opportunity to help Michal escape before the worst happened, and here she was, thinking about her own hopeless desires.

Ruth looked at her with something approaching compassion in her eyes. "Then go out and talk with Mr. Finnegan before I leave. He's pacing like the caged bear I saw in Lincoln." She bent over and whispered in Birdie's ear. "God will bless your faithfulness."

Birdie delayed a moment, checking the folds of her dress before going into the church. "Ned. . .Mr. Finnegan, I mean." The heat she had tamped down swept through her body.

"I like it when you call me Ned." An understanding smile tugged at his mouth. "You need to stay here with Miss Clanahan." Shifting his feet, he hesitated. "God is using you, Miss—"

"If I call you Ned, you should call me Birdie." Would he think she was too forward?

"Miss Birdie." His face broke into a wide smile. "Thank you for allowing me the privilege of using your given name." He leaned forward an inch before pulling back. "God has blessed your desire to help your friends. He has important things for you to do, much more important than anything I might want. With your permission, I will take you to dinner

232

at the diner one night next week."

The disappointment in Birdie's heart melted away at his kind words. "I would like that. Thank you for understanding."

"I will stay as long as necessary, in case Owen returns."

At the door, Ned turned around as if to fill his eyes with her image before he waved a final good-bye. Nodding, Birdie withdrew into the bedroom.

☙

The promised dinner didn't happen for almost an entire week, but Birdie didn't mind. Michal spent a couple of days in the back room while Birdie worked day and night finishing her dress. Last night, after Michal had donned a hooded cape, Ruth had walked with her to Miss Kate's boardinghouse, as bold as peacocks. The sheriff kept a close eye on them, making sure no one bothered them, and the move happened without incident.

Half an hour remained until Ned would arrive. Michal turned one direction and another, studying her reflection in the mirror. "Oh Birdie, I've never had anything so fine."

"All I did was show on the outside the beautiful person you are inside—a beautiful, innocent girl forced to make her living the only way she could." Birdie circled Michal, studying her work critically. Did she need to add another button at the back neckline? No, she decided. Finishing the dress had taken all the money she'd saved from selling eggs to Ned, and she hadn't even started on the long johns. Every day she thanked God for providing a way for her dreams to come true.

"I'll start on the long johns tonight." Michal had proven

as skilled with needle and thread as her voice was beautiful. At just the right time, God had given Birdie more work than she could do by herself.

"Thank you." Birdie spared a look at the mirror, wishing God had given her a different color hair. She had to cover it to walk anywhere without notice.

"Yoo-hoo, Miss Landry." One of Miss Kate's tenants called up the stairs. "Your young man is here."

"You'd better go." Michal threaded her needle and knotted the end. "I hope someone as nice as Mr. Finnegan courts me someday."

Courting? Something had given Michal the wrong impression, but Birdie wouldn't argue the point. "You will. God has just the right young man out there." Birdie spoke with an assurance she didn't feel, but for this young, unsullied girl, marriage was still a possibility. She tied a blue sunbonnet that matched the shade of flowers on her dress under her chin.

Ned waited at the bottom of the stairs. When the squeak of the top step announced her presence, he glanced up, joy shining in his eyes. "Birdie."

Birdie's tongue tangled. He had asked her to call him Ned, but that felt too informal. Her stuttering tongue stumbled, and what came out was "Mister. . .Ne–Ninnegan." She covered her mouth, embarrassed at the mistake.

He laughed. "Just Ned. Please." He placed his foot on the bottom stair and reached for her. "Aunt Kate has promised us a perfectly cooked chicken dinner."

"And no one cooks chicken like Miss Kate." Birdie accepted his arm as he led her out the door, where the same carriage Mr. Keller had rented on the day of the fair waited for them.

"You rented the brougham?" Maybe he *was* courting her. Fear sent cold tentacles down Birdie's arms, and she was grateful for the long sleeves in spite of the warm summer twilight.

"Of course." Ned helped her onto the seat as if he rented a carriage every day. "I felt bad for making you face down your former place of employment last Saturday." He climbed beside her, and they started forward.

"That's all right. If God hadn't brought us there at that time, who knows what would have happened to Michal?"

"We'll have to trust God has no one else for you to rescue this evening."

Birdie spotted Haydn Keller walking Gladys home. Gladys's face beamed total happiness, inviting Ned and Birdie to join the party.

The brougham took all the space in front of the diner. When Ned handed Birdie down from the seat, she half expected a red carpet to spread out under her feet. Never had she ridden in anything so fine. A couple of curious faces glanced at them then turned away, and she breathed a sigh of relief.

Ned led her to a table at the side of the diner, where she could sit with her back to the rest of the room, looking out a window. Miss Kate bustled out of the kitchen, carrying her coffeepot. "Oh good, you're here. I've got some fresh chicken fried up just now, and some of my best shortcake biscuits. Thank you for sending me the extra eggs today, Mr. Finnegan. I used every one of them in making the custard. Dessert's on me." She winked and bustled back into the kitchen.

Eggs? Dessert on the house? Fiddling with the strings of her sunbonnet, Birdie glanced at the chalkboard where Miss Kate had listed the day's specials. *Custard dessert 25 cents*— almost the same amount he'd paid her for a dozen eggs only a few hours ago. She folded her bonnet and laid it beside her.

"Aunt Kate likes to tell everyone what to eat, doesn't she?" Ned brought the coffee cup to his lips, oblivious to the anger coursing through Birdie's body.

"You sold eggs to Miss Kate. *My* eggs."

Ned's mouth formed a perfect O. "She ran out this morning and asked if I had any left. It's happened a couple of other times."

"How much did you sell the eggs to her for?"

Ned stared at the table instead of meeting her eyes. "Twenty cents a dozen."

"The same amount you pay me for eggs."

Ned's smile turned into a grimace, and he nodded his head.

Birdie wasn't sure who upset her more—Miss Kate, for buying eggs from Ned when Birdie would gladly have given her whatever she needed, or Ned, for charging the same amount to his customers that he paid her, not making any profit on their business exchange after all.

Miss Kate reappeared, chicken, mashed potatoes, and carrots steaming from two plates. She placed the first plate in front of Birdie with a flourish. Next she served Ned, but he didn't look at either one of them, his chin pushing against his chest. "Oh my. Let me pull up a chair."

No one disobeyed Miss Kate when she used that tone, and Birdie moved to her right. The cook plunked beside her and took both Birdie's and Ned's hands in her own. "You two young ninnies. You're not going to let any little thing keep you apart, are you?"

Chapter 7

Birdie's feet moved of their own volition, ready to take flight away from the mockery Ned and Miss Kate made of her efforts toward independence. Ned wrapped his intentions in a nicer package than Owen did, that was all. Like all the men she had ever known, he wanted to control her. What he and Aunt Kate didn't seem to realize was that if she accepted charity, if she depended on someone else, she would never know if she could make her own way. What if she were tossed out on the street again, forced to find work in another place like the Betwixt 'n' Between—or even worse? "I won't take charity."

The bell over the door jangled, and Miss Kate left to greet the new customer.

"I have to make my own way. Why can't anyone understand that?" Birdie glared at the butter melting on her plate. Should she be polite and eat the meal she now had no appetite for? Or could she simply walk out? She started to turn around to ask Miss Kate to wrap up her plate so the food wouldn't go to waste.

"Don't." Ned's voice dug barbs into her soul. "You don't want him to see you."

"Well, well, well. Look who's here, sitting as pretty as you please."

Owen. Birdie froze, the hair on the back of her neck standing on end. Why, oh why, had she agreed to come to the diner with Ned, as if she had the same right as anybody else to have a nice meal in a public place?

Silence fell across the diner, and a heavy tread crossed the wooden boards.

"Mr. Owen, why don't you sit over here?" Miss Kate did her best to divert his attention.

"Why, that isn't necessary. I'm sure there's room for me at Birdie's table."

Ned shot to his feet and blocked Owen's path to Birdie. "Miss Landry and I are enjoying a quiet meal. I suggest you do the same."

Birdie's nose wrinkled at the odor of stale sweat, whiskey, and cigar smoke that followed Owen like a miasma, and she choked as acid rose in her throat. She pressed the napkin to her mouth and willed herself not to turn around, but she couldn't stop herself.

Owen stood a little higher on his toes and peered at Birdie over Ned's shoulder. "I just want a conversation, real friendly-like, with the lady."

"She's with me." Ned's voice deepened until Birdie could hardly recognize it.

Neither man moved. Miss Kate went from table to table, refilling water glasses and topping off coffee cups. She spoke quietly to the customers, and slowly the chatter of conversation resumed. She squeezed behind the two men and whispered in Birdie's ear, "Eat. Don't let him rattle you."

Birdie didn't know how she could chew, let alone swallow the bite, but she knew Miss Kate was right. She dipped her spoon into fluffy mashed potatoes smothered in creamy gravy that would slide down her throat without effort.

Miss Kate stood by the table until Birdie took a few bites. Then, nodding approvingly, she faced the two men. "Mr. Owen, if you have no intention of eating here tonight, I must ask you to leave." For someone without a grouchy bone in her body, her voice bordered on angry.

With a single swift move, Owen ducked between Ned's slender frame and Miss Kate's more ample figure and came face-to-face with Birdie. "You can't hide from me forever, girl. I know you had something to do with Michal's disappearance, and you're gonna tell me where she is." Satisfied with his final volley, he swung in a circle and marched out the door.

The need for pretense gone, Birdie dropped her fork on her plate. She grabbed for the water glass to ease the dryness in her throat. A few customers sent surreptitious glances her way, but most kept their eyes on their plates or on each other.

Ned, her champion, sat, and the iron that had armed him gradually left. He brought a chicken leg to his mouth and crunched on the crispy coating. "I know you want to leave, and I don't blame you. But you should wait until that man goes back to whatever hole he slithered out of. And please, don't go anywhere alone for the next few days. He's angry and frustrated because you're winning skirmishes you and the

Almighty have started. He wants to strike back."

As much as Birdie wanted to make her own way, she recognized the difference between self-reliance and foolishness. Nodding her agreement, she dug her knife and fork into the chicken thigh. The flavorful dark meat went agreeably down her throat, and the sweet custard pie made from the extra eggs slid down without effort. Ned ate more than she did, chasing the crumbs around his plate. Neither one of them spoke beyond "Pass the salt, please."

Birdie took advantage of the quiet to formulate a plan. While Ned cleaned his plate, she folded her napkin in her lap and made herself look at him. "I know you want to help. But I have to make my own way. If you respect me at all, I beg you, let me do business in the way I see fit."

Ned's mouth opened and shut before he shrugged his shoulders in resignation. "I'll give you eighteen cents a dozen, if that will make you happy."

"Five cents for four eggs, or a penny an egg for less than that." She pinned him with her eyes.

Squirming at first, again he nodded his head.

Birdie had kept an account of every egg she'd sold to Ned, and the number stuck in her head. She knew exactly how much she needed to reimburse him. She had spent most of the money already, on the fabrics and whatnots to make another dress for Michal, as well as fabric for another dress for Shannon, another woman ready to leave Owen's employ. How could she pay Ned back?

As Birdie tied her sunbonnet under her chin, she

wondered at the futile gesture. Owen had recognized her on the street in spite of the hat. In any case, she couldn't have kept it on after she took her seat.

Once they made their way into the street, the setting sun continued beating on her head. Whistling softly, Ned used an alternate route to drive the brougham to the boardinghouse. When he acted like this, attuned to her inner feelings, protecting her, she could almost forget the things he wanted to do that threatened her independence. Part of her, more than she wanted to admit, hated to hurt him, to strain the relationship growing between them. Then she remembered the way his patronizing her had dimmed the shine from her new life. She couldn't afford to be that dependent on any man ever again.

They reached the boardinghouse before she worked up the courage to tell him her decision. The porch swing invited her to enjoy a few stolen minutes with Ned, but they would be vulnerable to watching eyes. Ned must have sensed her unease, because he guided her around the side of the house where beautyberry bushes hid them from passersby but kept them within sight of the house windows.

Ned dropped his hand from her elbow. "You're upset with me. I'm ready to listen."

Birdie took a deep breath. How could she explain her abhorrence of depending on a man when she couldn't quite explain it to herself? "This is something I have to do by myself. Not with your help or Miss Kate's. God's help, maybe." She allowed herself a small smile.

"But you yourself want to help your friends. We—I—care about you. You've come so far in the past year, all on your own. It's all right to accept a gift."

"I can't explain it." Birdie shook her head. "If I had the money to pay you back today, I would give it to you. But I spent it already, on the fabric I bought yesterday. I won't accept any payment for the long johns or the eggs until I pay you back."

❧

"It's not that much." *Weak, Ned, that's weak. Tell her you refuse payment of any kind.*

"I'll check my records to make sure of the amount." Her face relaxed a little bit. "But I've counted it over and over, every penny and nickel and dime."

Ned counted to ten. He could list any number of reasons, from spiritual to practical, to prove her wrong, but God's small voice told him to let it go. Staying silent was difficult when all he wanted to do was to take Birdie in his arms and beg her to let him help. "It's no hardship, you know. God has blessed my business." A previous discussion popped into his head. Following up on her suggestion could do no harm. "My business has picked up, and I could use a clerk to help me. Would you like the job?"

Before he finished voicing the question, color raced into Birdie's face and she backed up a step. "Not me. I'm busy sewing. But one of the girls is real good with numbers, and I think she's ready to leave. As soon as. . ." The same defeated expression he had seen on her face earlier returned.

"Would Miss Clanahan be interested?"

The expression on Birdie's face gave Ned her answer before she spoke. "She's shy, in spite of everything she's been exposed to. She's handy with a needle, though. She's already helping me with the long johns." A small smile lightened her face.

As long as the women lived with Aunt Kate, they wouldn't go hungry. Ned thanked the Lord for that much. "I will let you do this, Birdie. But don't you try to repay me one penny more than one cent apiece. You're not the only one who keeps records."

The window curtains twitched, reminding Ned of how long they had lingered outside talking. The sky had deepened to the dark blues of twilight. A single strand of red hair dangled across Birdie's forehead and cheek. His fingers itched to tuck it behind her ear, but before he could untangle his fisted hand, she found it and took care of it.

"Thank you for standing up to that man tonight." Birdie played with the strings of her sunbonnet, and he wished she would remove it and reveal her glorious hair. "I will see you in the morning, when I bring the eggs." A frown line creased the bridge of her nose. "The next time Miss Kate needs eggs, send her to me. Please. She should know she only has to ask."

Ned nodded in resignation. Even when he and Aunt Kate came up with the idea of her buying eggs from the store for the diner instead of asking Birdie for more, he had known this day would come. "I will."

"Until tomorrow, then." Walking away, she removed the

bonnet from her head, and the final golden fingers of sunset set her head afire.

Miss Birdie Landry might not accept his money. But there had to be something more he could do to help.

God would show him the way.

Chapter 8

"How's this one?" Ned held up an empty jar from the top shelf for Gladys's inspection.

"Perfect." Gladys accepted it and tied a bow in a red-and-white check around the mouth of the jar. On the outside she pasted a sign drawn on fine drawing paper that simply said: BUTTONS. She giggled. "Birdie will never guess what you have in mind. And she can't complain about this." She gave the jar a prominent place between the cash register and a container of lemon drops on the front counter. "Between Aunt Kate, Mrs. Fairfield, and me, this jar will be full in no time at all."

"And the button count will be a real contest. Everyone will win." Ned climbed down from the ladder. "I hope people will want to help."

"Mr. Keller has enough money to make things happen. In fact, he wants to be the first contributor. I'll buy some buttons, and you can put any change into Birdie's account." She pulled a ten-dollar bill from her pocket and studied the array of buttons with the sewing notions. "I know she loves pearl-like buttons, but they're a little more expensive. So I'll get wooden buttons in all different sizes and shapes, as well as in all different colors."

As soon as Ned counted out the buttons, Gladys dropped them into the jar, where they hit the bottom with a *ping*. "You said you have some buttons at home that you wanted to add?"

Emptying his pockets, Ned dropped a dozen or so buttons of assorted colors into the jar. "If I find more, I'll add them."

Gladys tacked another sheet of drawing paper next to the jar.

BUTTON CONTEST. BRING ANY BUTTONS THAT YOU HAVE AT HOME AND ADD THEM TO THE JAR. ON JULY 1st–3rd, GUESS THE NUMBER OF BUTTONS IN THE JAR. THE WINNER WILL BE ANNOUNCED DURING THE INDEPENDENCE DAY FESTIVITIES. GRAND PRIZE: A BAG OF LEMON DROPS AND A YARD OF YOUR FAVORITE FABRIC

"I never would have thought of lemon drops." Ned popped one in his mouth.

"The children will be excited. They'll pester their mothers, who will remember the buttons. Mrs. Fairfield said they've done the same kind of thing at church. Get the children to come and the adults will follow."

Ned scratched his head. "Did it work?"

"It must have." Gladys shrugged. "She wouldn't have suggested it otherwise."

The bell rang, and the door swung open. "Oh, you have a customer." Birdie spoke so quietly that Ned could hardly hear her.

"It's just me, Birdie, come on in. I wanted to talk with you anyhow." Gladys winked at Ned. "You're just the right person to help with this campaign."

"What is that?" Birdie came to the front. "Fifteen eggs today."

She waited while Ned counted them. "Fifteen it is." He nodded at the button jar. "I'm asking folks to bring whatever extra buttons they have, ones that they find on the ground or that they took off a shirt after it wore out."

"There are some in here already." Birdie leaned over and studied the contents of the jar. "You're off to a good start. Let me check and see if I have any. If I do, I'll bring them with me tomorrow."

Behind Birdie, Gladys smothered a laugh. "So you want the lemon drops?" She let out her laugh this time.

"If I win, I'll give the candy to Ruth for her school-children. And fabric always comes in handy." She tapped on the countertop. "I expect to have three pairs of long johns ready by Friday if anyone inquires after them."

"That's good." Ned nodded. "You're getting a lot done with Miss Clanahan's help."

That brought a smile to Birdie's face.

"God is already using you to accomplish the mission He called you to do. I'm happy for you," Ned said.

Birdie's smile dimmed. "I don't think there's enough sewing for more than the two of us. Girls leaving the life need so much—clothes, jobs, a home." She fixed her gaze at a point far away down the street, out to the farms lying east of town.

Gladys said with a smile, "I have an idea about finding jobs."

Birdie spun around. "What's your idea?" Turning to Ned, she said, "Gladys was the one who suggested the mission projects idea for our group. She's a bit of a dreamer."

Gladys laughed and hugged Birdie in a sisterly embrace. "I hope you approve of this new idea." She glanced at Ned for confirmation to speak, and he nodded. "Actually, this is Haydn's idea. Ned here needs help in the store a few hours a day." She lifted her hand and started counting on her fingers. "I'd like to stop working at the diner after I get married, so Aunt Kate will need help. Mrs. French just had twins; she could use an extra pair of hands. There are other people who are willing to pay a small salary for someone to help them out."

"But most people won't want to have a saloon girl helping them, will they?"

"We won't know if we don't ask. Pastor Fairfield is preaching about being salt and light in the world, so God is already preparing our hearts." Gladys bounced up and down in her excitement. "And Haydn would like to write articles about each girl."

Birdie shook her head sharply.

"Listen to her before you say no." Ned heard the pleading note in his voice. When she wouldn't accept his help, he had hoped she would accept a suggestion from one of the other circle members.

"Haydn will use aliases. He'd love to tell their stories, but that is up to each lady. And he won't describe them either, so no one will be able guess who is who."

"I don't understand. How does this help them find jobs?" Birdie hadn't run away yet. Ned took comfort in that.

"The focus of each article will be the life story of each woman, with perhaps a mention of the work they would like to do."

Birdie shook her head thoughtfully. "A lot of the girls are in that place because they don't think they have anything to offer. But maybe I could match the services needed and the girls' skills, since I know them."

"Yes!" Gladys clapped her hands.

"What if they don't want to speak with Mr. Keller?" Birdie was weakening! Ned cheered internally.

"He would tell you what questions to ask, and you could tell him the girls' answers. We don't want to make anyone feel uncomfortable. Mrs. Fairfield will speak with the people needing help to make sure none of the women encounters another Nigel Owen."

Birdie shivered, and Ned touched her shoulder. When she didn't shrug his hand away, he left it there as he breathed a prayer. *Please say yes.*

"I'll ask them." Her smile highlighted light pink dimples in her cheeks. "You've put a lot of thought into this. Thank you."

❧

Birdie splashed cold water on her face to wake herself up and pulled her hair back in a simple bun. Michal had already donned her new dress and was running a brush through her hair.

They heard a knock, and Miss Kate spoke through the door. "May I come in?"

"Yes," Birdie said.

The doorknob turned, and savory aromas accompanied Miss Kate into the bedroom. She set a steaming bag on the bed. "Ham biscuits and sausage rolls. I made extra, so you can take them for the other girls to eat."

For her landlady's sake, Birdie would try to eat. If everyone in Calico had Miss Kate's kind heart, Birdie wouldn't have any doubts about their plans for helping the girls.

But then, if everyone in Calico had Miss Kate's kind heart, the Betwixt 'n' Between would have gone out of business years ago. A piece of advice Mrs. Fairfield gave Birdie jumped into her head: look at others with God's eyes. That was the only way she could find her way to forgive men like Owen, men who had used and abused her.

"God sure has His hand on you," Miss Kate said. "The way Shannon came to church on Sunday, after the night she must have had. And then you could ask her to invite everyone who wanted to, to come to the meeting this morning."

The very hour of the meeting—four in the morning—spoke to the desperate circumstances of the women. It was late enough for the saloon to have closed down and its employees to be settled in their beds. And it was early enough that the girls hoped to leave without attracting Owen's attention.

Michal was already eating a biscuit. "This is delicious, Miss Kate. The girls will enjoy your home-cooked food." She ate every bite as if she didn't know when she would receive another meal. Meals were a haphazard affair at the Betwixt 'n' Between, cold leftovers snatched whenever they had a moment. Some girls turned to drinking their meals. Ones with an alcohol problem, like Michal's best friend, Susanna, would face even greater challenges than Birdie had if they were able to escape their present circumstances.

"Your three friends are all waiting in the kitchen. I gave them a bite to eat. Come on down when you're ready." The door shut behind Miss Kate as she left. For a woman of ample proportions, she was able to move quickly and quietly.

Birdie tied her blue sunbonnet over her hair and helped Michal into her cloak. Michal was still fearful to leave the safety of the boardinghouse. She hugged the bag of sandwiches and rolls close to her chest under the cover of her cloak.

Birdie's bag held only one item: the dress she had been able to finish. Only a single dress. Two more dresses were done except for the finishing touches—buttons and lace, matching thread for some invisible seam work. So little to show for so much work. Since she was now paying double for room and board—even though Miss Kate protested against it—she needed longer than she'd hoped to finish paying Ned back.

Candles cast a soft light on Birdie's friends' faces. Ruth hugged Michal as if they were longtime friends and introduced her to Annie and Gladys. Michal glanced up briefly from underneath the cover of her hood. "Glad to meet you."

"We are honored that you let us come." Annie's smile invited the world to join in. "Between the four of us, we hope we can address any concerns the ladies have."

Ruth gathered their dishes and put them in the sink. "Let's leave so we can be there when the others arrive. My mother is already at the church, ready to greet any early comers."

Her friends' kindness brought warmth to Birdie's heart but did little to ward off the chill of the early morning. She was grateful for the shawl draped around her shoulders. They walked in silence, Ruth, Gladys, and Annie surrounding Birdie and Michal, until they turned in the direction of the church side of the town square. A small light testified that someone in the parsonage was awake. "Papa said he would pray for us during our meeting," Ruth said.

So many people had helped to make this happen. Besides the sewing circle, Miss Kate, Pastor and Mrs. Fairfield, and Lieutenant Arnold had participated.

Ned. Birdie refused to think about him right now. One by one the women slipped into the side door of the church. Mrs. Fairfield rose from her seat on the front pew, embraced Birdie, and turned to Michal. "And you must be Michal. A shiny new jewel in the crown of our Lord. Please know how welcome you are here in our midst."

Michal colored, and Birdie remembered how uncomfortable Mrs. Fairfield's outspokenness had made her at first.

"And what is that I smell? Breakfast from Aunt Kate?"

"Ham biscuits and sausage rolls." Michal handed them to the pastor's wife.

"Excellent! I brought over a pot of coffee and some biscuits, but Aunt Kate's food is such a delight. Now, come this way. The room will be slightly crowded, but no one can see us in there." Mrs. Fairfield opened the door to the same room where Birdie and Michal had first taken refuge. "I'll stay out here in case anyone comes along later."

Birdie took the lead, entering the room first. One step inside transported her back to the Betwixt 'n' Between. Unwashed bodies, cloying floral scents, whiskey, cigar smoke—all of those smells and more, with girls in varying degrees of undress. She shut her eyes and stopped just short of pinching her nose, long enough for the unpleasant memories to diminish. Once again she repeated those beautiful words about God's love to herself. *For I am persuaded, that neither. . .things present, nor things to come. . .shall be able to separate us from the love of God, which is in Christ Jesus our Lord.* Mrs. Fairfield had added "nor things in the past." God wouldn't hold her past against her after she asked Him to forgive her. Something about her sins being buried in the deepest seas. She lifted her head high in the love of her Savior and prepared to meet the women He had called her to help.

Chapter 9

Ahandful of women crowded next to each other on the far bench. Naomi. Orpah. Both names, Ruth had told her, came from the book of Ruth in the Bible. Shannon, who was ready to leave today. Susanna, a Southern belle pushed west by the Civil War and its aftermath. She had taken Birdie under her wing, protected her as much as she could, and comforted her after customers got too rough. Michal had told Birdie that Susanna had also taken the blows dished out by Owen when Birdie ran away. Tears at the memories burned Birdie's eyes, and all her earlier fears fled, replaced by a courage unknown to her.

She glanced at the second bench, left free for the church ladies. She turned her back on the empty bench and laid a gentle hand on Susanna's shoulder. "Do you mind if I sit here?"

Eyes blurry from a night of excess peered at the sunbonnet on Birdie's head. "Birdie, 'sthat you?"

Here, in this room, Birdie had no need to hide herself. She removed the bonnet and shook her hair around her shoulders. "It's me, Susanna."

"I always did say your hair was like the sunrise." Susanna

lifted a tentative hand, and Birdie leaned forward, letting her friend run fingers through her hair. "All that color without help from the henna bottle. You'se a lady now."

With those words, the women around Birdie shrank back. She reached as far as she could in both directions, until she touched each woman. "I'm no more or less a lady than ever I was. What has changed is that God has made me new. I'm a new creation. Nothing from the past can hold me back."

"That's all good and fine for you, Birdie. But nothing's gonna change for a gal like me." Naomi shook her head, even though a hopeful light beamed from almost black eyes, her dusky coloring and dark features suggesting Indian blood.

Love flooded Birdie's heart, mixed with a desire for these women to accept the good news of Jesus as shown by the people of Calico. "God's love is for anyone, anytime, anywhere. The Good Book says we were still Jesus' enemies when He died for us. One of His best ladies was a prostitute once upon a time. He loves us, all of us."

Michal handed out Miss Kate's breakfast. Before long, a knock at the door interrupted her, and Mrs. Fairfield came in. Birdie introduced her two sets of friends to one another.

Shannon sank against the wall. It was almost time to go back.

Another time Birdie would tell more of the old, old story. Right now these women needed an escape plan. "This is what we have in mind. Miss Fairfield and Miss Polson came up with a plan to help you find work if you decide you're ready to leave the Betwixt 'n' Between. I'll let Miss Polson explain."

The women listened with interest until Gladys mentioned the interviews that Haydn wanted to conduct. "A man interviewing me? How do I know he's not fixing to run and tell Owen all about our plans?" Orpah's lips made a thin line.

Birdie met Orpah's glare. "If you don't want to speak with Mr. Keller, you can talk with me. We won't give out your names or anything else you want to keep personal."

Orpah frowned but didn't say anything further. Naomi voiced her objections. "I don't have any clothes I can wear in normal society. I can't wear something like this." She gestured to the dress she had arrived at the saloon in, only a couple of months after Birdie. The hem rose higher on her ankle than was considered proper, and the cloth strained across her chest. The clothes the others wore were in even worse condition.

Birdie hastened to reassure her. "I'm working on dresses for you so you have something decent to wear about town." The single dress in her bag seemed so small in comparison to the need. "I only have one ready now, but I hope to have more ready soon." As soon as she could buy buttons, bric-a-brac, all those finishing details.

"You always wuz right handy with a needle and thread," Susanna said.

"So can we all leave right now?" Naomi asked. "Or do we have to leave one at a time? Owen might take it out on whoever's left behind." Her voice wobbled, but her gaze remained focused on Birdie.

Fear and joy fought within Birdie's racing heart. This was what she wanted—wasn't it?—but whatever would they do with four women all at once? Five, if they counted Michal.

Be not afraid. Birdie took in God's promise along with Mrs. Fairfield's nod. "Anyone who is ready to leave right now can stay here at the church until we find places for you all to go." Miss Kate had said to bring anybody along to the boardinghouse who wanted to come, but she didn't know if even that indomitable lady could handle four strangers all at once. "You can stay here in privacy, and there's plenty of good food to eat."

Orpah stopped chewing on her sausage roll and nodded in appreciation.

"It will be one of us who brings your food and helps you get away to a safe place." Annie handed the bag of rolls around again.

"We'll get some menfolk to keep watch. The sheriff's a good man, and so is my fiancé, Haydn Keller." A smile of unbridled joy shone in Gladys's eyes. "And Annie's lieutenant and Pastor Fairfield. And Ned Finnegan."

"I'll introduce them to you so you won't get scared when they come around." Mrs. Fairfield crossed the room in a few steps and stood in front of Susanna and took her hand. "I'm the pastor's wife, Hannah Fairfield. I'm pleased to meet you, Susanna." Mrs. Fairfield didn't seem to notice the torn fingernails or the reek of whiskey coming from Susanna's clothes. She went down the line, greeting each woman by name. "The parsonage is right next door, straight out the side door. If something happens that worries you, day or night, come right over and tell us about it." She offered a cloak and bonnet she had draped across her arm to Naomi. "This is yours if you'd feel better about wearing it when it's time for you to come. I know it's hot in here, but you should be out of here in a day or two."

"What if Owen comes looking for us? He's already breathing fire after losing Birdie and his songbird." Naomi spoke as if Owen's violence was a fact of life. For her, it was.

"He'll have to get past a whole host of angels—human and heavenly—to get to you. And the church is a sanctuary even Owen won't violate." As she pressed each of their hands, Birdie saw courage rising in each woman's heart. "But we'd best leave for now, before someone has reason to question what all of us are doing at the church at this hour. Gladys, Michal, why don't you head out first?"

Birdie gathered her hair into a knot at the back of her neck and tied her sunbonnet on before draping her shawl across her shoulders. "I have one more dress that is almost finished. I'll bring it over as soon as I get the buttons." How she wished she could finish the other dresses more quickly.

She opened the door and slipped out after Gladys and Michal. A familiar figure waited at the front door. Ahead of her, Michal drew back, and Birdie touched her arm. "Don't worry. That's Mr. Finnegan."

✒

At the sound of female voices, Ned squinted into the early-morning sun pouring in the east-facing windows. *Birdie.* He hustled down the center aisle and met her halfway. "I thought I'd better come in case Owen figured out what was happening and tried to bother you."

Dependable. Kind. Brave. Any number of words could describe Ned Finnegan, even if the gun in his arm looked as out of place as a storekeeper's apron on a soldier. "Thank you, Ned."

The door opened, and Haydn scurried in. "Is everything all right?"

At Haydn's appearance, Michal drew back. Birdie said, "This is Mr. Keller, Gladys's intended. He's a good man."

Ned nodded at Birdie. "I'll walk you and Miss Clanahan home while Haydn escorts Miss Polson and Miss Bliss."

"Let's get moving, then, before it gets any later." But before Birdie could continue down the aisle, the front door opened and the preacher stood on the threshold. "He's on his way with his men."

Chapter 10

Pastor Fairfield didn't have to explain who he meant.

"I'll go get the sheriff." Haydn raced to the side door.

"Get back." Ned urged the women to safety.

Not quite steady on his feet, Owen pushed past the pastor, his men close behind. The gun he held was all the more dangerous in the hands of a drunken man.

"They're here. You can't tell me they're not. There's three of them right there, although what they're doing in church is a pretty story. Maybe your man of the cloth here isn't all you expect him to be."

"Why, you." Birdie spoke from behind Ned. She hadn't retreated to the room after all.

"Get down." Ned fought to keep fear out of his tone.

"I'll get 'er back sooner or later, but she ain't my concern this morning. Imagine my surprise when I headed downstairs for a pick-me-up, to find my faithful Susanna missing. Checked the cribs upstairs, and there's four gone, new this morning gone." Owen hurtled himself forward, almost falling down, righting himself when he grasped the back pew. "Bring 'em out nice and peaceable, and we won't have any argument between us."

"Over my dead body." Ned's voice rang out loud and clear. He might be a shopkeeper, but he had learned how to shoot on the farm as a boy.

"Nigel Owen!" Pastor Fairfield used a deep voice that could have scared the devil himself out of hell. "I have told you before. You have no business here. This is God's house."

Ned darted a glance at the pastor. Dressed in a pair of pants held up by suspenders, and with nothing more than a Bible in his hands, he still radiated unmistakable authority, the general of this spiritual fortress.

"Well, Pastor, so you keep saying. But you're interfering with a legitimate business. Those women signed contracts to work at the Betwixt 'n' Between. They have to come back."

Behind him, Ned heard Birdie grunt. She had told him about the marks the girls made on those contracts when they were too drunk to know what they were doing.

The side door opened and Sheriff Carter strode in. "Not unless I say so." He also trained his rifle on Owen. "In fact, I hear tell the town council is ready to put the vote to make Calico dry on the next ballot. If you know what's best for you, you'll skedaddle out of town before you lose your shirt altogether."

Owen stumbled forward a step, discharging his weapon as he flopped about. It hit a rafter high above him.

Ned's finger pressed on the trigger, and the bullet hit Owen right where he aimed it—at his right shoulder, to wing him, not to kill. Owen slumped on the floor and howled. "I wasn't shooting at you!" He screamed curses.

Sheriff Carter ran down the side aisle, keeping his rifle ready to shoot if necessary. He kicked Owen's gun away and handcuffed his hands together. "Tell it to the judge—after we all tell him how you started a gunfight in this house of worship. That'll be right after we get a doctor to fix you up." Dragging Owen to his feet, he paused by the door. "The rest of you better leave before I find a reason to drag you along with your boss."

"They all follow his lead." Birdie came up beside Ned as the men filed out the front door. "None of them has enough courage to come after us here without him. We're free." She pulled the sunbonnet from her head. "We're finally free. How perfect, to celebrate our personal freedom on the Fourth of July."

As the sheriff escorted Owen out of the church, Haydn headed for the back room and Ned crossed the front to the pastor. "I'm sorry for the gunfire, pastor."

"Don't worry. You were protecting what is most important to you except for the Lord Himself." He smiled at Birdie. "I'll join the ladies in the room."

Ned pulled Birdie close to him, closer than he ever had before, and she settled comfortably against his chest. He breathed in the floral scent of her brilliant hair. He could face a hundred lions for this woman.

Michal coughed, reminding him that although Ned had so much to tell Birdie, now was neither the time nor the place. He relaxed his hold on Birdie, and she took one hesitant step backward. "I need to get back to Miss Kate's. To let her know about her company coming." Even as she spoke, her eyes studied his features one by one, as if memorizing them.

✿

"You'll see me later today. I promise." A tenderness Birdie couldn't believe possible shone from Ned's eyes as he smiled down at her.

"Of course. When I bring you the eggs." Dropping her eyes, she stepped past Ned on her way to the door.

"And when I announce the winner of the button jar contest."

Birdie's laughter rang as she and Michal headed for the door. "I plan on being there."

"If you don't come, I'll come down and get you myself." She laughed again. "But now I'll walk you home."

Later that morning, Michal had no interest in the button drawing. "It's too soon for me, Birdie. But you go, with your Mr. Finnegan. Enjoy yourself."

Birdie walked down Main Street, striding confidently past the Betwixt 'n' Between. A good-sized crowd had gathered in front of Ned's store. He should be pleased.

Ned noticed her approach and motioned her forward. For some reason, he began to clap. Soon everyone joined in.

Birdie stopped in midstep. They couldn't be clapping for her—could they? Ned motioned again for her to join him in front of the store. "Now we can get started."

Light laughter rippled across the crowd.

"First I'll announce the winner of the counting contest. The person who will be leaving here with all the lemon drops she can eat, as well as a length of my prettiest calico, is the sheriff's wife, Enid Carter."

A young boy ran ahead and reached Ned first. "I'll take the lemon drops, please."

"That is up to your mother." Ned tossed a single lemon drop to the child, who caught it in midair.

"Thank you, Mr. Finnegan. For everything." Mrs. Carter walked back to her husband amid generous applause.

"And now. . .for the most important part of the day." Ned reached behind him and lifted the nearly full jar of buttons over his head. "Who gets to keep all these buttons that I've collected?"

Voices called from all over the crowd. "Miss Landry." "Miss Birdie." A few small children began chanting "Miss Landry" until everyone joined in.

Birdie looked at Ned, not understanding what was happening.

He handed her the jar of buttons. "Here is a gift from the people of Calico, to you. All of the buttons you'll need for a lot of dresses, as well as a sizable credit to your account for any other supplies you need, from concerned citizens."

The din of applause and hurrahs gave Ned and Birdie a cocoon of privacy. She found a tag attached to a red-and-white gingham bow around the top of the jar. She unfolded it and read the single sentence twice before looking at Ned.

"You don't think I'd let a few buttons come between me and the woman I love, do you?" Ned's grin was as spectacular as fireworks on the Fourth of July. "So. Will you marry me?"

All the defenses Birdie had built against a man's love crumbled. "Yes." Her answer was both a capitulation and an exultation.

Ned claimed Birdie's lips.

The crowd cheered even louder, their approval touching Birdie's heart like the ping of a button hitting the bottom of the jar.

A BLESSING
FOR BEAU

Pride goeth before destruction,
and an haughty spirit before a fall.

PROVERBS 16:18

Chapter 1

Ruth Fairfield rubbed her aching back. Cutting squares of sod used muscles she didn't need in the schoolroom. The people of Calico, Kansas, had gathered to build a home for the orphaned Pratt children. Now that their mother's brother had come to town, the three children and their uncle could spend the winter snug in their new soddy.

"What is such a pretty lady doing over in this corner, trying to break up the hard ground all by herself?"

Ruth held back a chuckle as she straightened. No one had ever mistaken her for a beauty. Pleasant, yes, and kind. But pretty? Even her mother reminded her that internal beauty mattered more than what could be seen on the outside.

She straightened up, up, up, taking in boot-clad feet and denim-covered legs, until she met brown eyes the same color as the dirt beneath her feet, sparkling like a fresh spring rain. A ten-gallon hat sat atop hair streaked with summer's gold, a little long. Everything about him screamed cowboy. Ruth herself was tall, taller than some men, but not this giant. Charlotte Pratt had spoken of her brother to Ruth, but she hadn't mentioned his jaw-dropping good looks. "Mr. Blanton?"

"As I live and breathe, but you can call me Beau." He swept his hat from his head. "And you are Ruth Fairfield."

"Please, call me Ruth. I feel like I already know you from what Charlotte told me."

"Uncle Beau!" Dru Pratt, a happy, gangly twelve-year-old who had taken the loss of her parents hard, threw herself at the cowboy. "This is my teacher, Miss Fairfield."

"We've already met." Beau's smile revealed even white teeth. "So how is my niece doing in class?"

Ruth relaxed a bit. Her students were her favorite topic of conversation. "She's doing very well, as are her brothers. I might even go so far as to say that Allan is my star pupil. I believe he would do well at the university."

"Don't know about that. He'll have work a lot closer to home." The cowboy's earlier cheer turned into a rumble of thunder.

When would Ruth learn to keep her mouth shut? Not everyone welcomed the idea of further education, nor could everyone afford it. Her gaze flicked to the spot where Allan Pratt worked side by side with Haydn Keller. To look at them, no one would guess at Haydn's college education. She peeled off the garden gloves she had worn to protect her hands. Teaching school didn't leave her with much time to tend to gardening.

Dru dashed away in pursuit of Grace Polson, the younger sister of Ruth's friend Gladys. The cowboy hoisted the squares of sod Ruth had cut to his shoulder as easily as he would a cornstalk. His eyes surveyed the horizon, as if envisioning the crops that would grow there someday. "Percy managed to choose a good spot for his homestead."

"Charlotte loved it here." She had loved Percy, too, in spite of his penchant for mishaps. "When she described their acreage, I could almost see waving wheat and rose trellises, fish caught in a favorite spot by the creek. We were all saddened when they died in that terrible fire." Ruth finished digging around the last square and tipped it so she could slip her hands underneath. A snake slithered onto her arm, and she flicked it off.

The cowboy laughed. "Let me get that." He staggered a bit under the weight of the third square. He nodded at the snake. "You and Charlotte sound like two peas in a pod. Most women I know would scream at the sight of that sand twister."

"We grow them tough out here." Ruth chuckled. "Although I almost screamed the first time one of my students gifted me with a garden snake. He was disappointed when I just took it outside and continued with class."

Beau scratched his forehead with the brim of his hat, holding back a grin at the picture of the proper Ruth carrying a snake by its tail and calmly dropping it on the ground. The children newly left to his care loved their young teacher. Allan raved about her with all the ardor of a schoolboy crush, she had found a way to make Dru enjoy learning her multiplication tables, and even Guy admitted she was "nice enough"—high praise from a fourteen-year-old.

"I'd appreciate anything you can tell me about those

three." He clapped the Stetson back on his head. "Charlotte saw them all with a mother's rose-colored glasses. As for Percy, best said that he was too busy to do much with them. I can tell they need a firm hand to guide them."

Ruth bit her lip. Although he appreciated a woman who could keep quiet, Ruth's silence didn't mean she didn't communicate her thoughts. Her open face betrayed her displeasure at his plain speech.

When she did speak, however, she addressed a different issue altogether. "You must have a lot to do to get started again here. And the children have settled in so well at the parsonage, we'd be happy to keep them awhile longer."

Another interfering do-gooder, like the ones who took him and Charlotte in when their parents died. He could have taken care of them on his own. He was as old as Allan was now and able to do a man's work. Watching his oldest nephew stagger under the weight of two squares of sod, Beau had doubts about how tough the boy was. But now that Beau was here to take a hand in his upbringing, he'd toughen up soon enough. He had to. Beau was determined to make his sister's dream come true: a homestead, proved up, ready to hand on to one of her children.

"That won't be necessary. The four of us will get along fine. We have plenty to do getting the soddy ready for winter and gathering as much food as we can. Don't worry, I'll get the younger ones to school when it starts next month."

A frown chased across Ruth's features. The liveliness of the emotions playing across her face made her downright pretty, softening the angles that would look harsh in an immobile face. He held out his free hand.

Her lips perked upward as she shook his hand. "You must know you don't have to worry about food. Everyone feels so bad about what happened. My mother organized the pound party going on in the wagon my father drove out here this morning. And here comes Sheriff Carter, bringing the rest of it."

Beau's antennae quivered at the words "pound party" and the even more ominous "rest of it." "Is that so?" He trotted to the place where people alternated squares of sod like fine bricks, placed the three he was holding on the ground, then paced quickly to the wagon. Food for dinner could be expected, but now he wondered if there was more. Flicking back the cover revealed flour, sugar, honey, cornmeal, canned fruits and vegetables, lard, dried apples—enough to last their family of four for the winter and beyond. Clucking alerted him to the presence of a rooster and five chickens in a crate. And more was coming?

Dust kicked up on the road subsided, showing a figure on horseback leading a cow. Did the people think he couldn't take care of his own? He walked to the spot where Ruth's father leaned over the sides of the wagon.

Pastor Fairfield looked up. "It's coming along well, Mr. Blanton." He clapped him on the back. "You'll be nice and snug in that place come winter. Our folks have become experts at this sort of thing."

Beau wouldn't admit that he only learned how to build a

soddy a few weeks ago, when he knew he'd be taking over the homestead. In his work as an itinerant cowboy, he'd always bunked at someone else's place. "So the children are getting the mud ready?" He looked over to where the children were working, just in time to see Guy fling a handful of gooey brown mess at Dru, who ran away, squealing. Those two needed to be brought under control.

The pastor smiled at the interplay, his grin echoing the same expression on his daughter's face. "Reminds me of the time Mrs. Fairfield made me mud pies back when we were children. Nothing like a good mud pie to cement a friendship." He chuckled, but then he returned his attention to the wagon. "You've discovered our little secret."

"Your daughter told me." Beau didn't like confronting a man of the cloth, but there were times. . . "I appreciate the thought, but we don't need your charity." He had to force that last word past his teeth. "You can return everything to the people who brought it, or put it in your church pantry, or whatever best use you can find for it."

The pastor rocked back on his heels. "I know you only accepted help with the soddy because you wanted to get settled as soon as possible. If it helps, I had nothing to do with this. The deacons asked their wives, and they put it all together. Truth is, this year's been pretty good to the folks of Calico, aside from the fire that killed Mr. and Mrs. Pratt. We can't think of another family as needful and deserving of help as yours." He spread his arms. "The Bible says it's more blessed to give than to receive, but my experience says both

274

sides need God's grace. Sometimes it's harder to receive than to give."

Especially when you've learned gifts usually come with strings attached. "As I said, I can afford to buy the things we need."

"You might as well accept it. My wife will make me drive back out here if I bring it home."

A rustle of skirts alerted Beau to the presence of a woman, and he withheld his answer.

"You might as well accept it," Ruth repeated. "Papa won't let you refuse a gift." Ruth hugged her father. "Mama says it's time for you to return thanks for our meal."

"Come along, son. We mustn't keep the women waiting."

Beau frowned at the grocery-laden wagon. Why did he have the feeling he and the lively Ruth Fairfield would cross swords over more than unwanted groceries?

He almost looked forward to it.

Chapter 2

When Ruth was a girl, the last few weeks before the start of school flew by. Now that she was grown, nothing had changed. Whereas in the past she enjoyed the last few days to play and spend time with friends, now she had to prepare for the next year's lessons.

With the addition of two new books for younger and older students, as well as several well-worn giveaways contributed by members of the community, the school library was off to a good start. She planned to make a soddy behind the schoolhouse to teach her students practical lessons on math and science. After she incorporated lessons on different building materials for homes, she'd add a timeline of American history. Building the new soddy for Beau Blanton and the Pratt children had given her the idea.

She couldn't get the Pratt children off her mind. Over the summer, Dru had a growth spurt, and she needed new dresses to accommodate her changing figure. Ruth was glad she had been there the first time the girl experienced her monthlies; she didn't know how the uncle would have dealt with such a thing. The very thought of it brought heat to her cheeks.

Ruth had finished another dress to give to Dru. She'd

even brought it with her to church last Sunday. But she couldn't make herself approach the uncle who had wanted to reject Calico's gift. If he saw the need for new clothes, he'd probably hire Birdie to sew something.

She tucked the material she had bought for men's shirts—sturdy brown cotton, buttons, thread. She smiled at the buttons. These days Birdie had all the buttons she needed for her seamstress business. She hadn't wanted charity either. Given her friend's previous occupation, Ruth could understand her reluctance to trust others. Why Beau rejected it made less sense.

Charlotte had spoken in high terms about her brother, how kind and thoughtful and protective he was, but she hadn't mentioned his pride. Ruth could only pray that he would accept the clothes she had made for the children.

If God didn't intend for Ruth to help the Pratts, He would bring someone else into her life who could use the clothes. Drifters stopping by the parsonage for a warm bite of food and a place to sleep generally accepted whatever was offered. If that was what God intended for her mission project, she'd accept it.

But all year long, Ruth had waited for God to show her that one special person or family He meant for her to help. After God led Gladys to Haydn Keller, Annie to Lieutenant Arnold, and even Birdie to Ned Finnegan, and thrown in Kate Polson and Norman Keller for good measure—she had hoped that maybe, just maybe, God had someone special for her. No one was ever going to marry her for her good looks, but she hoped to share in some special man's vision of helping people in the community.

No, Ruth had resigned herself to official spinsterhood with a bevy of students for children, until Percy and Charlotte Pratt died in the fire and the Fairfields took in their children. She couldn't pinpoint the reason, but somehow the three young people had burrowed themselves deep in her heart.

Since Ruth was an only child, Allan, Guy, and Dru might come as close to nieces and nephews as she would ever have. She bundled up her sewing supplies and headed for Annie's house. Rejoice, and again rejoice! In everything give thanks, even if everything for her included less than she dreamed of.

Her route to Annie's house took her past Aunt Kate's diner. The door swung open, and Birdie came out, waving at her friend Michal Clanahan inside. God had taken care of that detail, providing employment for every lady who wanted to leave the saloon.

Birdie still wore the sunbonnet that protected her from unwanted stares as much as from the sun, but she no longer kept her eyes trained on the ground. When she spotted Ruth, a smile brightened her face. "Ruth! I'm glad you're here. We can walk together."

Birdie's sewing bag overflowed with a dark blue calico.

"Who is that one for? Has Owen lured another victim into his clutches?" Ruth asked. "Mama thinks it's just a matter of time before the town council votes Calico dry and runs him out of business completely."

"A true miracle." Birdie hugged the bag closer. "But no.

I've started a quilt. I'd like to give one to each of my friends for their hope chests." She brought her free hand to her chest. "I've even thought about making one for myself. Who would ever have thought it? Birdie Landry, prime entertainment at the Betwixt 'n' Between. . .a merchant's wife." She giggled self-consciously, a carefree sound that brought joy to Ruth. "How about you?"

Ruth spared a brief thought for her own wedding quilt, tucked away in her hope chest for the past five years. "I'm working on clothes for the Pratt children. They lost everything in the fire, of course, and they've all grown over the past few months."

They walked at a leisurely pace, crossing in front of Finnegan's Mercantile. Ned waved at them through the window, and Birdie's face blossomed. As they made their way to Annie's house, Birdie floated as if she walked on air.

Rejoice with those who rejoice. "You're happy."

"Your father told me once about the difference between joy and happiness. When I read Paul's command to rejoice, I wondered what I had to be happy about."

Ruth nodded. "I've received that lecture before—after my heart was broken when my best friend moved away and I thought I would never have another friend." The memory brought a smile to her face. "What silly things upset us when we're children."

Birdie turned thoughtful. "After my mother died, I didn't feel happy again for a long time. Your father explained that I could always rejoice because God's love would never ever leave me alone again. . .and then I met Ned. I'm glad God loves me, but I'm thankful that a good man loves me as well." She patted the bag dangling from Ruth's arm. "Are you interested in the Pratt children—or in their handsome uncle?"

"Birdie!" The word burst out of Ruth's mouth at the same time heat rushed into her cheeks. "My only business with Mr. Blanton concerns the children."

"Uh-huh." Birdie sounded doubtful.

At times like this, Ruth wished she hadn't committed to this sewing circle. Nine months ago, they were all unmarried, with a common passion for helping others. They bonded together in spite of the difference in their ages. Now that she was the only unattached woman in the group, she felt her spinsterhood more than ever. Especially when they kept insisting God had someone special in mind for her.

Beau Blanton. She mustn't let her imagination—her heart—get carried away because he was one of the rare unmarried men to show his face in Calico. She would treat him like any of the fathers—the married fathers—of her students. Any basis other than friendship would crumble beneath her feet. Even friendship might prove difficult as long as he resisted "charity." As much as she'd like to avoid the confrontation, she should talk with him about the clothes.

"I can't go to school today." Dru remained in her nightdress while Guy was ready to leave for town in plenty of time for the first school bell.

"You have no cause to stay home. Allan and I will be busy

all day. I don't want you staying here by yourself." Beau wiped a weary hand across his eyebrow. "I thought you liked school."

"I do." A single tear slipped down her cheek, and she shuffled her feet without looking at him. "Uncle Beau, I only have three dresses, and two of them don't fit."

Beau looked at her nightwear. The hem hit her leg halfway between her ankle and her knee. It fit a little more snugly than most nightclothes. He tried to remember what she wore yesterday. It seemed to fit her fine.

"What about the dress you wore yesterday?" A pretty soft blue calico with small pink flowers, from what he remembered.

"I wore it all last week. It's in the wash. I can't wear any of my other clothes." Her voice wobbled. "I'll wash it today with the rest of our clothes. I can go tomorrow."

Peeved, Beau considered demanding that she get dressed so he could see for himself. But he couldn't blame her. All the children's belongings had burned along with the house, and Dru had obviously outgrown what people had given her. He stretched his memory back. Come to think of it, Dru had worn the same dress every day since his arrival. He had been too busy to notice. His mouth worked around the impossibilities presented by the situation.

"Very well. You can wash the dress today and return to school tomorrow. And I'll see about getting you something else to wear." Beau had seen some ready-to-wear dresses for sale at Finnegan's Mercantile. Maybe one of them would fit, or someone—the seamstress? Dru herself?—could adjust it to fit. "Allan will draw the water for laundry before he comes out to help me." Next Monday Beau would have to figure out a different way to get the clothes washed. Dru couldn't run the household and go to school. To respect Charlotte's wishes, Dru had to stay in school.

What Beau would do instead, he didn't know. He turned the matter over in his mind throughout the day as he and Allan worked on plowing up the fields. Even if they couldn't get a crop for the fall, the plants would help enrich the soil for spring.

"Uncle Beau?" Allan ran up the row to where Beau worked.

Working with his nephew didn't leave Beau much time for meditating. Before he came to the homestead, he figured nothing could be harder than the long, hard days of riding herds. Who would have thought that taking care of three nearly grown children would demand so much more of him? Why didn't Allan know more about the land that was his heritage?

"I found these by the river. I think they're wild onions, but I'm not sure." Allan held the bulbs up to Beau.

The aroma tickled Beau's nostrils. He grunted. "Onions. They'll taste good in our potato soup tonight."

Allan grinned as if pleased with bringing in something useful. He glanced down the road to town. "Guy's home from school."

More dust than a single horse should kick up flew through the air along the tracks made by wagon wheels. As they drew near, he could see that Guy was not alone.

Why couldn't Miss Ruth Fairfield leave him alone?

Chapter 3

"You did what?" Beau didn't touch the garments of folded cotton in the bag.

"Miss Fairfield!" Dru waved from her spot by the open campfire where she was cooking supper. The mild weather made a number of everyday tasks easier while it lasted. Winter fell early and hard in this part of Kansas.

Ruth must have caught sight of the scowl on his face, because she answered with a scowl of her own. A scowl that showed itself in stormy gray eyes, creasing the lines at the edge of her eyelids, but didn't erase the pleasant expression on her face. "Professional smilers"—that's the way Beau's father had characterized pastors one time. Unbidden, a smile came to his face, and the teacher relaxed.

With a glance at Dru, Ruth lowered her voice. "Dru in particular is in need of new clothes. Since you haven't been around them for a while, you can't know how much she's sprouted up." She looked as if she had more to say, but she kept her mouth closed. "The boys, as well."

Beau chomped on a blade of grass before he said something he might regret later. Why hadn't Dru mentioned her need for new clothing before Ruth had decided to intervene?

Ruth leaned a little closer. "I was concerned when she didn't come to school today. Guy mumbled something about her dress."

Beau's mouth tightened at that. Hadn't Percy taught his children not to blab about family matters?

Ruth must have caught his expression. "Don't worry. He didn't talk out of turn. I wouldn't last long as a teacher if I couldn't worm the truth out of a reluctant witness." She held the bag by the tips of her fingers, ready to drop it into Beau's hands. "I started the dress while Dru was still living with us. Please accept it."

She lifted one finger from the bag, and Beau almost reached out to catch it. On the top, he spotted brown cotton. It looked very much like a man's shirt. Instead of accepting the bag, he removed the shirt and shook out its folds. "This isn't for Dru."

"No." Her expression remained calm, but fire burned in her eyes. "The boys also lost everything in the fire. Most of what they have to wear are hand-me-downs. I thought they would appreciate something that fits right." Now worry wormed its way into those expressive eyes. "I didn't have their exact measurements, so I hope these fit all right."

Beau brought the shirt up close, studying the workmanship. The shirt was quality, made of good, sturdy material, with fine stitching to match. He grunted in approval. These clothes could withstand the kind of stress two youths could put on them. He had a couple of shirts Allan and Guy could wear, but they were worn out and torn in a few places.

"I'll be back in a minute." Beau motioned for Dru to join them. "I bet Miss Fairfield will be happy to tell you whatever you missed today." He didn't look back as he ducked into the soddy.

❧

Ruth stared at Beau's departing back. He had dismissed her, but at least he had taken the bag of clothes with him. She wouldn't allow her disappointment over his attitude to interfere with what Dru needed. She headed in Dru's direction and began taking down Levis hanging on the line. "I can tell you've been busy today with the laundry."

"Someone had to." Dru had internalized a lot of her emotions since her parents died, acting like the little mother of her two brothers—not that they always appreciated her interference. Ruth had hoped that the arrival of an adult relative would allow Dru to once again become a twelve-year-old enjoying her girlhood, but it appeared that hadn't happened.

When Dru stirred something in the kettle over a campfire, Ruth knew her fears were well grounded. No wonder the girl had almost fallen asleep in class a couple of times already.

Ruth spied a flat iron heating in the campfire and the pile of clothing needing attention. On top sat Dru's blue dress, which she had hardly removed since she received it. "I'll finish this for you while you take care of the Levis." She made a mental note to find someone to help with household tasks if Beau would accept the help.

"Can you stay and eat with us?" Dru sounded wistful. "It's

just beans with some salt pork."

Ruth made an on-the-spot decision. This early in September, she could join them for an early supper and get home before full dark. "I would love that, as long as I leave before evening falls."

Dru's step sped up at Ruth's words. She whisked up a batch of corn bread in the iron skillet. Last of all, she started coffee boiling.

The cow stuck her head over the fence and lowed softly. Ruth fed her a handful of grass and glanced at her udder. It was shudderingly full. She glanced around for a milk pail. Guy ran up. "Don't worry, I'll take care of her."

Allan followed at a slower pace. He leaned next to Ruth against the fence. Dark circles she hadn't seen before marred his face, and his shoulders slumped over. When he removed his gloves, Ruth could see the angry red on his blistered hands. He tried to hide a grimace, but she could read him as easily as her Bible.

"I've missed you in school." With only a year to go before he finished his public school education and hopefully headed to college, every day of school missed was a tragedy.

He shrugged, his silence saying volumes.

"I have a new book you might like." Although Allan especially liked mathematics—even at times exceeding Ruth's understanding of advanced geometry—he also won spelling contests and poetry recitation contests on a regular basis. He wouldn't stay away from school of his own accord. She was as sure of that as she was of anything.

She couldn't, she wouldn't, disrupt his uncle's authority with his new family. *Oh Lord, give me strength to hold my tongue.* "If you like, I can send it home with Guy tomorrow."

"Please." Much youthful angst and despair came through in that single word.

Ruth wished she could hug him to take the pain away, but she couldn't do that with the lad who was more man than boy. "I'm praying for all of you as you make this transition. But for now. . .I'll make sure you have books to read."

Ruth set up an ironing stand and finished the dress and one shirt before Beau came back outside. The bag hung limp from his hand. Good, he had accepted the clothing.

Supper passed pleasantly, and soon Ruth had started gathering dishes. Beau carried the last remaining platter to the sink. "I'd like to speak with you before you leave."

She nodded. "This won't take much longer. What is it about?"

He reached for his back pocket.

❧

Beau watched Dru and Ruth at work while he waited in the doorway. Dru looked livelier than she had since his arrival. Ruth had dived right into ironing. He grunted. Maybe taking on whatever task needed doing came naturally to a pastor's daughter. For Dru's sake, he was glad. All of them were working as hard as they could. Except maybe Allan. He was always a step behind. Beau had to work twice as hard to make up for his slack.

He needed to find a way to make life easier for Dru.

Ruth might know of a woman willing to take on some of the household duties. Which would take more money. Beau's new responsibilities ate into what he had saved to sink into a ranch of his own someday. Finishing his contract for the current season and collecting his full pay was the reason he had arrived so long after the fire.

The fire was the latest, and most severe, time he had had to rescue Charlotte and her family. Percy was a good-hearted sort who worked hard, but first he ran his father's business into the ground. Next, the small printing press he started didn't succeed. Beau had made it his mission to make sure Allan was better prepared for life than his father had been.

Ruth looked his way, the enthusiasm she must bring to her class every day evident in her face. If he'd had a teacher like her, he might not have disliked school so much. Maybe that explained the silly look that appeared on Allan's face when he mentioned school. Perhaps he liked the teacher more than the learning.

Ruth said something to Dru that Beau couldn't hear. Putting her fingers to her mouth, Ruth whistled—a shrieking sound worthy of a boy catching his first snake—or a teacher aiming to gain control in the classroom. Guy raised his head, then Allan, and she waved her arms, inviting them to dinner. Beau glanced overhead. Good sunshine would last for at least another hour. Beau kept an eye on the horizon, gauging when Ruth must leave to reach town before dark. Guy milked the cows while Allan talked with Ruth.

Supper ended on the right note, with a final bite of corn

bread and butter and a deep draw of cold water. By the time Beau's glass touched the table, Ruth was on her feet. She prepared dishwater while Dru shuffled their plates into a pile, added their forks and knives, and dropped them in the soapy water.

Beau moved into action before Ruth finished the last glass and rode off into the sunset. "I'd like to speak with you before you leave."

Her eyes brightened with curiosity, and she nodded. "This won't take much longer. What is it about?"

Beau wished he could stay and watch her work, but duty called. Last night's rainstorm had exposed a chink in the soddy walls, which he intended to fix before it grew bigger. "I'll be at the back of the soddy." His fingers brushed the seat of his Levis, against the comfortable bunch of his wallet.

Her eyes narrowed at the movement. Ruth's students might adore her, but any man interested in her would be subject to her strong opinions.

Why did the thought cause him worry?

Chapter 4

Beau didn't leave the ranch until Saturday, when he took the family into town. Allan disappeared in the direction of the diner, where Beau suspected he had his eye on a pretty young waitress. Dru hovered at his side, as if she didn't want to let him out of her sight. Guy had chosen to stay back at the ranch, offering to work on the fence. His willingness to undertake the task Allan hadn't finished impressed Beau.

First stop, the newspaper office. In the short time since his arrival, Beau had discovered the *Calico Chronicle* as a primary source for local happenings. One of Charlotte's last letters had mentioned the start of the paper and the romance blossoming between the editor and a local young girl as well as between the editor's once-reclusive grandfather and Miss Kate. Charlotte had used the outbreak of romance around town as an excuse to inquire after Beau's love life.

"That's the school." Dru pointed at the proverbial red schoolhouse that sat down the street from the newspaper office. The front door hung open, revealing a glimpse of Ruth at the blackboard, and he wondered at her working on her day off. Dru's expression said she'd love to say hello.

"Would you like to check on Miss Fairfield?"

"May I?" Dru pleaded, as she dropped her hold on his hand.

"Yes, but don't bother her too much." Dru disappeared so fast that he didn't know if she heard him. He almost wanted to call her back. He had parted with Ruth on a harsh note, his insistence that he pay her for the new clothes angering her.

Ruth came to the door at Dru's approach. Surprise mixed with genuine pleasure lit her face, and she embraced the girl. She waved at Beau, and he returned the gesture. At least she hadn't stayed angry with him. His steps trended in her direction until he remembered his purpose for coming to town today. In his new life as mother, father, and provider for three adolescent children, he found he had to make every minute count. If the sight of one pretty face distracted him from his goal, he had spent too much time with cattle.

Increasing his speed, Beau headed toward the newspaper, a small office crowded with a printing press and typesetting equipment. Peering through the window, he saw a man in the back sweeping the floor. A knock on the glass got his attention.

The lanky man with light brown hair opened the door. "Welcome to the *Calico Chronicle*. Mr. Blanton, is that it?"

Beau nodded. "Call me Beau. I wanted to place an ad in next week's paper."

"Come right this way." He gestured for Beau to enter the office and grabbed a yellow-lined pad of paper and a pencil. "The name's Haydn, by the way. How can I help you?"

"I have it right here." Beau unfolded the paper he had written out the night before. He wouldn't let Dru or Guy suffer the same fate he had, missing so much school he sometimes found it difficult to compose a letter. "Do you know of any woman who is looking for work as a cook or housekeeper?" The man sitting in front of him would know the pulse of the community better than anyone. "We need some help now that school's back in session."

Haydn made a note. "One of Birdie Landry's friends might be available. Or you could inquire over at the parsonage."

A trip to the parsonage would probably involve crossing paths with Ruth again. Dru would like that. For that matter, Beau would like that.

"If you find someone before next Thursday, let me know, and I'll yank the ad from the paper."

"How do I get in touch with Miss Landry? Does she live in town?"

"She lives at Aunt Kate's boardinghouse, but she'll be at the parsonage later today. The sewing circle is meeting there this afternoon."

"I'll head over there later." If he could get an answer before next week, it would solve a lot of his problems. He paid for the advertisement and headed for Finnegan's Mercantile.

Business was brisk at the store, so Beau browsed around the shelves. He noticed a sign advertising the services of a seamstress. Good, he'd found a solution to the clothing problem. Ruth wouldn't leave him alone until he took care of it.

The crowd thinned out, and Beau approached the pretty young woman at the counter. He handed her the shopping list he had written down. "I need these items. And are you the one I ask for seamstress services?"

"No." She flashed a shy smile in his direction. "Mr. Finnegan takes care of those orders."

"Shannon, did I hear my name?" A thin man, the perfect image of a shopkeeper with his glasses and pale skin, slipped behind the counter.

"Mr. Finnegan, this gentleman. . ." She looked at Beau.

"Beau Blanton."

"Mr. Blanton was asking about seamstress services. I told him you could help him."

"Miss Landry does beautiful work." Finnegan motioned him forward. "Did you see the ready-to-wear dresses on the table? If nothing there suits your needs, or if you're looking for men's trousers and shirts, I can arrange a meeting between you." He led Beau to the table. "What are you looking for?"

"A couple of dresses for my niece." Beau stared helplessly at the stacks. "But I don't know what will fit."

"My fiancée may be able to help you with that."

Perhaps she was a member of the sewing circle Mr. Keller had mentioned. "How old is your niece?" Ned asked. "Most of these clothes are for adult women."

"She's twelve. Not too tall." Beau indicated a height that didn't quite reach his shoulders. "She's in town with me today. Is it possible to meet with Miss Landry?"

"I believe she's hard at work this morning. She will be

heading over to the parsonage this afternoon for the sewing circle."

"Will I be welcome at the meeting?"

"The Fairfields never turn anyone away. Tell Birdie I sent you, and she'll take extra good care of you."

The clerk, Shannon, prepared his sack. Beau raised his eyebrows at the price but dug in his pocket and counted out the money.

Finnegan pulled his ledger out and entered numbers. When Beau handed the money to Shannon, Finnegan interrupted. "There's no need to pay right now. You can settle the account later."

"I'd rather take care of it now." Beau counted out his money. He'd find a way to cut costs. Maybe Guy or Dru could find a job after school. God could provide for them in a dozen different ways.

Finnegan maintained a neutral expression on his face. "I mean no offense. Most of the farmers around here keep an account, including your brother-in-law. Just offering to make things easier for you, with all the difficulties your family has been through."

"You'll soon find out I'm not my brother-in-law. I won't take things I can't pay for." Beau knew he was being less than gracious. He carried the sack out to the waiting wagon. Time to round up Dru and eat before dropping by the parsonage.

Where he would face the biggest challenge of the day so far: paying Miss Landry for work Ruth was willing to do for free.

"I'll see you on Monday." Ruth ached as she watched Dru walk away from the parsonage, where they had gone from the schoolhouse. Her new dress was wearing already, she wore it so much. Unfortunately, Charlotte's brother wasn't like his sister. She wouldn't have let pride stand in the way of her children's needs.

Standing in the doorway, she watched Gladys approach with Haydn. At the corner, he turned in the direction of the newspaper office, and Gladys walked toward the parsonage. Ruth opened the door for her first guest.

"Haydn says Mr. Blanton came into the office today." Gladys's sewing bag bulged with the squares for her wedding quilt. She greeted Ruth's mother with a kiss. While Gladys kept up the chatter with Ruth's parents, Ruth's mind wandered. In spite of weekly church attendance and Dru and Guy's regular presence at school, she hadn't spoken to Beau Blanton since the debacle of her visit to the soddy.

The gall of the man, insisting on paying her for clothes she had given to him. He'd held it out to her. When he tried to drop the money into her hand, she brushed it away and it landed on the ground. "You're welcome," she had said before she backed away from the embarrassing moment.

She later learned he'd given the money to her father. Papa had bragged on Beau's generosity and dropped the money into the box for missions. "He said he appreciated everything we'd done and to use the money wherever there was the most need."

Perhaps that was what God wanted after all. Even though she assumed God wanted her to help someone in Calico, maybe she was meant to help with overseas ministry, along with her mother and the other women of the larger group. Maybe she was getting too old for such girlish dreams.

She should accept her position as resident spinster of Calico, Kansas.

Chapter 5

Someone knocked at the door. Ruth's mother asked, "Ruth, will you get it, please?" She had her arms in dishwater up to her elbows.

A glance out the window revealed the guest: Beau Blanton. Dru and Allan accompanied him, and Ruth's heart lifted. If only Guy had come along. He needed tutoring in basic math skills, and she'd have squeezed in a few minutes before the sewing circle started. From what Dru said, all of them jumped into farm chores as soon as they arrived home and didn't stop until bedtime except for dinner and a chapter from the Bible.

Think happy thoughts. That would help Ruth keep a pleasant expression on her face, instead of imagining the impossible with Beau. Some might expect a pastor's daughter to want to marry another man of the cloth, but she didn't want that either. She couldn't keep the kinds of secrets her mother had to carry. As soon as her parents figured that out, they had done as much as possible to shield her from the more unsavory aspects of their ministry.

If the worst Beau Blanton had done was to value independence over offers of help and to fail to understand three young people, when he'd never had children himself, she had no reason, not to mention no right, to be upset with him.

After the scolding Ruth gave herself, she opened the door with a smile. "Gladys—Miss Polson—told us you might be stopping by. How can we help you?"

Beau removed his hat as soon as he entered the door, and Allan followed his example. Dru hung her cape on the coat tree. Beau shrugged. "I'm looking for someone willing to help us with the housework a few hours a day." He draped an arm around Dru's shoulders and hugged her. "Dru has been doing a yeoman's job, but it's too much for her, what with school and all."

At least he hadn't been blind to the dark circles under Dru's eyes. "Are you looking for live-in help?"

He frowned. "Perhaps. I'd offer room and board in exchange for a few hours' work, but. . .you've seen the soddy. It would be a tight fit. I know we're at a distance from town." His shoulders sagged. "Will that cause problems?"

"Not necessarily. I have some ideas, and my mother will probably know of more."

"Know what?" Mama came to the door, drying her hands on her apron. "Mr. Blanton, how lovely to see you again." The smile she offered their guest was wholehearted. "Since the sewing circle is meeting in the parlor, why don't you join me in the kitchen? If you need my husband, he'll be back eventually. He's over in the church praying over tomorrow's sermon."

Ruth said, "Dru will be visiting with us in the parlor, so

you can visit privately. Allan—you may wish to peruse the study. Papa brought home some new books when he went to Topeka last week."

"Thanks." Allan disappeared down the hallway before his uncle could call him back, and Dru followed at a slower pace, entering the parlor to warm greetings.

Beau didn't move in the direction of the kitchen, his eyes fixed on the floor. He rubbed the brim of his hat. Without lifting his head, he asked, "Is Miss Landry here? Mr. Finnegan referred me to her."

Ruth could think of only one reason Ned would refer Beau to Birdie. She tensed, grateful he wasn't looking up and so couldn't spot the anger she couldn't keep from her face. She drew in a breath before she answered. "Yes, Birdie is here. Come join us when you finish your business with my mother." She escaped to the parlor before he looked up and caught her expression.

From her spot on the sofa, Dru was rolling skeins of yarn into balls. Ruth was glad the girl had a day off. She'd make a good teacher someday if God led her that way. If her uncle allowed her to finish the additional schooling she would need. And if she didn't fall in love and get married, like most young women. Charlotte had strongly supported the idea, but Beau didn't value the same things his sister had.

Birdie pushed her needle in and out of the hem of a black gored skirt. "Dru says Mr. Blanton wishes to speak to me." She peeked up from the fabric in her lap. "Is that all right with you?"

Dru's eyes widened in surprise and her mouth opened.

"I suppose any way they get the clothes they need is acceptable." Ruth's throat tightened as she forced the words out of her throat. "It seems all God wants from me is to help people who come to us for help, but I was already doing that." How she wanted a chance to do something significant. Be a missionary to China. Run an orphanage. Even just marry a good man. She loved teaching, but some days she wanted more from life. It seemed instead of her helping Beau, he was helping her by forcing her to examine her life.

Birdie narrowed her eyes. "Mr. Blanton's arrival in town is timely. Naomi is ready to join Michal and me if we have enough work, and Orpah is in need of work until Gladys is ready to leave the diner. If he is willing to have someone with our history working in his home, that is." She secured the needle in the fabric and patted Ruth's knee. "You do the Lord's work every day. The other day I read in the Bible that the soldiers who fight in the battle should share the spoils of war with those who stay with the supplies. God knows each and every thing you do day in and day out for the needy around us."

She started working the needle again. Dru had finished balling the yarn and started casting stitches onto a pair of knitting needles.

Annie giggled. "If you really want to sew for Mr. Blanton, you could sew the clothes and Birdie could pretend she made them."

That drew an answering giggle from Dru.

Ruth took a moment to picture a dress made in a cheerful yellow calico before shaking her head. "It's not the same. He will still insist on paying you—"

"And of course I'll give you the money."

"But that defeats my reason for doing this."

"I could talk to him. . ." Dru stuck her needle into the first stitch, but the movement was awkward. The stitches were probably too tight, the way most of her knitting started. "No," the women chorused.

"I'll find a way to speak with him," Ruth said. "Just promise me you'll be praying for me."

"Always." Gladys smiled. "You don't have to ask."

❧

"Are these women"—Beau couldn't bring himself to call them "ladies"—"the only ones looking for work?"

"They are the ones most in need of gainful employment. God has been doing a tremendous work among the women who lived in that unfortunate place. No one was more surprised than I was when Miss Landry came to us, about a year and a half ago now, hungry for God and desperate to leave that life. Because of her testimony, we've seen at least one woman leave each month. They are willing to work hard and are thankful for the opportunity."

"But Dru. . ." Beau couldn't believe he was even considering the possibility. "She'd be a bad influence on Dru. I'm sure of it."

"She'd be an excellent example of God's grace and His transforming power. I agree that she should maintain her home in town. You both want to avoid any appearance of evil."

"I will think about it." Although Beau already knew he would rather accept Ruth's help than hire a former soiled dove. The longer he lived in Calico, the more strange facts about the town he discovered. Ladies on a mission to make a difference. A hermit brought out of self-imposed solitude. Prostitutes leaving their employment and being accepted as part of the community. An entire fort outfitted by a single woman. Not to mention an interfering schoolteacher, although that might not be so strange. As a cowboy, he didn't have exposure to towns much beyond trail drives, and Dodge City was nothing like Calico. No wonder Charlotte liked living here.

Asking Miss Landry to make their clothes didn't feel as out of place as inviting a woman to help with housework. Their business could all be conducted through a third party, such as Ned Finnegan. Now there was a strange pairing. He shook his head. If God had found such a—colorful—wife for the bland shopkeeper, maybe He had someone in store for Beau. Someone as spontaneous as Beau was reserved, someone as giving as he was cautious. . .someone like. . .Ruth. *Don't even think like that.*

After Beau finished the plate of cookies Mrs. Fairfield had served him, he ventured down the hallway to the remaining rooms. From the parlor, he heard feminine voices and soft laughter. He hurried past, looking for Allan. A door stood open to the left, and he poked his head inside. Allan's fingers traced the lines of text before he turned the page. Since he appeared unaware of his uncle's arrival, Beau cleared this throat.

Allan dropped the book on the desk. "Are you ready to leave?"

"Almost." Beau surveyed the room. He couldn't imagine a single person needing so many books, when he only had one to his name, the Bible his mother had given him. "I wonder if Pastor Fairfield has read all these books." He approached a shelf, studying the titles stamped on the spines. Some of them didn't even seem to be in English.

"Yes." Allan didn't seem to find that unusual. "Most of them he's read several times. He gave me a new book to read every week when we stayed here this summer. Today he said he had a new book for me to take with me. And we could talk about it when I come to church." He pointed to the book on the desk. "You don't mind, do you?"

Beau stared. Why anyone would choose to read when he could be outside under God's heaven baffled him to start with. But the wistful look on Allan's face stumped him. "As long as you read in the evening, after the day's work is done."

"Great!" Allan sprang to his feet, clutching the book as if he might lose it if he loosened his hold.

"You have a few minutes. I have some business to discuss with Miss Landry." At the door to the parlor, Beau paused. Dru was laughing. *Laughing.* At the soddy, she always seemed so serious. He had treasured the quiet, but laughter was even better.

He rounded the corner, and the smile disappeared from Dru's face. "Is it time to go?"

"In a few minutes."

"Have a seat." Ruth gestured to a comfortable-looking chair next to a table with a Bible, a book Beau didn't recognize, and a pair of reading glasses. "Papa won't care."

Beau studied the women around the room, trying to guess which name went with which woman. Ruth was the epitome of a schoolteacher. He'd guess either the blond or the redhead was the former saloon girl, although the brunette was pretty enough. This group had turned the town upside down. Only Ruth had remained relatively uninvolved, from what he had heard. As part of the pastor's family, she did a lot for others all the time. As a teacher, she exercised more influence on the future of Calico than almost anyone in town.

Given the fire in Ruth's eyes when Beau asked Miss Landry to sew for him, he knew she wanted more. For some reason unknown to him, she felt God had something else for her to do.

Beau had always trusted his own judgment. Only now, when a spitfire of a teacher challenged his long-held opinions, did he question himself.

And he didn't like it.

Chapter 6

I'm sorry, but I'm unable to take on your project at this time." Birdie Landry smiled as she said the disappointing words. "If you can wait for two months, after Miss Kate marries Mr. Keller, I can work on it then."

Since Ned had said she might be able to help, Beau found the situation confusing. Miss Landry exchanged glances with Miss Polson, who was engaged to the young Haydn Keller, from what he understood. "But Ruth has offered to make whatever you need, *now*, and she won't ask money for it." Her brilliant smile made it impossible for Beau to refuse without appearing mean-spirited.

Pleasure lit Dru's face, giving her a moment of carefree happiness. Cautious pleasure chased surprise off Ruth's face. "You might even say I consider it my mission in life."

Her mission? Beau's ire rose at that description. He wasn't a grumpy hermit, nor did he frequent the saloon. He was a simple, hardworking man, taking care of his family the best way he knew how.

But he couldn't sew. "You won't accept money no matter how much I insist, will you?"

Ruth shook her head. Miss Landry chuckled. "I did the

same to Ned. He kept looking for ways to help me, but I insisted I pay my own way. I didn't have the money to buy buttons, thread, and other sewing notions, so he had people drop buttons and other things in a button jar and fooled me into accepting the gift."

"In other words, you'd better accept the clothes before Ruth figures out a way around your objections." Gladys nodded her head emphatically. "She loves your niece and nephews. Let her do it for them if not for you."

"I give up!" Beau threw his hands in the air. "I accept whatever you have already made but no more. And actually, I have another area where I need your help."

What? Mr. No-thank-you-I'll-do-it-myself was asking for help? Instead of the pleasant expression she wished she could freeze on her face, Ruth was sure her shock at his statement must shine from every pore.

Beau laughed, a deep, hearty, masculine, happier sound than she had ever heard from him. "You are the only schoolteacher I know of in Calico, and I believe Guy could benefit from your help as he starts his job."

His words distressed Ruth anew. First Beau pulled Allan, who loved school, and now Guy would also work? Allan had motivation to learn on his own, but Guy needed a teacher's guidance more. What was next? Would he ask Dru to stay home to take care of the house?

As the daughter of a man who had attended seminary and a mother who taught school before her marriage, education had always mattered to Ruth. "I'll be happy to help Guy in any way I can." She felt compelled to address the issue of school attendance. "But at school the other students are also a great help. They explain things in different ways to each other."

"He's not that fond of school." Beau's face twisted in puzzlement. "That's no reflection on you. I'm sure you are a good teacher. He's looking forward to working where he can make a difference."

In Ruth's opinion, school attendance should be required and not left to choice. Not everyone agreed, of course. Charlotte had always insisted her children attend school, even when Guy swore never to return after sitting in the corner with a dunce cap on his first day.

Ruth blinked at the memory. "Tell me about this job."

"The bank needs a clerk. I know Guy's not that good at arithmetic, but I was hoping you could help him improve his skills. Then maybe he could take over the books at the ranch as well."

Ruth coughed and covered her mouth to hide her dismay. Maybe if she explained, Beau would understand. From what Charlotte had said, he was a reasonable man. "I'd be happy to help Guy keep up with his schooling. Allan as well. Allan was one of my best students last year. Charlotte and Percy had high hopes for him. In fact, Allan could tutor Guy."

A glimmer of something—disappointment? Discouragement?—flittered across Beau's face. "Allan already has his hands full with the farm. He was moping about school so much that I promised him he could continue lessons with you if he didn't go around quoting poetry all day long."

Ruth's heart sank another inch. Schooling wasn't the only problem. Allan's heart wasn't in the farm. Maybe Beau needed more time to recognize that. If she could get a job for Allan at the newspaper, Haydn could discuss subjects like philosophy and the classics with him as well as the prospects for this year's crops.

Beau's face darkened, and Ruth bit her lip. *Forgive me, Lord, for wanting to interfere where it's none of my business.* "Of course I will do everything I can to help. For any interested students, we offer a reading club, music lessons, a class in the wifely arts. We're also looking for men to teach our boys useful skills. The children are welcome to attend any of those classes, and I would be happy to tutor Allan and Guy two days a week." Ruth caught herself. The way she was prattling on, Beau would think she was as bad as the older girls in her class, who turned into chattering magpies as soon as a handsome lad caught their eyes.

Beau rubbed his chin. "I might consider teaching a boys' class next year. Right now it's taking twenty-five hours out of every twenty-hour for Allan and me to try to get some kind of crop out of the ground before winter comes."

Of course. "How foolish of me to suggest he do anything other than farm." Flames licked her face, a rare fit of anger building up in her.

"Ruth?" Mama called to her from the kitchen. "Would you come in here and give me a hand, please?"

"I'll be right back." When Ruth stepped into the kitchen, she didn't see any work to be done.

"Come over here by me." Mama stood by the window, looking out on the apple tree that provided shade in the summer, fruit in the fall, and preserves year round. "Sounds as though you need to go outside and look for any fruit that's ripened early. Unless you think you can bring yourself under control." She leveled a look at Ruth that could have sunk the Spanish Armada. "That poor man is our guest. He's just lost his only sister and found himself a father overnight. I know you don't like the way he's handling things, but don't you dare say a thing against him." Mama paused. "He's not doing any *harm* to those young folks, is he?"

"Not unless you call wasting a good mind harm, which I do." Ruth joined her mother at the window. "You're right; he's been gentle with them as far as I can tell. We just have different ideas about what's best."

"So did Barnabas and Paul about John Mark, and look what God did with that. Doubled the number of missionary teams. You just keep doing what God has called you to do. *Teach.* Sometimes it's in the classroom and sometimes it's by the side of the road." Mama broke a gingersnap in two and handed her half. "Maybe one day you may even find yourself teaching a certain farmer a thing or two about raising children."

Ruth almost choked on the cookie.

Mama hugged her. "Have you calmed down enough to go back in the room and be nice to Mr. Blanton?"

Ruth nodded. Shame followed on the heels of her earlier anger. Beau was standing, as if waiting for her return. Was it her imagination, or did a shadow of shame lie on his features as well?

"So can you tutor Guy and Allan on Mondays and Thursdays?" Beau repeated his earlier request.

"Of course." Ruth extended her hand to shake his. "It will be my pleasure. I love teaching."

His hand lingered on hers. "Once my life settles down, I'd like to teach the young men. I just can't do it right now."

"That would be wonderful if you want to. But not everyone is meant to be a teacher. Or a farmer."

After he dropped her hand and said good-bye, Ruth realized she hadn't thought about Allan once when she said not everyone was meant to be a farmer or a teacher.

She'd been too busy thinking about the tall, handsome farmer who was holding the teacher's hand.

Chapter 7

Guy stomped up the steps to the parsonage door. Allan followed right behind, shaking his head at his brother's behavior.

Not a good day. Today the boys might need more than Ruth's tutoring.

"I've got them a bite to eat. That might help," Mama whispered in Ruth's ear.

Ruth waved them inside. "Good evening, Guy, Allan." Ink and lead smudges darkened the knuckles of Guy's calloused hands. "Let's start in the kitchen. We can spread out our work there."

Guy slammed the textbook on the table. "It doesn't matter. I can't do arithmetic."

Ruth bit back her automatic response of "Of course you can." She had found that facts mattered little when a person's emotions were involved. "I know it doesn't come easy to you. I appreciate your hard work."

"Work." Guy made it sound like a curse. "The bank manager fired me today. I made too many mistakes in my figuring." He broke a gingersnap between his teeth with an angry crunch.

Allan held out the chair for Ruth, and she slid into it soundlessly. He quietly set his satchel on the floor. The silence lengthened as if the boys waited for Teacher to perform some kind of magic on Guy's situation.

"Oh Guy. I'm so sorry." Her brain stumbled for a response.

"And Uncle Beau, he's going to be mighty upset with me."

"From what I've seen, your uncle is a reasonable man." Ruth hoped one of the boys would speak up if they had a cause for concern.

"He would never hurt us." Allan must have sensed her worries. "But he does have high expectations of all of us. He keeps telling us how he's been a working cowboy since he was Guy's age." A slight shudder ran through Allan. Had his uncle been encouraging Guy to quit school and go to work?

She had waited long enough. She *had* to speak up.

"I'm coming home with you."

✥

"She's pretty nice." Dru spoke of the woman who had spent yesterday at the cabin tidying up and fixing a roast and vegetables they could eat over the next few days. Dru was kneading biscuit dough to eat with the leftover roast.

Beau grunted. He still was of two minds about hiring one of "Birdie's girls," as they seemed to be known. No one could deny the change in Birdie, but did that mean he should hire one of her friends to work in his home alongside his impressionable niece? Much better for her to be under the influence of someone like Ruth Fairfield, even if she did place too much value on school learning. Intelligent, kind, compassionate, someone who loved the Lord as much as her preacher father did.

Stop it. If Beau kept this up, he'd sound like he was describing the woman from Proverbs 31. While he admired many of Ruth's qualities, he didn't want to marry her or anyone else. He expected marriage to come before children, but God had changed the order in his case, and he didn't have time to court a lady properly.

Something rumbled outside, and Beau went to the door to check the sky. Even this late in the season, tornadoes were still possible. *Please, Lord, protect us from a bad storm while we still only have this dwelling of mud and sticks.*

Clouds scudded across the darkening sky, but no wind stirred the dead air. The rumble came from the ground, from horses' hooves and wagon wheels. The boys were back early.

The wagon came into view, a second horse in the harness and a third figure in the wagon—Ruth Fairfield. She held the reins, pushing the horses to a faster speed than usual. As they approached, she pulled on the reins and stopped their progress. Drawn almost against his will, Beau approached and offered her his arm. "Good evening, Ruth." Her name floated across his tongue like sweet honey. "Supper's warm on the stove. Come on in and eat with us."

Ruth took a seat on one of the rickety chairs inside the soddy. Allan took a seat on the single bed, and Guy sat beside him, his eyes trained on the floor. Allan tucked his book bag under the bed and fiddled with the strap, releasing it then cinching it again.

"Miss Fairfield!" Dru set down a plate of biscuits and flung her arms around her teacher. "I didn't know you were coming tonight. Let me get you some coffee."

"That would be nice, Dru." Ruth waited, her hands folded in her lap. She accepted the mug from Dru, who then served her brothers. Allan waved it away, but Guy gulped the coffee like an elixir.

As soon as Ruth sipped the drink, Guy spoke. "Uncle Beau, I lost my job at the bank."

Beau was flummoxed. He had never lost a job. The only people he had known to lose a job were either thieves or just plain lazy. Guy was neither of those things. Working his mouth, he came out with the words. "What happened?"

This time Guy looked at Ruth, who gave him a small, encouraging nod.

"I just couldn't do the numbers right. I've never been good with numbers. Ask Miss Fairfield."

She nodded regretfully. "Math has always been. . . difficult. . .for Guy. He's a fine young man but not suited to work at the bank."

Beau still didn't understand the problem. "That's why I asked you to tutor him at night, to catch him up on his figures."

Alan glanced at Ruth, who said, "That's not the answer. Guy can do arithmetic well enough for most things, but a banker needs a feel for numbers. Guy's interests lie in other areas."

Beau snorted. Guy's *interests*? Most of the time life didn't consist of a list of choices. A man figured out what he was supposed to do then went ahead and did it. That was it.

The two boys scooted closer together on the bed, and Dru joined them. This felt like a conspiracy.

Allan sat tall, his shoulders getting broad enough to equal Beau's own. "The thing is, I would love a job at the bank instead of working out here at the farm. You've seen me around here. I'm more likely to hit my thumb than a nail with the hammer. Sometimes I feel like I can barely tell the difference between a bull and a steer. But I'd do well at the bank, I know I would."

Guy looked up. "And I go to school 'cause Ma and Pa expected it, but my favorite times are in the fields." He dropped his gaze again.

Ruth drained her cup. "There is a simple solution. Let Allan and Guy switch places. I wish they could both continue in school full-time, but Allan doesn't need much before he's ready to apply for the university, if he has a mind to when the time is right. And Guy would relieve some of your anxiety about the farm."

"Do you have any tricks up your sleeve for Dru?"

The girl squirmed in her spot next to Guy.

"Unfortunately, no." Ruth turned a tender smile on Dru. "I think you are all coping admirably in very hard circumstances. My preferences, as you can imagine, would have all three in school full-time. But I believe my suggestions may help make the best of a difficult situation."

Anger stung Beau. He had managed to keep outsiders

from intruding on his life since he struck out on his own. Ruth Fairfield was determined to give him advice whether he wanted it or not. Not that advice was always unwelcome— he had asked for advice more than once—but never from a stranger and certainly not from a woman. Even a woman as sensible and as pretty as this one was. "We can try it your way."

Dru giggled, and Guy seemed to grow two inches.

"For two weeks. If things aren't any better by then, I'll decide what needs to be changed."

Ruth nodded, smiling, as if ready to join him for another conference in a fortnight.

"On my own. I don't appreciate interference in my family's affairs, and I don't believe Charlotte or Percy did either."

Ruth's smile dimmed. "Of course, the bank president has to agree to Allan taking the job, but I'm sure he'll be happy to do so."

We'll see. Beau took the coffee Ruth poured for him. *We'll see.*

A month later, Allan was happily settled at the bank, covering nearly as much in his biweekly tutoring as he had while attending school full-time. He could apply for university next fall—Haydn would love to write a reference for him— but Ruth knew Beau was opposed to that. He didn't have to say a word.

Guy was happier than he ever had been in class. His hours at the farm, doing work he loved, made him appreciate the breaks for classes. He would never make a bank clerk or a reporter, but he had a good grounding in reading, writing, and arithmetic, as well as American history and geography, and a natural knack for leadership that emerged as he found more confidence in his growing body.

The only Pratt child who still troubled Ruth was Dru. Beau was either blind to the physical changes in his niece or he hadn't found a solution that didn't offend his sensibilities.

Ruth brought up the problem with the sewing circle again. "I still feel like I should make some clothes, maybe even some unmentionables, for Dru. You should see her." At least the tears in her voice didn't drip down her cheeks.

"We see her on Sundays. Even the dress you made for her while she was living with you is getting small on her," Birdie said.

"I've been trying to think what I did when I was growing like that. I wore hand-me-downs from my sister and from Mama. But Dru. . ." Annie shrugged.

"Dru doesn't have any sisters, and all her mother's clothes burned in the fire. She doesn't have any family to give her things." Ruth fingered the sheet she was making for Birdie's growing group of girls. "You know I'm happy to make these, Birdie, but my mission is with the Pratts. I believe so now more than ever."

"Well, then," Birdie said in a matter-of-fact voice new to her, "you should just make her the clothes and let God take care of the rest of it."

"Thank you for reminding me." Ruth relaxed. "I'll do just that. I'll finish a dress for her this week. Maybe give it to her on Sunday. Mr. Blanton can't complain too much in God's house on the Lord's Day."

Ruth didn't have to wait for a trip to Finnegan's Mercantile to start. She had purchased the ideal calico weeks ago, the soft yellows and greens making her think of Dru as soon as she spotted it. She had even marked the pattern lines on the fabric, but then had stopped, not convinced that she should proceed with the project, waiting for clear direction.

That had happened after convincing Beau to let the boys switch positions and while watching Dru shoot up over the past four weeks. Now Ruth studied the pattern lines again. If she narrowed the seams and took out two darts in the front and back, it should fit. As for the hem, she had left it overlong until she could measure the correct length. Now that the girl had reached Ruth's height and passed it, Ruth made the hemline an inch and a half lower than those for her own dresses.

In fact, when Ruth finished making adjustments, she realized Dru's measurements came close to her own. The girl could wear Ruth's hand-me-downs, and she'd be happy to give her a few. Which would bother Beau more: hand-me-downs or specially made dresses?

Since either choice would test Beau's patience, Ruth decided to give Dru what would make a young girl the happiest. New fabric, a newer design, a few ribbons.

Taking her scissors, she cut the fabric. Soon her needle was flying through the fabric while the conversation turned in other directions.

Chapter 8

In fact, Ruth finished the dress right before the Thursday tutoring session. But she didn't want to create problems for the boys by sending the unwanted gift home with them, so she kept with her original plan of giving it to Beau on Sunday.

When Dru arrived at school on Friday, Ruth almost regretted her decision. The girl's dress dangled inches above her ankle and hugged her waist so tight that Ruth wondered how she could breathe. The pained expression on Dru's face and her general disinterest made Ruth suspect the girl had a worse than usual case of the monthlies.

When at last the class had a recess, Ruth kept Dru back. "Let me get you some willow-bark tea and you rest in here a spell. Unless you want to go outside?"

The misery with which Dru shook her head convinced Ruth she had the truth of it. Dru stumbled as she got to her feet then immediately sat back down. "Miss Fairchild."

That single mortified cry told Ruth what had happened. "Don't worry. I'll get one of the older girls to take over the class while I take you to the parsonage. We'll get you fixed up right away."

They headed out the door, Dru's coat hiding her embarrassment, and they arrived at the house within minutes.

Dru mumbled a few words that verified the nature of the problem, and Mama hugged her. "My dear child. I'll start some bathwater and salts for you. A good bath always helps me feel better when I'm hurting."

"I don't want to be a burden. . ." Dru started out in a good imitation of her uncle.

"Don't worry about that. This isn't the first time a girl's been caught unawares."

"I've got to get back to school." Ruth took the coat from the girl, her heart hurting for the motherless child. "But before I leave, there's something I want to give to you." She ran to her room and took the dress from its knob.

"But what am I going to wear?" Tears hovered behind Dru's words.

"We have some things," Mama assured her. "And it's early enough that I might be able to rinse this out and get it back to you before the end of the day."

Ruth set up the curtain around the bathtub in the back room so Papa would know to stay away.

Mama led Dru into the room and smiled. "And besides, I think you might have another choice."

Ruth held the dress up to Dru. "I made this with you in mind. And it seems that God's timing was perfect, that I would have this ready for you when you needed it the most."

Ruth didn't miss Dru's gasp of pleasure, nor the frown that followed it. "But Uncle Beau. . ."

Mama gently helped Dru slip out of her dress, clucking over her like a sympathetic hen. "The good book says to let tomorrow take care of itself. God has helped you today. We'll worry about tomorrow when it comes."

When Dru didn't come back to school that afternoon, Ruth hurried for home right after the final bell. Dru sat in the kitchen with Mama, looking a lot better than she had that morning. "I'm coming home with you. That way you can ride and not have to walk when you're already sore."

"Uncle Beau might not like that."

"Your uncle has never had to walk two miles when his insides hurt. Or at least not in the same way. And Mama is sending some food home with you so you can rest."

Some twelve-year-olds had to cook and keep house. Others had to deal with maturity and the challenges it presented all alone, without another woman in the home. Not many had to do both at once. Ruth's heart went out to her young student.

Dru didn't protest any further, allowing herself to be cosseted in blankets in the back of the wagon. Beau met them at the edge of the field where he and Guy were working. "You appear without warning, Ruth." He jumped the simple fence they had posted to keep deer and other grazing animals from the growing plants.

"Dru! What happened?"

❧

Beau had rarely spent such a sleepless night. After a few hours of forcing himself to stay still and not toss and turn, he went outside, pacing the perimeter of the cabin to keep an eye out for dangers he was more comfortable with than the ones he had encountered today.

He didn't know what to make of it all. Women's troubles, Ruth explained with little more than a slight blush. A new dress against his explicit refusal. Food from the parsonage. The Fairfields seemed determined to help him whether he wanted it or not.

But if the common lot of womenfolk was bad enough to send his niece away from school in the middle of the day, maybe he needed the help more than he knew.

For sure, Ruth Fairfield had plenty of gumption, but she exasperated him in equal measure. She'd plowed into his life like someone convinced she knew what was best, like the people who had tried to split him and Charlotte up after their parents died.

He'd seek out advice about Dru, although he couldn't imagine asking another female about it. There had to be books that taught about such things, some kind of medical manual. In fact, he might shut off all contact from Calico, aside from Allan's work. They'd stop the tutoring for sure, keep Dru home for a few days, until he could get their lives straightened out. Without the help of the interfering Miss Fairfield.

"Beau, what about asking Me for My help?" The Lord whispered to Beau as the night turned to day, but Beau turned a deaf ear. It seemed to him like God would be on the pastor's side.

Beau didn't share his plans with the family on Saturday. He allowed Dru to spend the day in bed and kept the boys away to accommodate her need for privacy. The problem was, he didn't have any of the resources a lot of homesteaders started out with, including a basic medical book. He'd had no need for such a volume in his travels, and he didn't know where to get one.

No one said anything about the change of schedule, although Allan had protested when they didn't go to church on Sunday. "Why, Uncle Beau? Dru is well enough to get up and about."

"It's okay to spend a day at home every now and then. We'll have our own worship service here, in the soddy." He pulled the Bible he'd kept in his saddlebag onto his lap. "I thought we could share some of our favorite verses or stories. You know, the Bible says wherever two or more are gathered in His name, He's there with them. That's us today."

Allan flicked a glance at Beau. "I might as well start. I've always loved Bible stories. David and Goliath and the ark are as exciting as anything I've ever read by Homer or Shakespeare. When I think of David going after the giant with only five small stones, I get more courage the next time I set out hunting." Beau had to answer Allan's small grin with one of his own. He had seen fewer young men less at ease behind a rifle barrel, although Allan could hit a target straight and sure. Percy had done one thing right. Shooting was even more necessary than reading for someone out on the western frontier, at least in Beau's mind.

Allan proceeded to tell the story with such imagination that Beau could almost smell the sweat, blood, and dust of the battlefield. After his start, everyone shared. Guy quoted John 3:16 and talked about the day he had asked Jesus to be his Savior. That reassured Beau's mind, especially when the others shared their testimonies as well.

"How about you, Uncle Beau?" Dru asked. "Are you a Christian?"

"Yes." Should he tell the long version or the short one? "I invited Jesus into my heart when I was just a little bit of a fella. I'm ashamed to say I drifted away." Mad at God for sending one of His "ministers" to split up their family. "But there's something about days on the open prairie, with only yourself and cattle for company, that turn a man's thoughts to God." More time than he had taken recently. He had to make spending time with God a priority, no matter how busy he was around the farm.

Dru shared a story next. "I like to read about Dorcas. She helped the widows and orphans in her church, and then she died and Peter raised her back to life. Miss Fairfield's friends are like that. I just hope one of them doesn't die, because we don't have any apostles around to bring anyone back to life."

Dorcas. Of all the stories in the Bible, of all the women in the Bible, why did Dru have to go and mention Dorcas?

"Didn't you invite Me to this meeting?" the Holy Spirit prodded Beau.

Just because Dru mentioned Dorcas didn't mean they were candidates for charity. No sir. Beau decided to break the news now. "You might as well know that you won't be going back to school in Calico. You'll either study at home or go to school in Langtry."

"No. If I can't go to Calico, I don't want to go at all." Dru jumped up, whipped her cape and bonnet from the door peg, and ran out the door.

Chapter 9

Beau thought about chasing after his niece but decided against it. Maybe all Dru needed was time alone. She'd had a difficult week. But after she hadn't returned half an hour later, he went outside to check. Dru was nowhere in sight.

"Dru!" He called at the top of his voice. "Come on back! Dru!"

Mist gathered above the ground, rising to meet storm clouds gathering overhead. It looked like fog was forming, making visibility difficult. A harsh wind whipped across the open ground, and Beau shivered with the cold. Although early in the season, snow was always a possibility.

His worry deepened as he checked the animal shelters. Everything was empty. He needed his coat, hat, mittens, gloves—maybe some extra cover for Dru. That cape couldn't keep her very warm.

"You didn't find her, did you?" Inside the soddy, Allan had prepared to leave. He handed Beau a mug of coffee and sliced bread and ham wrapped in a towel, unspoken accusations burning in his eyes

"It shouldn't take that long," Beau said.

"You don't know our Dru." Allan clipped his words. "And it's fixing to snow out there."

Guy added a sweater to the saddlebag with more food, as well as a blanket. He had chosen well. The boy had grown, putting on height and weight and muscle during the weeks he had worked on the farm, approaching his brother in bulk. They were both growing into good, strong men.

They finished up the leftover eggs in the skillet and ate a can of cold beans in about two seconds flat before heading out the door. They searched the yard and outbuildings for a second time. It didn't take long. The small lean-to they had built for the animals until they could finish a barn only took a minute, even with poking among the hay bales.

Next they checked the wagon. Beau had heard about secret places in wagon beds, especially in tales he'd heard about the Underground Railroad, but this one was solid wood.

All that remained were the open fields and plains. Dru couldn't have run far, but where was she headed? Did she even have a specific destination in mind?

You don't know our Dru. Allan's accusation repeated itself in Beau's mind. No he didn't. How could he? He didn't know much about girls, not even his own sister. He'd expected Dru to have returned by now, to have run out her anger. But she was still out there. He'd thought he knew boys better, but his nephews defied his understanding as well.

What was it David said in the Psalms? *O Lord, thou hast searched me and known me.* "Why don't you ask Me about the *children? I am acquainted with all your ways. I'll lead you to Dru."*

Beau halted his horse and looked up at the heavens, where the white ceiling was lowering close to the ground and cold air blew from the north. *Forgive me, Father, for thinking I know better. You made these young'uns. You understand them inside and out. You created women different from men, and I ask You to give me enough understanding of my niece so I can find her before she gets hurt.*

"C'mon, boys. It's time to extend our search." The boys mounted their horses. "Has Dru done this kind of thing before? Do you have any idea where she might go?"

Guy immediately shook his head, but Allan hesitated before nodding.

"What is it?"

The expression on Allan's face could have passed for a smile in other circumstances. "There were a couple of times Guy and Dru ran away and camped out by the river for a night. Ma had me keep an eye on them. Pretty much as soon as they ran out of food, they came on home."

"Oh yeah. I wasn't thinking about those times." Guy pulled the reins tight. "But those were in the summer. Not like. . .this."

"Take me to the spot by the river."

Five minutes later, they had reached the place. Beau could see how it would make a pleasant summer hideaway. Plenty of water, shade too, maybe good fishing. Next year he would check it out.

Although they dismounted the horses and searched

the banks on both sides, they found no traces of recent disturbance. They rode up and down the river from that favorite spot. Once Guy spotted something that turned out to be the beginnings of a beaver dam. Another time Allan found the remnants of a fox den.

With the storm hovering, the sky dimmed fast. They continued their search, knowing Dru might be only a few feet away and they wouldn't see her. At one point, Allan came to Beau and shared a slice of bread and a slab of ham along with a swig of cold coffee from his canteen.

The sky grew gray, then black, the soddy little more than a smudge on the horizon. Beau decided to call a reluctant halt to the search and whistled for the boys to join him. "We'd best get on back."

Both Allan and Guy nodded their acceptance. "I'd say to come out again with torches, but. . ." Allan shrugged. "We wouldn't be able to see very far."

"We'll start at first light tomorrow." Beau would pray all night long for God's protection of Dru during the long hours.

Even taking a straight path to the soddy took longer than expected, and Beau realized how far they had searched. How far could a girl in ordinary shoes and a long dress travel on foot? He didn't know. His last hopes for a happy ending to the day were dashed when they arrived at an empty soddy, devoid of light or warmth. Dru had not returned.

After they finished chores, they built a small fire and collapsed onto the beds without seeking further refreshment. Against all expectations, Beau fell asleep quickly, his rest punctuated with snorts of wakefulness. Each time, his chest tightened, and he sensed his heart had been carrying on its own conversation with God even while his body rested. He woke early in the morning and rustled up some eggs and hardtack that brought the boys to wakefulness. After a quick breakfast, Beau discussed what to do. "We didn't check much west of the yard yesterday. I thought we'd start that way today."

Allan shuffled his feet. "I was wondering if she'd circle back to the road once she got away from here. She might have gone into town. One of us should head that way in case she's heading home. I can ask when I get to the bank."

Allan had proven himself a strong presence in this emergency. He might never make a good farmer, but he had courage and common sense. "Tell you what then. Guy, you finish up the chores here and wait for my return." Cows had to be milked and animals fed, no matter what. They decided to meet back at the soddy at lunchtime. "And if it starts to snow. . ."

"Don't worry. I know what to do." Guy interrupted before Beau could continue his lecture. Revelation upon revelation about his nephews was piling up on this day.

✑❤

Ruth woke early Monday with a heavy heart. Every weekend since Beau's arrival, she had run into him somewhere. A couple of times he had dropped by Aunt Kate's diner. He had shown up at the sewing circle more than once, and he'd been mentioned every week. That thought brought a blush to her cheeks. Then there was Finnegan's Mercantile, the parsonage,

330

and even the school. His absence this past weekend troubled her more than it should.

She wasn't truly distressed until the family missed church. Was one of them sick? By Sunday, Dru's distress should have subsided. After attending each week as faithfully as the pastor did, their sudden absence created a void on the third pew on the left side of the church, their usual spot to sit. She checked it before the service started, glanced during the morning prayer—and caught the gaze of young Georgie Polson. Even though she didn't hear any opening or closing of the church doors, she kept hoping they had snuck in without her knowledge until at last Papa said the final amen and she made her way down the aisle.

The weather turned cold, hinting that the first freeze of the season would arrive before morning. But Beau didn't seem like the sort to let a little cold keep him from what he wanted to do. If anything, he'd plow his way through six feet of snow if he set his mind to it. Her concerns about the well-being of the family increased. All Sunday long she fought her conscience about making another unannounced visit to the soddy. Someone else should go, but she still felt like the "someone" meant to help the Pratts was her.

Monday morning dawned chilly, air whisking through the chinks around her window, and she dressed in underthings designed for cold weather. Hopefully the temperatures would rise as the sun came out. If the clouds covered the sky all day, sunshine wouldn't stretch the warmth very far.

Since the hour was early, she could go to the bank and

speak with Allan before school started. But what if he wasn't there? She discussed the problem with Mama.

"I'm truly concerned something has happened. A soddy isn't the best place to pass a winter, and Beau doesn't have much experience. I'm afraid something's happened to one or all of them."

"I pray you'll find Allan at the bank and everything is fine."

Bless Mama, she didn't tell Ruth her concern was unjustified. "But if he's not there?"

Mama took a seat opposite Ruth and looked her straight in the eye. "What do you want to do?"

"I want to ride straight out to the farm and check. A man probably should come with me. Except I can't go to the farm and start school on time."

Mama waved that concern away. "I'll stay with the children. You've planned your lessons so well, they're easy for me to follow."

Ruth sped from the parsonage to the bank, arriving at the same time as Allan.

"Miss Fairfield!" He looked flustered, and dark circles ringed his eyes, confirming her fears.

"What's happened?" Ruth stepped away from the entrance of the bank. A few children crossed the street in front of them on their way to school, and Ruth waved.

"It's Dru. She's run away. We haven't seen her since Sunday morning."

The first flat snowflake floated between them, landing on Ruth's coat like a strand of wool from an unraveling sweater.

Chapter 10

R uth glanced back at the bank. "You need to get to work."

Allan shook his head. "I'm going to ask them if I can take the day off and look for Dru. I know Uncle Beau is going to ask people to help search."

After his departure, Ruth glanced up and down the streets, looking for someone to come with her. Not seeing anyone, she decided she could make the trip on her own. She shouldn't have any problems if she left in time to get back before the snow made travel difficult. Backtracking to the parsonage, she saddled her horse and headed west down the rapidly disappearing road.

She kept her speed slow, in case she caught sight of Dru or the road grew slick underfoot. Each plop of the horse's hooves thudded in her heart. Dru, dear, sweet, Dru, who had trusted her like an older sister, had run away. In her heart, Ruth knew the way she had pushed Beau had something to do with it. Before she said one word to Beau about his niece, she'd better ask his forgiveness for interfering and for how that had led to today's events.

The flakes grew closer together and smaller, the kind

of snow that could end in great drifts. A coated and hatted figure emerged from the whitening horizon—Beau.

He saluted her with his hat. They both picked up speed and met, about a yard's distance between them. Ruth said, "Allan told me about Dru. Oh Beau, I feel like this is all my fault. If I hadn't interfered"—a lump formed in her throat—"this might not have happened."

𝒶❤

Allan must not have told Ruth the whole story. The fault belonged entirely to Beau.

"I'm the one who needs to ask your forgiveness. If I hadn't been so determined to do things my own way, this wouldn't have happened." Beau swallowed. "I put my pride ahead of my family's needs. I want to talk more about that with you later. But you haven't seen Dru?"

"No." The wind blew a strand of Ruth's dark hair away from her face, a whirlwind of white snow and dark circles of hair. "I want to help."

She would. Regardless of how little help a woman would be searching through a snowstorm, she'd think herself equal to the task. "But what about school?"

"Mama took over for the day. Although if the weather keeps up, she might send the students home soon. The one we have to worry about is Dru." Ruth paused. "I expect she found shelter somewhere. She's too smart to let herself get caught out in this." One bright red mitten embraced the gray horizon. "But we need help. We should—" She paused, her face flaring a pretty red like her mittens. "That is, if you agree with me."

He gestured for her to continue.

"I'm sure my sewing circle friends would be willing to help. And their beaus." Her voice stumbled at the wordplay between his name and the common usage of the word.

His heart surged with warmth in spite of the swirling snow. Could Beau be someone's beau? Could he be Ruth's beau? *Another time.* "That sounds wise. We could cover more territory that way."

He, Guy, and most of all, Dru needed help. Beau had already decided to drop his pride and accept the help a circle of good Christian people wanted to give him. "I'm supposed to meet up with Guy at the soddy at noon. Let's gather everyone and cover the town before we head back out this way."

As they rode back into town, the wind blew from every direction, pushing them first one way then the other. The horses plodded steadily along. Beau's stomach suggested the hour had reached midmorning, but he couldn't tell by the sky.

"We'll reach Finnegan's Mercantile first," Ruth called against the wind. "Mr. Finnegan can circulate word for people to keep a look out."

His family at the center of the town's gossip mill. *Your will, Lord.* Beau swallowed past his pride.

Ned hovered at the door to his store, Birdie at his heels, locking the door behind them. "You almost missed me." He unlocked the door. "What can I do for you?"

"We don't need to buy anything," Ruth started to explain.

"Come in out of the weather." Ned held the door open,

and Beau waited for the ladies before ducking his head under Ned's arm.

"My niece, Dru, is missing. She ran away." Beau stated the cold, hard facts, not caring what they might think. Pride was running away from him as rapidly as the snow accumulated.

"We'd like your help in looking for her." Ruth took off her mittens and rubbed her hands in front of the small fire Ned had left burning in the store. "We're going to ask everyone in the sewing circle to help get the word out. Can you get in touch with Annie while we go for Gladys and Haydn? Tell everyone we'll meet at Aunt Kate's diner in half an hour."

Thirty minutes later, they met in front of the diner. The doors remained open, Aunt Kate serving hot cocoa to anyone bold enough to brave the weather.

"I wonder what's keeping Haydn." Gladys rubbed a spot in the window. "He promised he'd come right away. We don't want to wait much longer."

In addition to the sewing circle, several other members of the Calico community joined them in the diner. Half of them, Beau couldn't put a name to their faces. Without his saying a word, the men organized search teams while the women decided which homes to set up as relay stations, places to return for warmth and refreshment. A few of the women, Ruth among them, wanted to hunt along with the men, and no one denied them.

Beau cleared his throat, and the room quieted. "I promised Guy I'd be back by noon. I'll head on out with whoever is coming with me."

"I am." Ruth's gray eyes met his.

Another man joined their party. They'd barely reached the town square when Pastor Fairfield clanged the church doors behind him, head lowered into the wind.

"Wait. Let's see what he has to say." Ruth nudged her horse forward toward the bent figure.

Pastor Fairfield lifted his head, hand clamped on a broad-brimmed black hat, and joy sprang on his face at the sight of Beau and the others accompanying them. "Good news, brother!"

Chapter 11

S it still, teacher!" Dru giggled. "That's what you always
tell us, and you're worse than the first graders."

Ruth smiled at the two of them in the mirror.
After Papa had greeted them with the news that Dru had
spent the night before safe and sound inside the room at the
church, they had reached quick decisions. Beau headed for
the soddy to catch Guy and hunker down before the storm
let loose its full fury. Everyone agreed that neither Dru nor
Ruth should face the weather without good reason. Once
again Dru was a guest of the Calico parsonage.

The snow continued unabated for the rest of Monday
into Tuesday. As usual, Aunt Kate and Mama and Papa took
in those schoolchildren who lived too far away to reach home
safely. Ruth had always enjoyed these times; they were part
of the reason she had decided to become a teacher. After
this most recent experience, she allowed herself to admit
that perhaps they helped reveal a desire for a family of her
own. A family with children of her own to love, special
ones like Dru. . .and Allan. . .and even Guy. With someone
like. . .Beau.

His name aroused a raging fire of emotions in her. She

must have mistaken the spark she'd seen in his eyes when they went looking for Dru. Silly woman, to mistake feelings stirred by the disappearance of his niece for romantic longings of a lonely soul. He hadn't even returned to town to take his niece home, although Allan had come by on his first day back at work to let them know the three menfolk had survived the storm.

"Now you've got that dreamy look in your eye." Dru ran the brush through Ruth's hair another time. "Do you want to keep it down around your shoulders? Or I could braid it and put it in a bun." Dru ran her fingers through the long strands. "Although that would be a pity. It's too pretty to hide. Or I could pile it on top of your head like a crown. . . ."

Ruth studied her image in the mirror. Not so long ago, she had worried about how to fix her hair. A simple bow holding her dark locks at the nape of her neck once brought her pleasure. Now she went with the most practical style for teaching, away from her face. During the summer, she kept her hair off her neck and let it down again when the weather turned cold.

But Dru was so eager, Ruth agreed to the experiment. "Whatever you like, as long as you don't cut it."

"I would never do that. It's too pretty."

Dru made a pretty picture herself. Now that Beau and Ruth had achieved peace between them, Ruth had finished another dress for Dru. This one was a soft green wool, one that would look lovely with her coloring, with white lace at the collar and cuffs, and a gored skirt in the back, flared just enough to look fashionable. Earlier today Dru had put the dress on for the first time, and Ruth had pinned her hair up in a simple bun. A little too grown up, too dressy for a weekday, but girls liked to dream.

Dru put a finger to her lips and turned Ruth around so she could study her face. "If you don't mind. . .I'd like to fix it the same way you fixed mine."

Happiness flooded Ruth's chest as if the girl had just said she wanted to become a teacher. "That's sounds wonderful."

Dru kept Ruth facing her while she led the girl through the steps. "That's perfect!" With a flourish, Dru held up the hand mirror for Ruth to see her reflection.

Ruth gasped. She hadn't looked so pretty, so young, so vulnerable since she began teaching five years ago. She touched the smoothed edges of brow and skin and cheek and hair. "You're a wonder, Dru Pratt."

The girl giggled again. "I'll remind you that you said that the next time I get into trouble at school." She tugged at Ruth's arm. "C'mon, stand up. I want to see us side by side."

Their hair was different colors. So were their eyes. But something—the joy in their eyes? The laughter on their lips? The shine of their hair?—made them look as alike as sisters.

"I wish you were my sister. Or my mother, since my ma died." The young lady slipped into a child again as she flung her arms around Ruth's neck.

"I am your sister in Christ. And you can always come to me with questions you don't feel comfortable asking your uncle." Ruth wondered whether she was wise to make such an open-ended invitation. If—*when*—Beau married, Dru should go to his wife with her questions.

"Everything would be perfect if you would just marry Uncle Beau. Then I could have you all to myself."

Ruth turned away before Dru could see the telltale heat streaking across her cheeks. "He has caught the attention of several ladies of the church. It won't be too long before you have an aunt you can go to with your questions."

Dru's mouth drooped. "I want you for my aunt."

"What you want and what God and your uncle Beau want may be different things. I'm where God has placed me, teaching the Calico School. I don't expect marriage to be part of my future." She reached for her hair, ready to ruin the fancy hairstyle. With a look at Dru, she dropped her hand and sighed.

❧

Beau waited in the parlor for Mrs. Fairfield to call Dru. He leaned forward, not meaning to eavesdrop but unable to close his ears and unwilling to move where he couldn't hear.

I don't expect marriage to be part of my future.

The words hit his soul like a death knell. Dru appeared in the doorway and squealed, and Beau hastened to paste a smile back on his lips. She must have seen his unhappy frown, however. "Uncle Beau, are you mad at me?"

She wore a pretty green gown that showed a lovely young woman, one who was growing into the image of her mother. Beau blinked at the tears the memories of his own dear sister brought to his eyes. "Mad at you? Yes, and worried and relieved and. . ." He drew in his breath. "Mostly, I'm mad at myself that you felt you had to run away rather than stay with me."

Dru looked at the floor. "I acted like a child. All you wanted me to do was to get my schooling someplace else. You weren't sending me off to someplace like the Betwixt 'n' Between, like the fathers of some of Birdie's girls did."

Of course Dru had heard some of the stories, as much as Beau wished he could shield her. "I was treating you like you were still seven years old and didn't have any ideas of your own. Expecting you to run the house and then not respecting your opinion about what was best for our family. . .that wasn't very smart of me."

"Maybe." She dragged her gaze to look at him. "So we're all right, then?"

"More than all right." He opened his arms, and she flew into them. He hugged her to his side, feeling once again the sizzle of joy he had felt each time he had reunited with Charlotte. He took a few steps with her. "Come outside with me." When he whispered in her ear, she followed with wide eyes the snow-packed path leading from parsonage to church. Once he found a secluded spot, he shared his plan with his niece; he had already talked it over with Allan and Guy. When a fit of girlish laughter collapsed her, he led her into the church. "Why don't you wait in here? I'll come for you soon."

"Of course. And Uncle Beau?"

"Yes?"

"Don't hurry back."

Ruth caught sight of Beau and Dru hovering behind the back wall of the church. Young couples who thought that was a good place for privacy didn't know that the parsonage bedrooms looked over their hideout. Most of it was innocent enough, although once or twice Papa had to step in.

Whatever Beau wanted to discuss with his niece was none of Ruth's business. She shut the curtains against the sight and rustled through her closet instead. Over the months she had filled a box with things she had made for the Pratts. The bed quilt wasn't quite finished, so it lay on top where she could grab it and work on it during odd moments. She had shirts and pants for the boys and a skirt and blouse for Dru. Annie had added socks. After she finished reviewing the contents, Dru and Beau still hadn't come back inside. She twitched the side of the curtain; they had disappeared from view. Frowning, she pressed her head against the glass but didn't see either one of them. He hadn't taken his niece home without saying good-bye, had he?

"Ruth." Mama knocked on the door. "Mr. Blanton would like to see you in the parlor."

Ruth's heart leaped at those words in a way that didn't reflect well on her continued peace of mind. "Coming, Mama."

Beau stood at the entrance to the parlor. Something about the way he held his hat in his hands, hope shining from his eyes, made her glad for the extra pains she and Dru had taken with her appearance today. "You're looking mighty fine today, Ruth."

Heat rose in her cheeks as she entered the room. He rushed to the back of the chair closest to the fire and held it for her. "Let me take that for you." He took the basket of shirts and household goods from her with a glance. "Let me guess. Your needle's been busy again."

"Yes." Ruth studied his face, nervous that he might reject her gift. She held her breath.

"Good." He smiled.

"So you're not mad?"

"How can I be mad at you for blessing me even when I was too stubborn to accept help when we needed it?" He set the basket beside him, on top of his coat, where he could easily pick it up when he left. "Mad? I should be offering my gratitude as well as asking for your forgiveness."

"Given. And I should ask for yours as well."

"We've already discussed all that." He didn't speak again for the space of a few seconds. "That's what I want to talk to you about. You've already forgiven me for being a stubborn fool. But I was wondering if you could do more than forgive me." His eyes searched hers. "If you could, perhaps, even. . .love me? Love me enough to marry me, to raise three children and any others the good Lord sees fit to give us?"

Mama poked her head around the corner. "Your father has already said yes." With a wink, she disappeared again.

Ruth blinked, certain Beau could read the answer in her eyes. . .her mouth. . .even in the way her ears reddened. "Yes yes yes!"

She couldn't wait to tell the Calico Sewing Circle that their mission was complete.

Matchmaking and all.

ABOUT THE AUTHOR

Award-winning author and speaker **Darlene Franklin** recently returned to cowboy country—Oklahoma. The move was prompted by her desire to be close to her son's family; her daughter, Jolene, has preceded her into glory.

Darlene loves music, needlework, reading, and reality TV. Talia, a lynx point Siamese cat, proudly claims Darlene as her person.

Darlene has published several titles with Barbour Publishing.

JOIN
US
ONLINE!

Christian Fiction for Women

*Christian Fiction for Women is your online home
for the latest in Christian fiction.*

Check us out online for:

- Giveaways
- Recipes
- Info about Upcoming Releases
- Book Trailers
- News and More!

Find Christian Fiction for Women at Your Favorite Social Media Site:

 Search "Christian Fiction for Women"

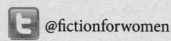 @fictionforwomen